A Cleansing of Souls

A Cleansing of Souls

A Novel

Stuart A. Ayris

iUniverse, Inc.
New York Lincoln Shanghai

A Cleansing of Souls

Copyright © 2007 by Stuart A. Ayris

All rights reserved. No part of this book may be used or reproduced by any means, graphic, electronic, or mechanical, including photocopying, recording, taping or by any information storage retrieval system without the written permission of the publisher except in the case of brief quotations embodied in critical articles and reviews.

iUniverse books may be ordered through booksellers or by contacting:

iUniverse
2021 Pine Lake Road, Suite 100
Lincoln, NE 68512
www.iuniverse.com
1-800-Authors (1-800-288-4677)

Because of the dynamic nature of the Internet, any Web addresses or links contained in this book may have changed since publication and may no longer be valid.

This is a work of fiction. All of the characters, names, incidents, organizations, and dialogue in this novel are either the products of the author's imagination or are used fictitiously.

ISBN: 978-0-595-45479-2 (pbk)
ISBN: 978-0-595-69583-6 (cloth)
ISBN: 978-0-595-89791-9 (ebk)

Printed in the United States of America

England

1961

Spring

Michael Parrish woke up in bed with his sister, Jennifer. He was seventeen years old. She was fourteen and dead.

There was a smell of dread in the air.

What do you honestly do at times like this? What do you honestly do?

Well, Michael, he just grinned. And he kept on grinning.

They took him to the Psychiatric Hospital, the Lunatic Asylum, the Nuthouse—whatever you want to call it.

He was there for 28 days, time enough they thought to get inside his head, his mind, his soul. But a thousand years would not have been enough, not for Michael.

So they let him go.

And he floats and he floats and he floats.

The world is real and it is not real. It moves and shifts and envelopes us. What you see is not what I see. And that is the wonder of this life.

But time catches up with us all …

England

1989

Summer

THE SOULS

Chapter One

The sun is high and blazing. I wish you could see it raging up there, swathing the small town below in pure heat. And that town, the town of my birth, can but hang a head of shame as we follow the light above through the sultry mists of our time. We can feel only humility on this, the most baleful of summer mornings.

People tread their weary paths to the station or to the office blocks that rise up, dull and wracked with the remorseless onslaught of monotony. Row upon row of small windows are lit like candles, set afire and aflame by the burning sun, flickering amidst the charred bricks that so dutifully house them. But in the harsh, torrid seasons when wind and rain are king and queen, the blackened bricks are cleansed pure, leaving the once resplendent panes to be shrouded in a veil of mist, hiding real tears.

This town, which was once just a market place, is home now to insurance companies, fast food restaurants, bargain shops and pubs that change in façade and content with equal regularity. There are multi-storey car parks in various states of decay, back alleys, subways of gloom, broken paths, needles and cans and bottles and shattered glass. The market place is still there though, bullish and archaic—and may it always be so. But I know one day it will not be there at all. I can see the traders arriving in their ramshackle vans and the lads, pulling the palettes on wheels upon which lay the bones of the stalls all ready for construction. Arriving at a place that is no longer there but in memory. And they will stop together, staring into the void, before scratching their heads and wandering back into the darkening dawn.

There are huge buildings that lurch from the dry ground, breathing austerity and throbbing with a dull foreboding. Where once there was a park, lush and tranquil, there now is just all this grime and this concrete and this suspicion. All within a four-lane ring road.

And what makes it all so much worse, so frightening, is that this change happened without you even noticing it. Your memory of what it was like before is not even there, simply because there is no before and there is no after. And the present is just the blink of an eye. What we have about us in this town, this town that is so much a part of me, is an aching, soulless grind to a picture-perfect world.

It is hard to say whether the people changed as their town changed. Perhaps they just adapted. Still, in this town, as in any other, they somehow get through to the end of each day. They come to find that there is an intense feeling of safety in the routine, the banal. Those that do not have that feeling are scattered in pieces across the town desperately searching for something to hang onto, to get a foothold somewhere that will deliver them to a safe place to be. For at the core of each man's heart must surely be a belief in the profound, unconscious truth that the struggles of his existence will one day be replaced by an ease of living that will wash over him like a summer rain. If that is not true then for what other reason would we put up with all of this?

So the town and its people begin another day on this humid morning. The ring road shudders beneath its thunderous load and the early blue of the sky is streaked by the excrement of pollution with which it is so often regaled. Fumes rise from the streets as if the pavements themselves are creeping smouldering upwards and about us. Oh talons of dark wonder.

It is upon these streets that Tom Spanner ambles along his wayward path to one of those faceless, nameless buildings. Tom Spanner—insurance clerk—a young man with hopes and dreams yet to be fulfilled.

Tom is just a little less than six feet tall, though his sloping, awkward gait lends him neither presence nor authority. He is slim and gaunt—a man of pipe cleaners and tissue paper. His suit just hangs off him and the tail of his white shirt, even this early in the day, peaks from beneath the back of his jacket like some ignoble gesture of surrender to all that lies behind him. His wide shoulders rise and fall to a tortuous rhythm as he shuffles down the street in the manacles of his own agony. The skin of his face is pale, almost grey in places, but that only serves to emphasise the beauty of his eyes. Those eyes just engulf you for they are the eyes of pain itself, deep, childlike, ageless. I could not tell you all that they have seen.

The grey building looms before Tom now. He affords himself one last backward glance before he is consumed by the lumbering mass of concrete and glass, reality fading away for another day.

Ah, Tom. Nineteen years old. I remember when you would laugh. The way you used to look up from the tangled dark hair of yours and smile the smile of the devil, your eyes aglow with rebellion and love and a raging fury just to live and experience life in all its glory. I remember those days, Tom, those days before Little Norman. Ah, Tom. Tom.

The darkness of the foyer was unnerving. They dimmed the lights just as you entered. It happened every morning. It was like stepping bewildered through the rear of a creaking wardrobe. As Tom's sunken eyes began to adjust to the lack of light, the white desk of the receptionist faded into view. The face of the woman behind the desk glowed in the dull blackness of it all, glowed like a pale three quarter moon. Her face was huge and ephemeral, flickering in and out of vision. There was a plug socket behind her.

The glowing, humming receptionist was able to receive incoming calls, type letters and admire herself in the mirrored tiles on the opposite wall simultaneously. Being in no way adept at the first two of these tasks, the third was generally considered to be the one to which she gave her most careful attention. Often, though, the mirrored tiles would slice her face in two or four, leaving her to writhe in her rotating seat in complete terror searching wildly for completion. She was sad even when she smiled. And when she laughed, you could almost taste the tears.

Tom allowed himself to be pulled into the gaping mouth of the lift and he closed his eyes as he was dragged in.

So the receptionist was left alone once more. A switch was flicked somewhere up above or down below and her faced began to melt, melt with a velvet ease as all the mirrored tiles became as one. And thus she disappeared from view just as the light of the falling moon does sink beneath the waves.

Mirrors. Mirrors.

There were mirrors in the lift too. They followed you. This was their way. There was a camera in the ceiling. Only once had Tom seen it flash, preferring since then to keep his eyes closed. They wouldn't get him that easily. Among the many things he hated, mirrors were foremost, for it always shook him to be reminded so abruptly of his own complete frailty. He knew the man he was and it was a different man from the one that gazed at him with such dismay within the frame of a mirror. There were some people who used this particular lift instead of the stairs purely for the perceived pleasure of their own visible company. At one time, vanity such as this would have made him laugh out loud. Not any more. Not since Little Norman.

The things that once had humoured him now filled him with a dark and debilitating sadness.

Tom opened his eyes as the lift doors slid gently back to reveal a short corridor at the end of which was a set of thick double doors. It was on the other side of those heavy doors that he would spend another long day. He stepped out of the lift and walked along the corridor, peering through the glass at the top of the doors, patches of mist forming on the pane as he breathed upon it. He wiped away the vapour with his hand and saw that the clock on the far wall allowed him three more minutes—enough time for a cigarette and the dubious pleasures of sanity.

The men's room was clean and white and fresh and an open window let in a cool breeze. There was a distinct clarity about the air in there.

Tom took a cigarette from his jacket pocket and lit his first of the day, inhaling deeply as if he were drinking the nicotine through a dirty paper straw, the pale skin of his cheeks clinging to the bones of his face like pastry stretched too far. Gasping, he blurted out the smoke and a rasping cough shook his whole ragged frame. The lungs took note of the burden they were once again to endure and furtively revelled in the sweetness of revenge.

The smoke curled high to the white ceiling, following a path entirely of its own. And Tom closed his eyes once more, wishing earnestly to remain in this precious state forever, this pure, absent blissful state. But he knew he could not. For he would surely be found, found upon the floor in a beautiful daze.

There was no time.

There is no time.

The office was massive. All the walls sloped outwards and the floor crawled up to meet the ceiling. There were no colours—not even shades of grey. And the air was almost too thick even to breathe.

Tom walked over to his desk and draped his jacket carelessly over the back of his swivel chair into which he slumped down and leaned back, surveying the mess before him imperiously like a fallen officer gazing upon the battlefield of defeat. Blank sheets of paper had floated down from the sky overnight. Files had arranged themselves across the back of the desk, rotting paper squeezed from their depths by dirty thick elastic bands. And empty plastic cups lined the tops of these files like ramparts on an old and forlorn cardboard castle. He switched on the computer before him and it squealed in response with a vindictive cry that seared right through him. He leaned forward and mournfully gathered up the plastic cups and crammed them into the bottom drawer of the desk. The computer squealed again, waiting for the entry password. Tom told it to fuck off before typing in the same seven letters.

The morning dragged on interminably. A minute was an hour. An hour was more than a lifetime. Conversations droned on in monotone—unlikely tales of weekend bravado suitably rewarded with contrived interest and canned laughter. Sometimes an argument would punctuate the proceedings, an argument about politics or religion or some other great theme during which feigned outrage would soar like a bird of ignorance, leaving honesty itself to lie wide-eyed and bleeding amidst the empty rhetoric of the apathetic.

It was just another day.

At eleven-thirty, William was crucified.
William was the Eternal Clerk. He loved his job, and had done for the past twenty-seven years. His work was his life, the embodiment of his personality. He left the ambition and the aggression to others. His voice was a single on 33rpm, his skin doughy and his eyes a watery blue. Every evening, he would arrive home and tell his mother of his day in the office, of calculations and phone calls, of photocopying and faxing. She would just sit quietly in her damp armchair and listen to her little boy.
William was a large man.
At the appointed time, William's telephone rang and he answered it in the slow, methodical way in which he did everything, reciting the words like a litany—'William Clapworth, Pensions and Deaths, good morning, how may I help you?' As he listened to the voice on the other end of the line, a red cape was draped heavily about his shoulders. The receiver became cold and unwieldy in his hand, dragging him downwards. At last, with a huge effort, he arose, only to stumble backwards like some grotesque, wounded bear. The room enveloped him in a dense silence as he lumbered over to the small man behind the big desk at the far end of the office.
Lead was licked.
Mmmmmm.
Suddenly, the heavy silence was split by a loud, high-pitched whine, like that of a dog with a broken leg. The small man behind the big desk was letting off steam. The whine became a screech cased in glass, glass that shattered, as it had to, splintering into William's distraught and sagging body.
Tom saw the blood that trickled from William's hands and he saw the blood that seeped from William's feet. And he saw him return to his immaculately ordered desk and stand upon it, his arms stretched wide, his great head falling to his chest, the only true sound being the pitter-patter of blood on the crisp white paper below. Tom saw all of this.
The sun began to burn into the blackness, only to be met by the swift snapping of a Venetian blind in every window. Blind, blind, forever blind.
William was a large man.
William is not large any more.

As for the small man behind the big desk, he will continue to get smaller and smaller, until finally he slips in terror between the cracks of his own heart.

It was just another day.

On returning from lunch at two o'clock, a lunch that consisted of two double whiskies and a bag of chips, Tom found a note taped to his computer monitor. It informed him that he should present himself before the General Manager at three-thirteen precisely. He took the note from the screen, screwed it up and dropped it onto the floor. He then spent the intervening hour compiling a meaningless list of all the files that cluttered his desk. It was at small, ineffectual tasks such as this that his aptitude for endeavour was at its peak.

At ten past three, Tom picked up a withering cigarette from his ashtray and eased it between his dry, cracked lips, ash spraying onto the newly written list. Yellow eyes blinked slowly in the darkness as he walked towards the double doors and there was a low rumble as the floor moved a couple more inches closer to the ceiling.

In the lift, Tom gazed at his now spent cigarette, twisting it aimlessly between his fingers. He then let it fall to the floor and as he dragged his shoe over, he felt the temporary thrill of temporary power.

The General Manager's office was opposite the typing pool and the view through the ever open door was one of which the great man never ceased to tire. They were such lovely young girls. They were so pretty—a blessing from above indeed.

There glowed within the office itself a light so unreal, so entirely manufactured, that you felt upon entering that you had just stepped into a light bulb. All was brightness. The glass-fronted photographs on the walls were positioned in such a way as to reflect one single beam of light, stronger and brighter than all the others, onto the General Manager himself—as if that were really necessary. For not only was he a man who illuminated himself, he had actually created himself. Many years of early mishaps and failures had led him in later, more successful years, to assume a figure of majesty and legend. His life had become one great monologue of the gods. Each waking moment laid claim to his greatest performance. And through it all, he ran his company with as sure and cynical a hand as greed this side of the law would allow.

Charles Grandon—General Manager. This man loved an audience. In fact, he employed one. They worked, of course, or else they would have been cursorily dismissed, but their primary function was to witness the incredible oratory skills of their self-esteemed manager. In his younger days, he had been a truly bizarre member of an Amateur Dramatics company on the south coast and there still resided in his top drawer a brittle clipping from a local newspaper of the day extolling the virtues of his King Lear—these being primarily eagerness and punctuality.

Mr Grandon insisted that his employees call him by his Christian name. No formalities with our Charles, fine, down to earth, honest to goodness chap. He is one of us. Calls a spade a spade and isn't afraid to get someone to use one. That's our Charles.

Now, Mr Grandon had a limp. When the rumour circulated that he had sustained it whilst fighting on the beaches of Normandy, he of course did little to discourage it. The truth was slightly different. If he had been fielding perhaps deep in the covers rather than at silly mid-off in the Scouts versus Scoutmasters annual cricket fixture, his left knee may well, to this day, still be in one piece. From square cover drives are heroes born.

"Ah, come into my light-bulb, lad. Sit down."

"Thanks," said Tom, sitting himself as comfortably as he could on a curiously formed wire chair. "Shall I close the door?" he added, hopefully.

"No, no, lad. Nice to have a view every now and then, that's what I say, eh, eh?"

Charles Grandon chuckled, looking every one of his sixty-five years. "And what's all this 'sir' business?" he continued, "I've not been asked to see Her Majesty yet you know, not yet!"

A large picture of Her Majesty appeared briefly on the far wall and Charles Grandon ran the tip of a bony yellow finger across his thick, grey lips.

"Well, Spanner, back to business. You've been with our little set-up for some time now. Are you happy here? Are you enjoying yourself?"

Tom yelped and nodded like a small puppy and Charles Grandon looked across the room at him through sallow eyes. Tom felt unable to return his gaze and took to picking at a loose fingernail—click, click, click. And that was when he noticed the complete absence of any other sound. The typists had stopped typing. The telephones had stopped ringing. Just click.... click ... click ...

At that moment, the loose fingernail twirled to the floor, twisting in the air like a sycamore leaf before embedding itself in the thick carpet. As this happened, a stage eased itself from the floor, fronted by reverent footlights that were surely the gleaming eyes of the adoring typists. And with a swish and a clank, a spotlight picked out The Great Thespian, centre stage....

"Far be it from me to assume omnipotence
But I have seen much in my life
I have seen Death and I have seen Despair
But also have I known great Pleasure.
I have seen the weak rise up to conquer the wicked
And I have seen the wicked stoop to vanquish the weak.

If I had built this Company with mine own hands
It would have been with these two hands I hold before you now.
But it was not to be
For my role was not to be that of Architect
I was to be the Custodian—the Keeper of the Castle.
And I have pursued my task
I have worked
I have toiled
I have lain to waste, waste
I have relieved this Company of its burdens
But I have remained a Man's man
Men respect me and I in turn respect that respect
I have clung to my roots with such ferocity
I almost wrenched them from the soil

But now I begin to hear news
News that troubles me
News that something is amiss
Something is rotten
In a state
And this news saddens me
For I am a fair Man
But also I am a harsh man!

I employ people
Employees
They work for me
I pay them money
It is simple
It is a chain

A chain that must be preserved
Each link is vital
I am the Guardian of the Chain
And if a link is broken I must act
I must act ...

You, Spanner, have broken that link
Your work, when you produce any, is Untidy
Your relationship with your colleagues is Abysmal
Your attitude is Deplorable
You look Disgraceful
You put filthy cups in your drawers
You drop cigarettes in the lift.

This, Spanner, is your first and final warning
You are to be a new man from tomorrow morning!"

And on this stupendous rhyming couplet, Mr Charles Grandon, thespian, genius and wanker, forfeited the use of his left leg and fell off the stage.

Tom left the General Manager to his light bulb and wandered towards the lift, feeling unwell. He had been in that office for just four minutes. As the lift doors slid open slowly to greet him, a crushed cigarette winked up at him slyly. He gazed at it for just a moment, leaned against the wall and closed his shattered, bloodstained eyes.

That it had come to this—the dreams of youth, the beauty of a child-like hope. Ah, Innocence. That it had come to this.

So get the camera out of here lads and leave this boy to his tears.

Chapter Two

Tom's bedroom ceiling was scribed in circular patterns that rolled above him like tumbleweed. The patterns seemed to alter their shape as he stared up at them from his bed, breaking and re-uniting, incessantly in search of form, pulsing with some vibrant energy. And beneath it all, the young man just lay there, broken.

Wispy talons of curling smoke stung his eyes so he closed them, blindly stubbing out what was left of his cigarette in the full ashtray beside his bed. It was just six-thirty in the evening and the weariness that stalked him constantly had finally caught up with him. He had neither the instinct nor the will to resist. Will and Instinct, those two keystones of youth, had left him, left him stranded. They had slipped away one winter's evening to be replaced not even by bitterness or anger, but by a tedious ennui that had smothered him since. Ennui, that Baudelaire state that pounces upon you in the guise of self-pity and fits you oh so well.

In the years since Little Norman, a routine had enforced itself upon Tom's life but only recently had he succumbed to the force of its domination. It ate away at him like waves of despair on the once golden shoreline of his dreams. Time had fallen into itself and appeared as abstract as surely it is. Minutes, hours, months, years all meant nothing. All that was left for him were sharp, stabbing memories of his childhood, memories that taunted him with their clarity and burned him with their innocence.

Just three years ago. Sixteen. Your sixteenth birthday—opening presents in the dawn light … Little Norman squealing with glee amidst that sea of wrapping paper … listening to that Otis Redding album for the first time … standing by his birthday cake, grinning inanely whilst Mum took serious photographs … smiling from afar as he and Dad watched Mum scamper around the kitchen trying to catch Little Norman who was clinging to that last roll of film … sitting down in the evening to watch a video of the hundred greatest goals ever scored, Little Norman cheering them all until Geoff Hurst cracked in his glorious third whereupon that crazy little fan just keeled over on the rug and fell fast asleep, maybe knowing before everybody else that it would soon all be over…. and that terrifying, overpowering sensation as he had lain in bed that night, that terrible notion that, at sixteen, his childhood was now gone, that he was a child no more….

These images pasted on a wall in the long, dark corridor of his reminiscence, a corridor that grew longer and darker with every dream.

A knock on the bedroom door tried to nudge him back to reality. The visions in his mind merged with one another until they were just one sweeping watercolour wash behind his eyes, devoid of form, replete with emotion. He made not a sound. He did not move. And you would have said he was sleeping the sleep of a child.

Tom's mother knocked once more, waited, and entered quietly. She sighed as she saw her son there on the bed. He worked so hard, too hard. He was such a good boy. She had worried more than he could ever have thought that he would not find a job on leaving school, but he had. And she had been so proud of him. To see him in his suit and tie that first time was seeing him change from a boy to a man overnight. People who used to be good friends, but whom now only spoke to her in embarrassing chance meetings, they would always comment on how much Tom had grown or how handsome he was. And for that brief, sparkling moment, she would be alive again. You would be able to see it in those dark eyes of hers. And she would stand just that little bit taller. Tom, Tom I love you. I need you so much. We both do, your Dad and me.

She stepped softly across the room to the window and pulled the curtains together before retreating and gently closing the door behind her to put Tom's dinner back in the oven. He could have it later, poor love.

Tom heard the click of the door as it closed and he opened his eyes, immediately grateful for the half-light in his room. Everything was bathed in a scarlet glow as the evening sun seeped through the thin red curtains, creating an intangible aura. Beyond the bedroom door, another soap opera trundled along, peddling the tales of everyday folk, but here in the bedroom, there was silence, silence and safety. He could not be harmed in here, not from the outside at least. But thoughts, you know what they are like, those nagging, devious creations that bring doubt and fear. Those thoughts can take you anywhere.

The reds, the blues and the yellows had fallen from Tom's life. The burning righteousness that once had held him in such wonder was gone. It had raged, flickered and then, well, just died. The naive hope of youth had given way to the cruel cynicism of adulthood, leaving the child within the man to shiver in the dank corner of his own petrified soul.

In short, he had lost his spontaneity, his love of life. Each day differed from the last only by what was on the television or a change in the weather. Numbers meant nothing at all. People were just shapes. The world still turned, but inside him, Tom was static, lifeless, without motion. Monday was so far away from Tuesday. He was just living the same day over and over again. He was in a well of his own anguish and was barely able to look above for the light that surely beckoned him. Look at the light Tom. Look at it now, for there are inexplicable things that happen to all of us.

And the light burst into the room, shooting through a gap in the curtains and exploding onto an object that leaned against the foot of the bed. There it stood, glowing, as majestic as if it had been dispatched from heaven that very moment. Just look at it. Caress those curves, feel the power within it, the taut strings, the perfection of that long, slender neck, the splendour of the body. There it stood—the Beautiful Guitar.

We all need a crutch at certain times in our lives, all of us. We all need something or someone to lean on, to help us to stand straight, to help us to walk unbowed in this frantic world of ours. Some of us choose people, some of us whisky. There are all kinds of crutches out there. Tom's was the Beautiful Guitar. It soothed him. It calmed him. It had stayed close to him always, never letting him down or betraying him. So precious was it to him, that it had never left his room. It was the looking glass through which he would lightly glide into his own private wonderland.

So Tom stretched towards the hovering light at the end of his bed and picked up the Beautiful Guitar, holding it close to him. And he began to play. The notes danced slowly around the room, sweating, oozing from the fingers of this tortured young man. They floated in the red air, changing even its colour, slipping in and out of reality, and hanging on forever before wavering and finally easing into the night. Tom's eyes were closed tight as he played and he winced as that most recognizable of pains broke from his big heart. Tears bit into his eyes and he could not hold them from streaking down his face. We had all loved Little Norman.

Sometimes, all we can do is to keep on moving. Our mind and our heart deceive us into thinking that what we seek is out there somewhere, just waiting for us. And to a young man, who feels his life drifting away from him, the dreams of his youth tarnished and rotting, this desire to physically break free, to effect change is as inevitable as it is destructive.

So the following morning, just as the sun was rising, he left.

It was as simple as that.

He just left.

The sun shimmered on the horizon and a slight breeze cooled Tom's neck as he walked to the station. The pavement was cracked and uneven, the road hard and remorseless. Cars sped past on their way to work or returning home from the night shift. The houses that lined the road had stood there forever, observers of every season, every change, every wilful movement. And so many times had they seen a young man with a bag in one hand and a guitar case in the other, walking to the station, an expression of fear and hope on his face, an expression that not even the greatest actor could portray.

It was as if a physical weight had been lifted from his bony shoulders. He felt light, inebriated. Thoughts were coming clear in his mind now, one after the other, unrestrained yet almost tangible. He began to look around him as he walked, looking above the cars and the buses, the smoke and the pressure. And he beheld the sky and the earth.

The pigeons beneath the railway bridge bickered and shrieked, offended by the invasion of their territory by this curious young man. Tom though heard neither shrieking nor bickering, but merely a sweet song of nature. Inside the station itself, there was barely a sound. The noise of the pigeons faded away. And Tom stood there alone, quite, quite still. Then suddenly, two large birds swooped down from high above issuing loud, bellicose cries before escaping into the brightness of the morning.

Bold shafts of light shone through gaps in the station roof, waltzing on the stone floor. Tom was serenity. A calmness of disposition enveloped him like a silken sheet. And for just a moment, as he made his way up the stone steps to the platform, he heard a choir singing.

Tom, I pray for your safety boy.

The next train was due in five minutes, so Tom sat down on a low plastic bench and prepared for a long wait. He was not worried though. Time was not an issue. He was not on his way to work or to meet anyone. There was no deadline. He was responsible to no one; for he was writing his own script now.

Tenuously suspended from the platform roof was a large clock that clacked away the time until, finally, a low drone could be heard. Then with a clattering roar and a painful screech, a train came to a stuttering halt. Tom picked up the Beautiful Guitar in one hand and his bag in the other and boarded. The train ground reluctantly into motion once more, shaking and rattling, coughing and wheezing, down the crooked line to Big Town.

Tom had not been altogether practical with regard to his preparations for leaving. Having made the decision to go, it had all seemed suddenly so simple, so easy. Sitting on the end of his bed, he had placed the Beautiful Guitar gently in its hard, black case and fastened the catches. For the first time since it had come into Tom's life, it would be leaving his room. They were both on their way. He had then searched the various pairs of jeans and trousers that lay strewn across the floor, retrieving any money he could find and cramming it into the back pocket of the jeans he was wearing. At this point, he had paused to think for a moment. But a moment is no time at all. After a glance through the curtains at the rising sun, he had taken his old school bag from the bottom of his wardrobe and thrown in a sweatshirt, a book and what was left of his packet of cigarettes. And then, ever so carefully, he took the small, framed photograph of Little Norman that he kept by his bed and eased it into the folds of the sweatshirt, wrapping the cloth tight around it as if the photograph itself had just been bathed. You would have thought he was handling his own shattered heart, so careful was he.

Tom, if just then you had taken the time to gaze into those wide blue eyes of your baby brother, had allowed the tears to truly fall, let your anger, your guilt and your fear overwhelm you, perhaps then your story could have ended here.

Having sat down on the train, Tom tried to stand the Beautiful Guitar between his knees, but it was too uncomfortable a squeeze, so he placed it in the empty aisle beside him, putting his left arm around it as if it were a loved one. Settling back into the torn seat, he closed his eyes and felt a wonderful peace within.

Barely had a second passed, when he heard the primitive sound of a gnarled knuckle rapping the guitar case.

"You can't leave that there, son. It's blocking the aisle."

Without looking up, Tom shuffled across the seat until he was by the window and hastily moved the case to the seat next to him.

"Not there, son. Not on the seat."

So he was left to stand the case, with much discomfort, between his knees.

"Right. Tickets."

It took Tom a moment to realize that this utterance was actually a request and not some expletive that had up to now eluded him. He cautiously peered out from behind the guitar case.

"There was no-one in the ticket office and the machine was broken so I ..."

"Heard them all son. Where are you going?"

"Big Town."

"Single or Return?"

"Single."

"Single, eh?"

Tom nodded.

"Two-thirty."

"Sorry?"

"Single. Big Town. Two pounds thirty pence. Now don't mess me about, son, not with me, not today."

Tom stood up from his seat and wedged his hand into the back pocket of his jeans, battling against the lurching train and the gaze of the inspector. Eventually, he pulled out a crumpled note, handed it over and slumped back down.

The machine that hung from the inspector's neck whizzed and whirred before producing a small ticket that was proffered to Tom between blackened fingers. He took the ticket shamefully as the inspector counted out the change into his hand with a paucity of speed that indicated the need for a battery change.

The land of hope and glory was unfurled before Tom's eyes, rolling by like a home movie shot through a train window. He had only ever been to Big Town before on lonely drinking sprees and had never looked towards the windows except out of maudlin curiosity when confronted by the reflection of a particularly attractive woman or a singularly strange looking man. Either way, he had never focused any attention on that which streamed by outside. Now, on this beautiful morning, he gazed in awe and let his soul take hold.

Those fields are incredible. If any proof were required of man's complete inferiority to nature, you need only look out of the window of a screaming train as it rips through the countryside—crops standing tall, spiky, course and bristling, soft purple heather spreading out in a deep, rich ocean of decadence. Fields replete with stacks of pure sustenance, bubbling under the surface with life and virility. The hedges and the stone walls, walls put together stone by stone by stone, a contribution of man almost on a par with the natural, ragged perfection that surrounds them. The brick farmhouses stand there cowering, sterile and lonely amidst all that rampant beauty. And the sheep and the cows and the horses that have surely stood in that very place forever as if they too were the products of the very soil beneath them.

There is life.

Man had once lived by the land, nurturing it, working with it, reaping its good and suffering its failures. It had been a vast and wondrous task.

As Tom stared out of the train window, he tried to imagine how the land had once looked, free from all the blemishes of progress that were becoming more and more prevalent the closer the train got to Big Town. With each scene that passed, he tried to consciously remove the steel pylons, the telegraph poles and the golf courses. He discarded the aircraft that flew so slowly overhead, the black smoke that billowed from all around and those strange, squat buildings with the barbed wire and 'keep out' signs.

And there before him lay a sight profound. Stretches of unbroken forest, dark and green, strolling majestically into the distance; people in the field, writhing with the earth until sweat stung their eyes; and sheaths of corn in giant, endless rows, marching in time to empty stomachs and blistered skin.

Tom was sure that man had once sought merely to live—to eat, to live, to survive. Just to live. He had sought not to conquer nature but to exist with it, respecting it, fearing it even. But little by little, this basic simplicity had been stripped away to reveal burns and scars and scorched hearts. One insistent word had precipitated the fall to enrichment—'more'. This unbridled yearning had ensured that with each improvement in productivity, in economic management and in streamlined efficiency, so there would be born upon this earth a new generation of the deprived.

So this young man's agrarian vision was infiltrated by dirty grey buildings with jagged windows and factories left to rot beside rivers and streams that had themselves turned green and black with the excrement of failure. Foliage crawled over the rusty corrugated roofs, forcing its way into the bleak interior. Rows of houses like rabbit hutches filled the train window, each back garden separated from the other by a rickety wooden fence to which was attached what seemed to be one continuous washing line from which damp clothes hung limply. No sun ever dried these clothes, not even on the hottest of days. That task was left to the rattling wind that tormented these dwellings day and night. Each garden contained more stone than grass, more shadow than light.

And the train roared on.

Tom became shocked by the squalor and the coldness of all he saw as he approached Big Town. He as much as passed judgement on the people, with one fleeting thought condemning them, for he had to protect himself. But in that instant, he learned his first lesson. For as the train edged into the final tunnel on its approach to the station, it was his own face that he saw reflected in the black window, his own face. And in that face fluttered an expression of aloofness and subdued contempt. These were the subconscious feelings in the man whose pale face looked back at him. And as the train came out of the tunnel and eased into the station, Tom felt ashamed. The feeling hit him in the stomach and almost wrenched it out. Shame, shame is as good a place to start as any. Try it some time.

So the train hissed and shook, stuttering to a stop, having delivered Tom Spanner to Big Town.

Tom's father sat at the kitchen table, both hands around a mug of coffee that he had no intention of drinking. The thin, aromatic steam drifted into the air and produced moist droplets on the distraught face that gazed into it. How could he tell her? How could he tell his wife that their son was gone?

There had been no note, no goodbye. Tom's clock radio had gone off at the usual time and half an hour later, the fabulous DJ was still spewing out fabulous details of another fabulous competition. Tom would be late for work. His father had gone into wake him but he had not been there. Gone. And that was when he had noticed it. The guitar was missing too. No guitar. No Tom. The guitar never left the room. Tom always turned the clock radio off. He had intentionally tuned it to a station he despised in order to ensure he didn't lay in bed listening to it. Perhaps he had just gone out for the day, had taken the day off, had gone to meet some friends? There was something in the air though, a finality, a strange emptiness. The father and the son were a part of each other, yet neither really knew it, not yet. You or I may have jumped to a different conclusion, but the father knew. It felt somehow inevitable. And that was it. Gone—a terrible, empty word.

So here he sits, waiting for his wife to come downstairs and ask him why he has been crying.

"Have you seen this, love?" came a voice from the hallway. "It's a bill from the electric people. I thought we had sorted that one out. We did that one didn't we?"

Tom's mother shuffles into the kitchen in her long pink dressing gown and the fluffy pig-shaped slippers her son had bought her last year for her birthday. She is holding a brown envelope lightly in her hand.

"We did, didn't we?" she asks again.

"Did what?" replies her husband, his voice barely audible.

"Pay it, the electric"

He looks up at her now and sees how strong she looks yet he knows she is forever on the verge of breaking apart. And she sees his raw cheeks and the way his jaw just seems to hang so loose. And she is scared.

"George, what is it, what's happened?" Her words are quick, urgent. Her heart is thumping, thumping, punctuating the words.

There is a pause, a terrible pause that lingers in the air.

"George?"

"I think Tom's gone."

Freeze Frame.

Bang.

George moves his arm to reach for his wife but he is moving now in slow motion. The mug of coffee by his elbow rolls onto the linoleum floor with a clonk that rings out deep and solid like a church bell. And this is the cue that sets his wife moving. She turns and runs upstairs with a heartbreaking awkwardness, her slippers dragging her down, sticking to the stairs as if there were glue upon them.

And, arriving in the bedroom, it is not just the absence of the guitar that hits her, but the missing photograph of Little Norman—those two cornerstones of her son's soul both gone. She screams a loud, guttural scream that causes her husband to physically flinch downstairs in the kitchen where he sits, so terrified.

They had both gone through too much, what with Little Norman, and now this. Yet, deep in their hearts somewhere, there had always been lurking the knowledge that Tom would one day leave them too. And that was what really hurt. On this evidence alone, evidence based purely on love and instinct and despair, they had both arrived at the same conclusion, the right conclusion. Their son, Tom, was indeed gone.

So as the coffee drip, drip, drips onto the faded tiles of the kitchen floor, George Spanner prays for the first time in his life. He just closes his eyes and prays. Sometimes it's all you can do.

And far, far away, somewhere across the other side of Big Town, a young girl weeps beneath the sweating body of her father.

Chapter Three

So here we are on the streets of Big Town, where people scurry about like ants searching for scraps on a rotting corpse, though it be the corpse of a king. They know where to go and they know where not to go. This is their town and these are their secrets.

Buildings looked down upon Tom as he passed them, his eyes big and wide. There were massive hotels fronted by nothing but glass, a doorman outside each one, stately and demure, benign acquiescence in every twitch. There were huge shops that glowed and buzzed, music pouring from them, squeezing people in and squeezing them out again. But on this day, the illuminations of the shops were as nothing compared to the sun. They were but pale imitations. For the heat of that sun, especially in Big Town, could burn the very streets upon which you walked.

Some of the structures in Big Town were so elegant, so impressive, that Tom would just stand before them and gaze up at the stone carvings around the windows, those elaborate, tortuous designs, and he would touch that dusty façade as if some of its splendour may pass into him. Then he would look up further still only to see the top half of the building encased in steel restraints, gripped fast in silent anguish by the iron claws of modernity. Was it the eradication of history or the preservation of it? Tom wasn't sure. Of one thing, though, he was certain—he would not be contained or held or restricted. He was free now.

The people in the street along which Tom walked kept their heads bowed, as if by instinct. It was unwise to catch the gaze of another and it seemed so much easier to make your way looking down rather than ahead. They were a people of generations, of tribes; a constitution of disparate parts that combined to comprise the inhabitants of Big Town. Each was alien to the other. It was in their attire, their gait, their fear and their anger.

Big Town had always been a sombre town and Tom saw it now, in the character of the people that he passed and in the buildings about him. It was a desperate town, a sinister town, a town that harboured all the excesses of the human from.

Be careful, boy.

Some of the people looked quickly at Tom with a wary eye as he approached them and they stepped just a pace wider than was really necessary in order to get by him. And they would glance back furtively over their shoulders at him when they were a safe enough distance away.

Tom began to feel a growing sense of uncertainty as he walked on. Big Town was a strange place and he was a stranger. He felt eyes upon him from every direction. His first thought was of blood. Maybe he had bit his lip. Perhaps his nose had started bleeding. He knew how blood disturbed people.

There had been a time when he was younger when he had taken to reading as he walked, on his way to the pub or to the park. It had been his way of denying the world. Books were real to him; they were his guides, his way of rationalizing his feelings. It had been whilst deep in a book on Lenin that he had walked almost directly into a stone pillar. He had entered the pub some moments later to have people stare at him, fear upon their faces. And on checking, there had been blood oozing down the side of his head. He felt now, walking through Big Town as if he had just stepped into that same pub again.

So Tom put down his bag and felt his face with his fingers. No blood. He then turned and looked at his reflection in the tinted window of the shop beside him. And at once he saw a dangerous man, a man with dark, straggly hair, unshaven face, oversized denim shirt that hung loose to the knees of his torn and faded jeans and a guitar by his side. The window could not even begin to reproduce the aura of yearning and desire that emanated from this young man—that indefinable presence of a man in search of his life.

The image in the window was the image of himself that Tom had always looked for. All those nights panicking in front of the mirror before going out on one more drunken evening, trying in vain for that smart unkempt look. Being ready too early and pacing up and down in his room, waiting for the poor bastard that had to drive that night. Ah, all that contrivance. All that wasted energy. And now, here he was, gazing into a window in Big Town, gazing at the man he truly believed he was, proud and scared and honest. He was living from within now.

Throughout his life, Tom had been on the edge of things. He had been the perpetual substitute, the twelfth man, the could-do-better, the must-try-harder. He had been the boy at school whose nickname was so frequently and indiscriminately used that when his name was called each morning in the register, his classmates would scour the room for the newcomer. And he had accepted all this as being just the way his life was. There are some who shine and achieve and there are those who just get by. And there are others within whom there dwells a steady, sullen rage. With each cold Saturday morning on the touchline, with each fresh humiliation, so grew Tom's rage, though never had it overwhelmed him. Still, there it dwelt. There it simmered.

Of all things, Tom Spanner was no rebel. He did not possess that paradoxical coldness of heart so inherent in the rebel. He considered the feelings of others even to the detriment of himself sometimes. Any token act of revolt was commonly tempered by multiple acts of meek abeyance. The cause of the rebel may be just, but someone somewhere must suffer the pain of the rebel's fury.

So, looking in the window at the man before him, Tom saw neither a confused man nor a frightened man. He saw a righteous man, a man of bounteous humility and goodness, kind and forgiving. He was tranquil and at peace. It was as if he had finally come to rest.

"From now on," he said to himself, "I will be a good man."

The angels sang.

Flowers bloomed.

And you know now that this boy is surely heading for a fall.

The sweat, the fumes and the clatter of machinery played like an orchestra of the age, crashing and discordant. Big Town was just a vast piece of tragic music, awesome, incomprehensible. The notes, the instruments and the tunes are ours and ours alone.

So as the flutes and the clarinets soothed the harsh violins, the resonant hum of nature made its mellow entrance. It was a silent explosion, an effusion of greenery. Tall conifers lined a gravel path, their wiry frames resplendent in such verdant finery. The path opened up into a circular gravel clearing that was ringed by wooden benches and punctuated at intervals by bright yellow litterbins that looked truly alien in so luscious an arena.

The birds twittered and warbled as Tom walked slowly across the gravel, feeling it crunching satisfyingly beneath his feet, to one of the vacant benches. It was two o'clock in the afternoon. He had been walking for six hours—yet he was still just a forty-five minute train journey from home. He sat down on the bench, Beautiful Guitar leaning against him, and drifted into sleep with only the imperious sun to watch over him.

As Tom slept, small birds fluttered down to spy upon this newcomer, their sweet chattering ranging from the melancholic to the exultant. Each sound emanating from each tiny beak was entirely of its own. At one stage, a whole throng of birds gathered on the gravel in front of him, babbling and chirruping, strutting and dancing. It would not have been at all surprising if they had laid him on the ground and secured this sleeping giant with ropes. Eventually, they dispersed in threes and fours emitting salutary chirps and strangled farewells as they floated back up to the clouds.

When Tom finally awoke, he was no longer alone on the bench, though all the other benches remained vacant. Beside him was a man. The man smiled. He wore a dark pinstriped suit that was crumpled and marked and his shoes were drab and dirty. His hair was thin on his head, possessing a translucent quality, yet it did not age him. Pale blue eyes seemingly forever on the verge of tears gazed at Tom above cheekbones that could at any moment have broken through the pallid skin of his face.

Tom did not meet the man's gaze. In truth, he was still not fully awake. He was in a strange place and felt an aura that was not at all familiar. It was so quiet and somehow delicate and forlorn. As these thoughts eased in and out of Tom's mind, he felt a need to break away for a moment. He recalled a hamburger van just outside the entrance to this sanctuary, a simple burger van. Familiarity. Normality. So he got up and made his way towards it, his legs betraying him a little with their stiffness. He was hungry anyway.

The hamburger squirmed within the soggy bun and the onions slithered free onto Tom's hand only to scamper clean up his sleeve. Eating with speed, the burger was gone before he arrived back at the bench. Then he felt a sudden, sickening fear—the Beautiful Guitar. But there it was, on the gravel, leaning against the bench. He picked it up and sat down, placing it between his knees. It was awkward, uncomfortable. But it was his. Remember Humility, Tom—keep hold of your visions, mate.

And the man beside him looked on.

"You play?" asked the man, softly, his voice kind and reassuring, almost childlike in its sense of wonder.

Tom looked across at him and looked away again.

"It's a fine thing to play an instrument," continued the man in that same melodious, engaging voice, "a fine thing. A gift, I'm sure."

The man mused for a while, intent, thoughtful. It was as if he were listening to the most wonderful piece of music right there, right then.

Tom's eyes turned briefly to the stranger. He was of an indeterminate age. Tom couldn't decide how he felt about him. And as he turned away again, the man suddenly spun around as far as he could whilst remaining on the bench and leaned over to Tom offering his hand.

"Oh, I'm so sorry," said the man, "how rude of me! My name is Michael. It is a pleasure to meet you. Ah, to expect you to converse with me with such a lack of introduction. Well, so far have I sunk perhaps."

Tom did not turn towards Michael, though he had flinched with the sudden movement. He just stared at the ground ahead of him.

"I'm Tom," he murmured.

Michael mirrored Tom's posture and sat too leaning slightly forward, elbows resting on thighs. Tom was his friend. No question. No doubt about it.

"Good, good," he said softly, smiling with a sad affection.

There was a moment of almost complete silence in this natural haven that even the birds observed. The only sound was of Big Town imploding across the horizon. And there were the two men, two strangers, side by side on a park bench, both with more in common than either could have imagined.

At last, Michael sat up and spoke, his voice mellow and smooth. It could soothe you with a mere syllable.

"May I see it, Tom, your instrument? It's just that things of beauty do fascinate me."

Tom was grateful for the intrusion into his thoughts—the Beautiful Guitar. His coolness melted a little. Some control had been passed back to him. The ethereal ground upon which he wavered became more solid now. So, slowly, he laid the Beautiful Guitar across his lap and unsnapped the catches of the hard case. He lifted the lid delicately, as if unveiling a lost treasure.

"My, my," said Michael with due reverence, "well, well." He looked at the Beautiful Guitar closely along its entire length, studying it with those pale blue eyes, barely breathing. "Do you mind, do you mind if I hold it?" he asked. "Of course, I'd understand if you felt unable to allow me to. It is such a wonderful instrument."

Tom felt all the pride of a father with a newborn child.

"All right," he replied, looking now at Michael.

Tom passed the Beautiful Guitar to Michael who held it gently with hands soft and white, fingers thin and light. "Exquisite," he murmured to himself, "quite exquisite." After a few moments of staring into the guitar, he handed it back to Tom who put it back in the hard black case and returned it to its former position.

The Beautiful Guitar was Tom's chink of light. Michael saw that immediately.

"Well, Tom, what do you do from day to day, I mean, in this life of ours?"

Tom did not reply immediately. He was a little thrown by the question. But Michael allowed him time, for they had plenty of time. He just sat there in the sun waiting for the young man to answer.

"I'm a musician," replied Tom, eventually, looking into the distance, trance-like, heart weary and mind trying to make sense of so many things.

Michael looked at the boy, studying his frame, getting a feel for him.

"Why, a musician. That's wonderful. A musician. A star."

He beamed at Tom, who suspected he was being ridiculed. But there was no ridicule, nothing but wonder and honesty. Tom did not know at that time that Michael was incapable of any form of derision. There were a lot of things of which Michael was capable. But Tom did not know that then.

"I think," said Michael, grasping Tom's left hand with both of his own, "I think that you and I are going to get along just fine, just fine."

Tom withdrew his hand slowly but was unable to smile. The rigors of this his first day of freedom, as he perceived it, had left him overwhelmed and exhausted. So he rested on and off throughout the remainder of the afternoon, floating in and out of reality in this garden of Gethsemane.

The sun gazed down in wonder upon the man and the boy, now and then peering closer. They seemed so incongruous—the young one with the countenance of an old and battered soul, the elder serene and youthful.

Whilst his young friend slept—and he was so very young—Michael's mind was elsewhere, in another place, another time. So much had happened in his life and time was surely drifting from him now. He was just waiting, waiting for the next stage. He had given up trying to rationalize why all these things had happened to him. But it was no good. At least he would be found in a place of calm and beauty. That thought alone sustained him for the present.

Michael tried not to dwell on past events, or for that matter, on the present, for he existed not upon our earth but deep within his own mind. He warmed his soul on the burning fires of his own innate faith. His journey was inwards, not outwards, inwards to the eternal world. Only seldom had he ventured beyond the walls of his own design and on each occasion he had returned butchered, helpless. All that was left for him now was this sanctuary of his where he knew he must remain. He had no choice. Not this time.

So he sat there on the bench as Tom slept. He let the glorious flowers and the towering trees wash over him. He watched tiny insects scour the blooms, gathering what they could from the most delicate of benefactors. The air was as clear as it was ever going to be and in a few short hours, the pale moon would be rising up to greet with solemnity the smouldering sun.

"Ah, awake at last," said Michael as his young friend rustled into life.

It took Tom a moment to adjust. He had expected Michael to be gone when he awoke.

"What's the time?" he asked, drowsily.

"Around six I think, Tom, although I couldn't really be sure."
Tom nodded and leaned back, yawning.
"Still on the tired side?" inquired Michael smiling kindly.
"I'll be all right."
And thus each man leaned forward simultaneously. There was a profound silence as their bodies, slightly hunched but perfectly still, shook within.

The sky is a perfect blue. The flowers, the grass and the trees have leapt straight from Vincent Van Gogh's soul.
Man is so small, so slight.
Man is surely the thorn upon the rose.

The afternoon had played tricks with Tom's mind. During his sleep, a frightening vagueness of purpose had crept up on him, blurring his ideals, muddying the clear waters of his optimism. And he couldn't shake it off. The sun and the hamburger had combined to add a feeling of nausea to his already unsettled state. As he sat there on the bench he felt fear and loneliness. He also felt a little foolish, but most of all, he felt alone, terribly alone.

Tom's loneliness was compounded by an empty sensation within him, a dense void, and a heavy, indefinable pain that stung him with images of earlier times. He was in bed, wrapped in cold blankets on a winter's evening, twelve years old, his homework still to be done and school again tomorrow. His mother had kissed him goodnight and walked to the door to turn off the light, leaving him in darkness and silence. And as she had opened the door to leave, he had closed his eyes, praying so hard that she would turn back and just hold him for a while. 'Mum, Mum just hold me please. I'm scared and confused. And I know everything will be all right if you just hold me.' That was a long time ago now, but those feelings cruelly returned to him now. He just wanted to be held.

Michael was perceptive. He could see into your soul. For it was the very plane upon which he himself lived.

"Well, I'd best be off now," said Michael, gathering his energy. "I'm going to the library. Bit of a read, you know, before they close. The papers, that sort of thing."

Michael rose from the bench. He looked down upon the head of the young boy and put his hand upon his shoulder, squeezing it gently, massaging it almost.

"You can come too, Tom," he said softly. "If you want to."

Tom offered no audible reply. He just stood up as if he were being lifted, guided. And he could see himself from above, guitar in hand. For this crucial moment, every movement was scripted, written in parenthesis. There was nothing for him to do but to watch and let it all happen—to watch and to wonder at the heavy beating of his own heart.

The evening sun began to quail beneath the smoke and the fumes of Big Town. The visible cloud of pollution filtered the falling rays of sunlight until they were weak and dim, barely able to light the way of the man and the boy who wandered out of the park onto the ragged streets upon which they both were strangers.

The library was divided into two floors, the lower for borrowing and browsing, the upper for study and research. Books lined the walls opposite the entrance and continued down both sides of the ground floor. Michael led Tom to a rising stairway in the centre and they both ascended to the haven of learning.

The door to the upper floor study area was heavy and stiff and Tom needed all his strength to hold it open whilst Michael slipped through, and just avoided the snapping jaws himself as the door slammed shut behind him.

Indignant eyes were raised.

There were twenty-four tables across the floor, aligned in uniform rows. Huge wooden bookcases rested against every wall and a small reception area, just in front of the door through which Tom and Michael had just entered, abounded with leaflets, posters and advertisements for various local community groups and activities.

Students, both mature and immature, occupied all but one of the desks, some there to study, others for more spurious reasons. The tables had been designed to comfortably accommodate four people—two either side of a low partition. But the ugly instinct of the learned had been at work. Open books and bags lay strewn across the desks, taking up space, ensuring that the lone occupant of each desk remained undisturbed by intruders, undefiled. The territory had been marked.

There is so much to learn.

There is so little that can be taught.

Silence returned to the library, though the slamming door could still be heard reverberating dully against every wall. And those eyes that stared at Tom and Michael on the moment of their arrival and continued to stare at them as they stood before the reception area, those eyes were so cold.

The librarian appeared from below the counter like some slow motion jack-in-a-box, wavering slightly as he gained his full height. He was a tall, thin man wearing a beige suit that had perhaps been designed for somebody slightly shorter. He had large, sad eyes and a voice that sounded like wood cracking.

"How may I help you?" he asked.

"I would like to see the newspapers, please," replied Michael.

After a suitably studious look at the two men before him, the librarian turned and walked slowly to the rear of the cramped booth. He came back after some moments with a stack of newspapers, his sandals slapping on the tile floor and his head bobbing up and down in sympathy with the agonizing oratorio of his life.

"Well, Tom," said Michael as they sat down opposite each other at the vacant table, "what do you fancy?"

He lined the newspapers up for Tom, presenting them to him as if they were great sketches.

Tom shrugged his shoulders. He didn't care. He was just glad to be around people. He was glad of the light and of the normality of the place. He took a newspaper anyway and began to flick through it with little interest.

Michael gathered the rest of the newspapers together and arranged them neatly on top of each other on his side of the table, taking care not to take up too much room. He then reached into a canvas bag, his only accoutrement, and took out a small notepad and pencil. After a moments thought, he rose, scanned the bookcase behind him and returned to his seat with a small hardback book. A final flash of sunlight reflected off the book's laminated cover and dazzled Tom's eyes. He was thus provoked into watching Michael.

Arriving at the page in the first newspaper with the crossword on it, Michael used the pencil and the spine of the hardback book to transcribe the crossword grid onto a clear page in the notepad. Once the grid was complete, he flipped over to another clear page, took the next newspaper, found the crossword and repeated the process. It was only after Michael had drawn the third grid that Tom noticed no attempt had been made to either number the squares or copy out the clues. It was just the columns and rows of black and white that seemed to matter, particularly those black squares that were shaded in with such force.

Tom had only once been to a library before of his own volition. He had skulked amongst the shelves during school hours but his first willing foray had been when he was sixteen years old.

Between the ages of thirteen and seventeen, he had fallen in love so many times. He had loved each girl more than the last, and each in turn had repaid him by being more and more oblivious to his undying affection. In his mind, he had gone through all the stages of love, from initial infatuation to eventual disenchantment. In his mind, he had experienced warmth, loss, longing and desire. In reality, he had barely spoken to any of these girls. He had just made them too big, too special even to approach. They had become angels in his eyes—and why not?

Ah, what a woman can do to a man.

Rebecca had been Tom's last and fondest love, preceded in this most tortuous of adolescence, by Paula, Natalie, Gaynor, Juliet, Ruth, Susan and Charlotte. But they had been as nothing compared to Rebecca. They had been the prelude, she the finale.

He had loved Rebecca for her pure and natural ways, her innocence and her charm. She had possessed none of the petty affectation of her classmates. She was gentle and kind.

Tom had followed her home once, from a distance, in the cold rain. He had followed her through the park and out onto the street where she lived, waiting there until she had gone into her house. He had resisted the temptation to do it again, but to have tasted just a part of her life, to have walked for just a moment where she had walked, seen what she saw every day, had been beautiful to him.

Rebecca had worked in a shop on Saturdays that sold records, tapes and videos and Tom had become a frequent, if furtive, visitor. He would roam the aisles in search of her and, having located her, would gaze at her from behind the records. The snapping of that price gun in her hand mesmerized him. Bang. Bang. Bang...

But one day, he had been unmasked for the lovelorn fool he was. That fateful day, he had been unable to find Rebecca in her usual place on the ground floor, so he had made his way cautiously up the stairs to the first floor where the videos were displayed and sold. On arriving at the first floor, he had been struck by how much quieter and open it was. He had been in the process of finding cover behind a display of videos when he saw her, not five yards away, talking to a customer.

To his eternal credit, he had not panicked, and to his huge relief, he had been sure she had not seen him. But what was that, footsteps coming closer and closer? Clack … Clack … Clack … beautiful perfume wafting nearer and nearer. He had known instantly that it was her. No one clacked like she did. Thinking frantically, he had decided on the casual approach. Be cool. Be the tall, dark stranger in town.

So, there he had stood, legs wide, feet firmly on the ground, hands clasped manfully behind his back—at ease, sir. And as Rebecca had come around the corner to say hello to that sweet boy in her class that she was so secretly in love with, there he was. He was cool. He was sharp. And he was gazing in abject horror at row upon row of naked women sprawled across the covers of the pornographic videos before him, all huge breasts and red lips …

It had been that afternoon that Tom had felt the need to visit the public library. He had needed a quiet place to think. For a re-appraisal of strategy had seemed in order.

And now, here he was just a few years later, leaving a library in Big Town, stepping into the fading light with a man he didn't know, on his way to who knows where.

The little girl is no longer weeping beneath the sweating body of her father. Michael is in Big Town now.

Chapter Four

Two days later, in a large house in the country, a bronze letterbox snapped shut. Christine was drinking a cup of tea in the study when she heard the noise. Although she had been waiting on that sound and reacting to it every day for the last week, it still startled her each time. She was a tall woman with long, dark wavy hair that had not yet given way to the grey strands of age. Her face was slightly angular, though softened by her brown eyes. Those very eyes, usually so bright, were now tired and sore, her face sallow and weary. The natural strength and purpose that had always pervaded her was daily faltering.

The study was a room in which she had always been reluctant to spend time. Her husband insisted on calling it a study—as far as he insisted upon anything—but what he actually studied in there, she was never sure. There were no books, no writing equipment, no journals, computers or any other signs of learned endeavour, just a large wooden desk with a telephone on it set facing the patio doors and the garden.

For the last three days, Christine had woken early, sat in the leather chair behind the desk and gazed into the garden as the sun lit up the dew like tiny torches and the birds heralded the morning. On hearing the crack of the letterbox, she put her cup and saucer on the desk and went out into the hall, trying to suppress the curious mixture of fear and resignation that was gradually becoming so much a part of her. She bent down. Another bill, another circular. Please let there be something from him.

On the doormat was a small, white envelope, so small in fact that the postmark had almost entirely obliterated the address. Recognizing the handwriting on the front, Christine tore it open hurriedly. Then just for a moment, time stood still as a thin piece of paper slipped out, swaying from side to side, floating to the floor beneath some invisible parachute. She crouched down and picked it up and holding the small piece of paper between thumb and forefinger, she gazed at the words that been written so precisely between the black squares.

She felt her knees crack as she rose and she winced a little. She took the piece of paper into the study and, brushing the cup and saucer inadvertently as she sat behind the desk, picked up the telephone.

"Ron, it's Chris. Can you come over?"

"Is he back?"

"No, no he's not back. I've just received a note from him through the post. Can you come round? I know it's early."

"I'll be as quick as I can."

Ron was a stocky, muscular man with sturdy legs and a thick, strong neck. He was fifty-five years old and had been married to his wife, Diane, for seventeen years. He was a man of order and a man of reason. And thus he lived his life. Even now, following the early morning call from his close friend, he dressed slowly, meticulously. He was in no hurry. Time was his to command. Patience. Composure. At last, combing some oil through his already lank hair, and applying after-shave as if he were washing his face with it, he stepped into the day.

"What do you think?" asked Christine as she and Ron sat beside one another on the sofa in the beautifully ornate lounge.

"At least we know he's all right," replied Ron. "It could have been worse." As he had walked the short distance to Christine's house, he had imagined perhaps a more tragic message.

"Who's to say it's not going to get worse? That, that bastard has kept me waiting here day after day, just waiting. I don't know where he is, what he's doing. He hasn't even phoned. And when he does deign to get in touch, he can't even bloody do that normally." Christine paused, angry, tearful. "He doesn't even say when he's coming back," she added, almost to herself. She lit another cigarette and smoked in agitation. "I thought I knew him," she said softly, staring straight ahead now, the pain of the last few days clambering over her crumbling defences. She shook a little and turned towards Ron, her face that of a child, a child that has been betrayed for the very first time. "I thought I bloody knew him."

Ron continued to look at her face before averting his eyes.

Christine was thinking now of the moment she realized he had gone. That evening three days ago when he didn't come home from work, she had waited up until gone midnight in sullen anger, before falling asleep on the settee where she now sat with Ron. And she had awoken with spiteful anticipation, ready to curse him for his lack of responsibility and his complete lack of awareness of how a married man with a child should conduct himself. But he had not been there at all. So all that rage, that violent energy, was left to churn within her where now it just ached and throbbed. Two days had passed then two nights, then another and another. It was a gradual realization, a feeling of deep fear. A part of her world was gone. And this fear, this foreboding gripped her from the depths of her stomach straight through to her heart. It was debilitating and crushing. And she had become angry, irritable, not consistently but at times when he should have been there—when she was doing a puzzle in one of her magazines and she couldn't ask him the answer or when Laura wanted to play one of those games he had made up for her. Or when she got out too many plates for dinner. Or when she awoke in the night so cold even at the peak of summer. At these times, she had been acutely, unbearably aware of his absence. His presence had almost seemed insignificant, but his absence left a huge gap. She was angry both with him and with herself. But it was anger that could not find expression. For he had always been that subservient well of tranquillity into which she would discharge her rage.

"It's just his way, Chris," said Ron, putting a hand on her shoulder.

"Don't touch me!" she replied sharply.

Ron withdrew, stung, sitting stiffly once more.

There was a silence, a dark, heavy silence.

Footsteps clumped along the pavement outside, quietly at first, then more loudly, before fading into the air. They were accompanied by the rhythm of Christine's tattered heart, beating faster as the steps grew louder and just throbbing as they drifted away. The waiting was destroying her in as much as she was soon going to have to look at herself, apportion blame perhaps. She did not know how much she had needed him until he was gone. She had not known how much he had meant to her until he wasn't there at all. These thoughts settled in her mind now like vagabonds, tormenting her with their sense and clarity.

"Ron," she said finally, "you've known him longer than I have. What is he doing? Why is he doing this to me?"

Ron waited before replying, deliberating over his response.

"I would say we just have to be patient, Chris. You know how he is, his ways. And you know how much he loves you. He needs you, Chris. He'll be back soon. We just have to be patient."

Christine looked deep into Ron's face. He was always so sure, so dependable, and so different to her husband. She looked down at her slippers, staring as if awaiting advice from them. And then a thought crashed into her mind, blazing, urgent. She looked at Ron, fear all over her. But Ron met her gaze with calmness and assurance. He had been there. He had experienced that intense fear; for a thought just as explosive, though very different in content, had occurred to him the day he found out Michael had gone. Guilt shows no compassion.

"Chris, he loves you. And he loves Laura."

There, there.

As he was walking back home, Ron felt he had done enough to reassure Christine, though he was having difficulty convincing himself that all would turn out well. Through all the years he had known Michael, he had never quite been able to work him out, had never really been able to say 'yes, this, this and this are what Michael is made up of and this is what he is all about'. There were problems posed by Michael's character to which answers appeared wilfully elusive. Ron found him at times impossible to comprehend. Perhaps that was part of what sustained their apparently incongruous relationship. He didn't really know Michael. He just knew more about him that was all. He had helped to steer him through the cruelty of children. He had guided him, looked out for him. And now he was gone.

Michael's disappearance was just one issue on Ron's mind though, as he opened the door to his house. There were different scenarios evolving in his head, each with their own consequence. So he had to do what he did best. And that was to look after himself.

Diane was in the kitchen when her husband came in, listening to the radio and frying some eggs. The music that permeated the smell of the sizzling breakfast could have been Bach or Mozart or frankly anybody as far as Ron was concerned. It all sounded the same to him. He was strictly a Sinatra man. Diane loved all sorts of classical and other types of music and secretly appreciated the interest her husband tried to show in it. He would always have a guess as to the composer in a manner that suggested he already knew and was in fact testing her. That was so like him. He couldn't just ask.

"Hello, love," she said.

"Hello, dear," replied Ron, sitting down at the table, thoughtful and subdued. After a moment, he spoke.

"Haydn?"

"No, love. Humperdink."

"Ah, Humperdink."

Ron closed his eyes for a second.

"Christine rang," he said, his eyes still closed. "That's where I've been. She needed me to talk to her."

"Has she heard from Michael?" asked Diane, looking up from her gently fizzing eggs just as Ron opened his eyes.

"He sent her a note."

"What did it say?"

"Nothing really."

"Well, at least he's had the heart to finally get in touch. If I were Christine, I'd be going out of my mind by now. How is she?"

"She'll be fine. Everything will be fine."

"Has she phoned the police yet? She told me yesterday she would if he wasn't back soon."

"No, we discussed that. He'll be back soon."

Aware now that the conversation was to come to an end, Diane nudged the eggs from the frying pan onto her husband's plate to join the sausages, tomatoes, beans and toast, and began tidying the kitchen.

Ron drank his tea and ate his breakfast, deep in thought. An unpleasant feeling was building up within him, a nasty, acidic taste that crept into his throat. Maybe it was the whole situation that he could foresee developing. Maybe it was just the eggs. He could see everything moving too fast. He had become so accustomed to the easy, predictable swing of his life that he was having difficulty accommodating the sharps and the flats that were being injected into the music of his middle years.

He was a man who bled confidence. He was seen as loyal and trusted. Friends confided in him knowing they were safe to do so. He was a man for whom people believed temptation was anathema. Surely it would not dare even to approach his door. He was surely not a man to fall victim to its seductive tones. But Ron knew more than most, and at this time in particular, that temptation succumbed to in a life of hard conformity is liable to take advantage of its oh so privileged position.

"Have you finished, love?" asked Diane as her husband examined his empty teacup.

Ron looked up at her and smiled as well as he was able. She came around to his side of the table and picked up the cup and saucer and his plate.

"Don't worry, love," she said to him. "He'll come back and Christine will be happy, Laura will be happy and it will be like it all never happened."

But Ron knew that things could not be the same again. Things had got out of hand. It was time to take control again.

"Tom," said Michael, "do you ever think about the stars?"

Tom had just woken from a lengthy, faltering sleep and weariness still clung to him like irritating cobwebs. He had been away for three days now and it seemed that all he had done was walk, sleep and listen to Michael talk. His energy was leaving him, his dreams becoming cloudy, the brightness of his vision and purpose losing its clarity beneath hunger and damp nights.

"What do you mean?" he managed to respond.

"Don't they amaze you, Tom?"

"Why should they?"

"Do you know how many there are?" continued Michael.

"How am I supposed to know that?"

"Have a guess. Go on. Just guess."

"I don't want to have a fucking guess, all right?"

The silence that followed berated Tom. The evening was becoming colder. He shivered.

"Thousands?" he muttered, more as an act of atonement than of genuine interest.

Michael, temporarily quelled, sprung back into life.

"Millions," he responded, proudly, "billions even." It was as if he had fashioned each one of them himself, such was his sense of wonder. "Billions and billions."

Tom stared mournfully upwards into the black sky before curling himself up again to try and retain some warmth. He felt so old as he lay there.

"I sometimes think about the stars, Tom. I like to lay back and look at the sky as if I am on some great hill in the country, just lay back and look as far into the sky as I can. I look at the stars, day and night. Just because we can't see them so easily during the day, it doesn't mean they're not there. They're just a little harder to find."

Michael's melodic voice continued on like a gentle stream as he lay back on the cold ground.

"You know, Tom, some stars are bigger than the earth, much bigger and they move terrifically fast, so fast that we can't even see them moving. That's how they shine. It's because they're actually moving, moving and glowing like a huge fairground ride. Ah, Tom, those stars."

But Tom was asleep, his eyes close, his mind heavily vacant.

Michael smiled a clown's smile and nodded his head very slowly. He looked with tenderness at the boy beside him. An urge came over him to kiss Tom's grimy forehead, just gently, softly. But he resisted. So he began to talk again in that wonderful voice, whispering almost.

"I sometimes close my eyes and imagine myself in a dark room. I don't know the size of the room; I just know that I am at the entrance to it. The door closes tight behind me and I feel alone. And I realize soon that with each step I take, I could be a yard from the other side of the room or I could be a thousand miles away. But I know deep within me as I stand there shaking that my dark room is everybody's dark room. We are all here together somehow. And as it is so dark, so very dark, the clever people close their eyes so they may pretend that it is they who are creating the darkness. They just close their eyes and strut quickly to the other side, leaving this place in seconds. They learn nothing and they experience less. But me, I keep my eyes wide open. And I realize I am the only one there. For the others have gone, not seeing me at all. And it is light and it is beautiful all around me."

Chapter Five

Tom's father, George, was forty-eight years old. He was a tall man with a pallid complexion and greying hair that hung well past his neckline and was forever flopping across his grey eyes.

By trade, George was a carpenter. From the start of his apprenticeship at the age of fifteen, he had manufactured a world entirely of his own. It was as if the practical skills he was taught were translated into metaphysical techniques. With each new skill acquired, mastered, he had added one more insulating layer between himself and the world outside.

George had safety and surety in wood. Where most people saw the picture, he saw the frame. And in a timber yard, there was paradise. The soft texture of fine sawdust in his palm, the smell of the burning wood as the drill bores through it, that beautiful acrid smell, the sound of the hammer on the cold nail head and the rasping of the saw as it wobbles and bursts its way through. These were the elements of George's fragile existence, the corners of his earth. He was an introspective man who found comfort and peace in dreamy solidity. And there exuded from him a childlike awe of all things, a seductive innocence so natural as to be perfect. Some would call him a dreamer. Some said he was sweet, others thought him just plain odd.

George had met his wife, Elaine, at evening classes. He had gone to learn French polishing, she car maintenance. Both sessions took place on the same night in adjoining rooms. After the classes, some of the students would gather at the village pub for a drink before heading home. For many of them, it was the only socializing they engaged in. George, at twenty-eight had been the youngest and most dedicated in the French polishing class, his passion shining through.

When George first met Elaine, she was small and thin and had the most beautiful long dark hair. She had always worn tight jeans, trainers and baggy jumpers that, although they added bulk to her slight frame, did not detract from her petite figure. She had enrolled in the car maintenance course as a result of having then recently bought her first car. She had purchased it from a friend of a friend and was soon to discover that she had shown perhaps a little too much faith in this extended acquaintance than had been fiscally sound. In short, she had been ripped off. Unable to easily afford mechanics' bills, she had decided to learn to take care of her car as much as she could. It couldn't be that difficult, she had reasoned. She had come to know a few mechanics since buying the car and their attitude had instilled within her the resolve to deprive them of her custom.

The pub in which the students would congregate was small and gloomy and quiet, untouched by modern extravagance. It was an Inn, an Alehouse. There were no bright lights, lurid colours or loud, searing music. There was just a bar, some tables and benches, a dartboard and a fire. And George would sit there alone at a corner table, gazing up through the smoke at the blackened timber beams above his head.

It had been one such evening, as George sat transfixed by the ceiling accoutrements that Elaine had sat down opposite him. He had turned and looked at her, at her smooth, youthful face, her green eyes and her long hair. And he had fallen in love with her hands, her small, gentle, perfect hands. She had looked into his wide, timid eyes and fallen in love with his fragility. A year later, they were married. Take away the worries, the deceit, the fear and the jealousy and there is love, simply waiting for you to happen upon it.

The wedding had been a small gathering attended by close family and a few friends. The couple returned from a short honeymoon somewhere not very far away and began their married life in George's flat in the village. They would walk for hours in the evenings and at the weekends, through lanes and fields and woods that eased on forever. They would become lost and enraptured in their surroundings as they followed hidden paths together. He trusted to fate, she to her sense of direction. And they would barely speak during these times. Just to be in one another's company was enough. Love is simply the pleasure of experiencing another—oh, so simple. Yet, I feel my heart beat dull within me as I write these lines.

Those first few years of marriage had been idyllic for George and Elaine. They had both in turns felt the responsibility and irresponsibility of partnership but had remained close. Looking back now at that time and all that happened over the ensuing years, it had indeed been an idyllic period. It is a torment of time that we only realize how precious is a moment once that moment is long gone, a true torment.

At the age of twenty-two, Elaine gave birth to their first child, Tom. Fourteen years later, almost to the day, would come the birth of Little Norman.

Moving from the village to the town shortly after Tom's birth, George had joined a large building company as a carpenter. All those things for which he had secretly hoped had come true. His days were spent amidst the smells and the sounds of creativity. He would breathe it in, inhaling it all deeply. And he would return home to Elaine, exhausted and elated. No man cherished his work more than George for everything was wonder to him.

Elaine had, in almost every respect, brought Tom up by herself. When her husband wasn't at work, he was in the small shed at the end of the garden hammering and sawing. For a while, she had accepted all of this; but as time wore on, resentment wove its way into her mind. The reasons she had given herself to justify his behaviour such as his sweetness, his boyish innocence, now seemed trite to her. She was being asked to change and adapt, manage the house, the family. It was hard for her. They would argue frequently, or rather she would scream at him until tears streaked down her face and he would look back at her scared and truly bemused, like some puppy that was being chastised for muddying the carpet with his sodden paws. He really did not grasp how she felt during this time. And it had been then that Elaine had sadly realized that she and her husband occupied different worlds. They saw things from different angles, one incapable of understanding the other.

But, as happens, Tom grew to love and admire his father and to take on his persona. George would make toys and games for his son and they would play together for endless hours. So Elaine saw her son grow up to be a dreamer for which she blamed her husband. Communicating with Tom became ever more difficult. She saw how he struggled so hard to understand why she shouted at him. She couldn't answer him when he would come to her as she stared out of the kitchen at the vibrating shed, tears in her eyes. And she saw that he really did try to get close to her, but there was something within her that was forming, something cold and hard that prevented her from showing the pleasure and affection her son so innocently craved.

Elaine loved George and Tom deeply—her 'two boys' as she would call them in uncommon lighter moments. From the confident, pragmatic girl who had enrolled in that car maintenance course to teach all car mechanics a lesson, she had grown into a formidable housewife and mother. And thus she worried and fretted more than she laughed. She became easily irritated and upset, found it harder and harder to relax. She regretted almost everything she said. She had watched herself receive heavier and heavier burdens until her once shining green eyes became shrouded in lines of doubt and despair.

Little Norman had come to save Elaine. He could have saved us all.

Elaine gave birth to Little Norman at the age of thirty-six. Tom was fourteen. The bitterness and reproach of the previous fifteen years that had covered her like a blanket of cobwebs left Elaine in an instant as she held her tiny baby in her arms. Nobody had ever seen a woman more transformed or more joyful. She was young again.

The night Elaine brought Little Norman home from hospital had been a triumphant time for George. He had been decorating what would be Little Norman's room for months. Tom had helped a little but the adolescent disaffection for all things family had begun to nag at him. This new baby would be nothing special.

Little Norman's room had been George's masterpiece. He had stripped it bare, completely removing the carpet and rubbing away the existing paint until the whole room breathed relief, fumes wafting to the open window thick, heavy and delightful. From the skirting boards to the coving from the walls to the ceiling, George performed magic. He crafted mobiles of clowns and cars and animals from balsa wood and suspended them from on high where they would dance and twirl in one heavenly, dismembered frenzy. The paint was applied everywhere with a gentle touch and a subtle hand. Everything was perfect. But there, there in the middle of the room rested George's heart. He had designed it himself, built it with his own hands. His sweat and his blood were in every dovetail joint, in every rounded corner and in every brush stroke. The tiny crib in which Little Norman would lay his sweet head was wonderful, magnificent.

One morning, some weeks after the birth of Little Norman, George had arrived at work to find he was to be made redundant. It had hit him like a train. To be without work had never been a contingency that he had really considered. To be denied the right to work. He was forty-two years old, a skilled craftsman. None had ever worked harder. 'The world will always need its craftsman', he used to say to himself. He doesn't say that anymore. For that was his world. The world into which he was from that day thrust was one where Beauty and Imagination are subservient to Expediency and Conformity, a world that had finally caught up with him, had leapt upon his back from behind as he looked up in wonder at the tall, tall trees of his own heaven.

Thus the days had stretched before him yawning wide and eternal. He would find himself gazing at programs on the television for hours without really watching them. They were just moving pictures. But at least it was motion. Countless times, he would pace from one end of the front room to the other just to see if anything outside had changed. Maybe a car had been moved. Maybe a 'For Sale' sign had been erected or taken down. Or maybe Tom was coming home early from school.

When the telephone rang, he would let it ring and ring just to hear a different sound. And when he did finally answer it, it was never for him. He had given up answering the door entirely.

George had lost so much when he had lost his job—confidence, motivation, self-esteem, and human contact. Mutual friends of himself and Elaine would bury him deep beneath excuses and embarrassment. He was alone and ostracized. And he had never been so scared in all his life. Each day, he would hear on the radio or sometimes read in newspapers that he was now one of a large group of people who were a burden to society, who wanted something for nothing, who were undermining the infrastructure of the country and that measures would have to be put in place to streamline the system that so magnanimously supported him.

Ah, sir. If you could only live my life for a while, I would show you my very soul. And then may you weep.

This initial period of despondency had eventually given way to a rush of enthusiasm. He would get another job. He knew it. He was still over twenty years away from retirement age. And he had a skill to offer, a specialized craft.

So, George had visited the job centre every day, scanned the ever-decreasing Careers Section in the local newspapers and even put a card in the window of the local shop advertising himself, somewhat modestly, as an 'odd-job man'. There had been some posts for which he had applied to which his experience and abilities were eminently suited. He would write lengthy applications detailing his career, his skills and his virtues. Time after time, he would make a single spelling mistake and screw up the whole letter before starting again. It had to be perfect. And he would wait like a child for the postman to come each morning.

But gradually, ever so slowly, one basic truth began to sink and embed itself into George's heart—he had actually ceased to exist outside of his family. It had been a long process but the final realization came to him in a sudden flash, followed almost by relief. He was no more. He had faded to nothing in the world. Gone.

Nobody returned his telephone calls. Bright young voices asked for his name and then promptly forgot it. Letters he wrote, so many letters, received no reply. He became confused as he tried to make sense of it all. What had he done wrong? For what was he being punished? He had never harmed anybody, never even insulted anybody. He was a kind and gentle man, thoughtful and hardworking. He had never taken a day off sick, had always been on time, and had always done whatever was asked of him. As such, he was an easy victim of the fabled Market, pure and simple, a casualty of an economic situation. He was the price paid for another man's mistake.

As time wore on, the creative stimulus that had fuelled George's being was replaced by a dull void. And it was within this void that this quiet, gentle man lived out his days.

Elaine's hands had been full during her husband's early months of unemployment. Her tired eyes and restless nights were due as much to the broken man who lay awake beside her as to the midnight yells of Little Norman. But although he kept her awake, Elaine was unable to think one bad thought about her new baby. He was beyond joy. There were, of course, some days when he would just not stop crying and George would be sitting there in that bloody armchair as another Open University tutor lectured backwards through a ragged beard. At these times, Elaine would become angry and miserable. And she would just stand and wonder at the lines on her face, feeling them with her fingertips. But then, just at the darkest moment, Little Norman would stop crying. He would look at his mother and smile, perhaps giggle, chuckle in a way you wouldn't believe. Elaine would cling to him with raw hands and clutch him to her shoulder as if trying to absorb him into herself. And he in turn would look past her through his beautiful eyes at the sad and tortured figure of his dazed father.

When Elaine had found that Tom had left home, her mind had burst. She had suffered too much, been pushed too far. The intensity of her love for her two children had left her maimed. It had been just over a year since Little Norman, and now Tom too was gone. Her love had undone her.

There has always been a market for those who love too little and who think hardly ever. It is the only market that will ever flourish in times of austerity. Just let the rest of us burn.

George took Elaine to stay with her sister in the north. No other mind could have withstood what she had been through. Her boys had left her, one after the other—gone. It has nothing to do with strength and less to do with gender. It has nothing to do with spirit or character or desire. She just fell apart. When the object of love departs, neither man nor god has right to pass judgement on the reaction to that loss.

Two days after his son's disappearance, George reported him missing to the Police. 'Ah, missing person, I see. Young lad, maybe in Big Town? Well, Big Town is a big town. If that's where he's gone of course. Most of them go there,

Lord knows why. Could be anywhere. Not much hope I'm afraid. But, we'll do our best … Next … Ah, missing person, I see. Young lad, Maybe in Big Town? Well….'

George telephoned Charles Grandon's office, but he was in hospital having a footlight removed from his head.

So, here we are. Almost a week has passed. George sits down in his armchair. He is alone in the house. It is dark and it is quiet. And he feels something within him, deep within. He cannot describe the feeling because he has never felt it before this moment, this strange moment. It just grips him and takes hold, shaking him, jolting him until he leans sharply forward as if released from the taught bow of his own anguish. And he smashes his fist through the glass top of the coffee table before him.

Silence again.
Darkness still.
A torn hand trembles a little.
And a father resolves to bring home his son.

Chapter Six

Tom felt Michael's lips close to his ear, not touching it, but close enough to make him instantly withdraw.

"You know, Tom," said Michael, himself straightening up, "I've not heard you play your guitar yet. You must play for me."

Tom sat up and edged away a little from Michael so he was now resting against the arm of the bench.

The guitar, oh the Beautiful Guitar.

Tom awoke from his torpor, the thick curtain that had fallen across his dreams lifting a little. The child within him stirred momentarily, that child that had remained so silent for so long—the Beautiful Guitar.

"What do you want me to play?"

For a moment, he was the expert, the master.

"Anything, Tom, anything at all. But please play for me."

So Tom played the Beautiful Guitar. The notes crept deep and lonely, flattened and saddened, exuding despair and loneliness, fear and rage. The arena into which the notes were set free gave them vitality, meaning and body. Progressions that he had played in his bedroom through mechanical, tedious hours were now emboldened with a fundamental depth and spirit, sweet, sultry and fantastic.

The birds shuffled about on the grass, listening to this strange and lonesome sound. The anguish deep within the boy's soul was being drained through his fingertips, emerging from the very heart of the Beautiful Guitar.

And after what may have been hours, one last, long, lingering note was carried away on fragile wings and swept down to the muddy waters of the Mississippi River.

Within the frame of a twelve bar blues, Michael learned more of how Tom felt than he would have learned through any form of speech. Neither of them spoke. The silence was too precious. For where the soul is King, words are mere vagabonds.

The evening sun gracefully faded behind the trees, going down in a blaze of pink and orange, and the birds staggered and stumbled to their treetop homes. A slight breeze sighed about the park and the long shadows of the trees struck out across the gravel, intertwining to form some huge, darkly intricate, woven basket.

Tom and Michael left the park, crossing the black strips of gravel, and walked the short distance to where they had been spending their nights. This place of rest was behind a skip at the end of a dank alley between two desolate office buildings. No light shone upon the two men and even though it had barely rained for a month, water dripped incessantly onto the stone floor upon which the two ghostly figures would curl themselves up and somehow make it through the night.

As he tried in vain to find comfort on the cold, damp stones, Tom's mind was filled with the names of the old blues men he had read about and whose music he so loved, those men who suffered but played on, whose lives bled sorrow and destruction. He imagined them roaming the Southern States in all weathers, with just a battered guitar and sore fingers, entirely at the mercy of the world. And for a scintillating moment, he felt akin to them—Tom Spanner—blues man.

They had lived in a world of primitive social deprivation so bitter as to leave them with little choice but to survive on the wings of their own souls. Their music was their rebellion, their guitars their sole means of expression. They had lived, suffered and died. But on the way to their mournful graves, they had given of themselves to this world. Throughout their stricken lives, they had searched intently for a haven, a place of comfort where they would be neither judged nor castigated. And they had found it—there within themselves.

Now Tom, Tom was an office clerk with a three hundred pound guitar and vague ideas about living a life of freedom. The choice had been his. It had been there for him to take. He had committed his fatal error the moment he stepped out onto the street in the half-light of the morning ten days previous. The day he left had been the day of his condemnation. He had aspired to physical freedom and hoped to attain some form of spiritual emancipation as a direct consequence. The former necessarily requires riches extreme; such excess can only hinder the latter. He was a boy in search of himself and anyone who begins that long and lonely journey is nothing but courageous. No medals are handed out, nor honours bestowed for the reward can only be eternal.

Tom had, in a moment of pure insight, caught a glimpse of the man in his mind and had set out to pursue him. The journey thus far had brought him to a place of fear and dirt and despair. But the journey is long my son, and you are so young. Remember that as you lay there in that alley, barely awake, brown water dripping onto your cheeks like tears. Remember that as you try to find peace on this the blackest of nights.

That week, the people at Tom's workplace mocked him. Word had got around, as it does. Each ugly faculty was given the chance to reveal the inherent sickness within. There was an insipid cowardice in the air above the desks, hanging there, swirling above everybody, choking them as once it had choked their own dreams, dreams long abandoned. A life of vicarious enjoyment was all that was left to them now.

"He'll be back in the morning begging for his job back," they all squealed from their processed song sheets.

And so what if he was.

So fucking what.

Saturday morning was fresh and tranquil. As Tom awoke from his bed on the ground, he felt somehow relieved. It was indeed the overwhelming feeling that had assailed him each of the previous few mornings—relief. He had given himself up to the world and had survived another night. He could never work out how or even why. Time would be his saviour. Time would see him through. During the daylight hours, he could take in the sights around him, let them fall into him, for he was a part of them now and they a part of he. He could live by the minute, thinking not of yesterday or tomorrow, in fact, not thinking at all. It had been so easy to slip into, this drifting state of just being, existing. And he had fallen into the trap. With no structure, he was lost, beautifully, transparently lost.

Tom had always cherished Saturday mornings. He would leave the curtains open and let the Summer birds in the garden tease him from the depths of his warm quilt with their irritating though captivating sounds. But always, as he was just coming to terms with being awake, about to creep from beneath his soft shell, Little Norman would burst in, clambering onto his big brother like a soft, fat puppy. Tom, beneath the quilt, barely attuned to the day, and Little Norman trying to prize him out, falling on him, giggling gorgeous, alive, just so alive with an indefinable glee. Tom could almost feel his baby brother on him whenever the scene was cruel enough to establish itself in his mind. And he knew that he would never again feel such honest love.

Each day had been the start of a great new adventure for Little Norman. Each object he spotted with those dark brown eyes was an object of wonder. To be so young, so enamoured with life itself. Bring it on home to me.

The birds in the park greeted the daily arrival of Tom and Michael with a piercing aria that tested even Michael's adoration of them. The grass that had been so green during the spring months was now yellow in places, reduced to blunt shoots. Only the grass beneath the moving shadows of the trees retained any kind of juice. In one sense, this was a living place. In another, it was surely dying.

Sitting again on the wooden bench, Tom longed for Little Norman. The park was peaceful and quiet and allowed him the chance to catch up with the sleep he had missed each night. But the whole place was so old, so ancient and sedate.

If only Little Norman could just waddle out from behind the trees covered in dirt and grinning like a madman.

The memory of Little Norman always made Tom's heart beat that little bit faster.

He is on the edge now.

Chapter Seven

There is something disturbing about a man with ideas of peace. It usually ends in violence. Michael did not believe in violence—as a rule. Just as this world may not be free for the individual, so it is unreceptive to the dreamer. The wheels of a harsh society grind into motion and the dreamer is no more.

Incompatibility with those around you can drive a man insane.

Michael had come to Big Town to recover and to wait. It had seemed the right thing to do. Nature, both in its depth and in its beauty would reconcile in his mind the scene that he had left behind. It would allow him to clamber back on to that great stage of reality upon which he had performed in so tragic a fashion. Or it would let him go.

"Ron," pleaded Diane as she stood on the driveway in front of their house, her husband in the car, struggling with his seat belt. "You said yourself that he'd be back within a few days, that he'd come home when he was ready. That's what you told Christine."

"No. That's what you told me," replied Ron pointedly.

At last, he succeeded in snapping the seat belt into place, the activity having caused him to perspire. He told himself that he must not lose his temper with Diane. She didn't know the whole story as he did. This situation called for the calm assurance and the steadiness of hand for which he was renowned.

"Look, love," he said, "I've told you once already. I'm just going to go to Big Town to meet Roger and find out how Michael left things at work. If he had booked any time off then Roger would have had to have ratified it. If he's called in sick, Roger would know. That's all. And, if you'll excuse me, I'll be going now."

Ron just wanted to get away now, to sort this whole thing out. It would suit everyone for Michael to be found, particularly himself. That was his priority—to find Michael. Bringing him back may be a different matter. Perhaps it wouldn't be necessary. He just needed to speak to him.

Diane realised the futility of questioning her husband. Even across the length of the driveway, she could see him reddening.

"Okay, dear. Take care," she called. "I love you," she added, quietly.

But Ron heard nothing but the rumbling of the car engine.

He was gone now, gone to Big Town.

The motorway rapidly filled with vehicles until the immense convoy of metal and abuse merged into one long, snaking line. Ron shielded himself from the fumes by winding up his window, but this only served to intensify the sticky heat that smothered him as he drove. The seat belt irritated him and the odour rising from the smouldering upholstery left him nauseous. He had only bought the car four weeks ago and already he hated it. Frantic to escape from the horns and the exhausts, he allowed his mind to slip for a while into past, present and future.

From early on at school, Ron had been recognised by his teachers as one upon whom they could depend. His quickly developing athletic stature and oddly deep voice for one of his years had marked him out from the other boys, none of whom would ridicule him for the latter, due to the imposing nature of the former. He was, by way of his build and his demeanour, on a different plane. He was maturity personified, old before his time. And nobody had ever bothered him. He was surely never young. Or perhaps his pre-school years had simply been repressed, as dark times so often are. We will never know.

One of Ron's duties at school, as he progressed through the years, had been to ensure that the young first year pupils were not bullied by the older boys. An added difficulty in the management of this task was that the school had consisted of two distinct elements. There were the local children—products of semi affluent families—and there were the children from the Children's Home that was physically and metaphorically on the very edge of town. Friction was constant between these two groups of children, fear and ignorance being their only common factor.

Michael was from the Children's home.

It had been clear to Ron on seeing the frail figure of the new boy that there was someone who was going to have a rough time. Michael would just stare at people with those large, timid eyes and his whole face seemed to move precariously whenever he spoke. His hair was so fair it could have been white.

At the age of four, Michael's mother had left him at the Children's Home. Events had conspired to force her to give up her children.

Four years old. The world is just opening up to you. All is grand and important. You are so excited and so readily excitable, learning new things every day, finding your place and living one long, wondrous day. For each day is full of wonder. You bounce and charge about, frantic for experience, holding on to those you love and who love you more than you are able to imagine. And you know so clearly that things will always be like this. But there is your first blow. Mummy is gone. You saw her crying and you didn't know what was happening. And your little sister who had not long been in your life was in your Mummy's arms when she left you standing there—though you would see that lovely little girl again soon when she too was left at the open mouth of this world like yourself.

This big place is not your home. It is cold and full of strangers. Your room with your bear and your train is gone. I don't like it here. I don't like it at all.

As Ron was jolted back into the present by a blaring horn from behind, he was left with a fading image of a young boy in a crowded playground, lost, confused and entirely out of reach.

On reaching Big Town and calling at the office, Ron learned that Roger Peacock, Michael's boss, was due back from a meeting at two o'clock. He decided therefore to take advantage of the time available to him by searching for Michael in likely places. He knew Big Town well and also thought he knew the sort of places to which Michael may go. If he could find him by luck or coincidence, then so be it. There were no such things as long shots for people like Ron, people in control. It would be reassuring to just clarify one or two things with his old friend.

Time. Ron could do with it stopping still whilst he looked for Michael. In a second, his life could change—a phone call, a letter, Michael arriving back home. Perhaps he was worrying about nothing. But he was not a man to take chances. Christine had hinted to him that there had been signs that Michael had been becoming unwell in recent weeks, not like before though. It had been nothing as bad as that.

Time. Time. Time.

So, that morning, Ron scoured the museums, the churches and other places of solitude. He felt momentarily at peace as he wandered from silence to silence. He had not been to a museum for years, having once made the mistake of visiting one in the middle of the school term. On that occasion, he had angrily fled the undisciplined hordes with their clipboards and their packed lunches. It still made him uneasy to think about it. But there were things of greater import to moisten his brow now.

As each of the preceding days had passed, so had Ron's control of his life become ever more tenuous.

He had a brief lunch in a restaurant off the main street and mulled over the relative lack of success the morning had brought. He thought about ringing

Diane to apologise for the curt nature of his manner when he had left, though his thoughts swung now from rational to irrational and back again. The wine he consumed at the corner table instilled in him some strange, alien sense of puerility. He felt for a moment as if he had been let out to play. It was a dangerous, unsettling feeling and one that, despite the encouragement of the wine, he swiftly laid to rest. It was however replaced by an overwhelming sense of guilt that made him feel ill. Childishness and guilt were two states that Ron had kept shut away deep inside him. The former was a strange entity that surprised him on occasion. That latter was only every a momentary lapse in one such as Ron.

Diane had always been the perfect wife for Ron. She ensured he had someone to return to. Hers were the arms in which he would lay contemplating. She was the shade of grey that smoothed the edges of his black and white soul. And they would talk about the begonias often.

Outside the restaurant within which Ron had indulged himself, a man lay on the pavement. Many people strode manfully by, convincing themselves that it was but a pile of rags. Ron emerged into the afternoon sunlight and almost stumbled over the dark, ragged mound, having to step back sharply in order to retain his balance. He was just steadying himself when he saw the fingers.

The man was wearing a long, black coat and heavy boots. A dirty beard pulled at what little could be seen of the cracked face, and tiny insects made their busy way across the limp left palm, following each other in streams up the sleeve. This man could have been ninety years old. He could have been twenty-five.

Ron stepped around the man and, in doing so, was gripped by a chill. Was this what death looked like? He couldn't be sure. Somebody would call an ambulance soon or maybe the Police would come alone and deal with the situation. Anyway, this was probably a drunk or one of those 'addict' people.

That cold, lifeless man could have lay there for a hundred years. Nobody would have helped him. And all who passed, well they would just bare fleeting witness to the steady decay of the remnants of a man's life. The bones would turn to dust and the beard would grow and grow until it enshrouded the whole grimy face. Through rain and snow it would have lain there, through hail and storm.

But Ron knew, knew instinctively, that Michael would have been the exception. Michael would have knelt down beside this man from whom he himself shamefully walked. He would have taken him in his arms and softly brushed the scurrying creatures from the deep folds of the black coat. And he would have cradled him like a baby.

The proposed visit to the area by vague royalty ensured the removal of the wretched body some days later. You see, these scenes never happen, never occur. In a flash they are gone from sight and from conscience forever.

A tall man in a perfect suit stands erect before his peers. His limbs are strong. His back is straight. He is a proud man. And so is his wife. He is well respected by all about him. He knows what is best for you and he knows what is best for me. With a majestic stride, he mounts the box of my dreams and with a long finger gestures at the crumpled heap of a dying man.

"These," he proclaims in a voice loud and brave, "These are the people one steps over when one comes out of the opera."

Oh, what cheers there are.

And amidst the roars and the adulation, the crumpled heap turns to pure light and surely enters Heaven in glory.

As Ron had been preparing to go to Big Town, Tom was waking from another dream. He had begun to sleep with some regularity the last few nights and was becoming used to his new routine. He was beginning to accept the strictures. It was all a case of focussing the mind. Forget this. Remember that. It was as if he had just been born, his first nineteen years on earth being nothing but a prolonged labour.

It had not occurred to him to call his parents. He had told Michael they were dead. He was in a new role now. He could be whoever he wished to be. Except, perhaps, himself.

But dreams, dreams were bringing him down. He had no control over their content nor over the feelings they left him when he woke. Before going to sleep the previous night on the cold ground, he had put on his black sweatshirt; thankful for the warmth and comfort it gave him. As the summer wore on, the evenings were becoming cooler. And that night, as the stars and the moon looked down upon him, Tom dreamed his dream ...

... the car speeds along the road following the twists and turns as if upon a rail. The moon is high and shines upon the fields, illuminating them, igniting them, inciting them to flame. In the driver's seat is Tom and beside him is a beautiful girl. The car is red and silver, cutting through the night like some bloodstained knife. There is rock and roll music on the radio and the girl taps her sweet feet to the beat ... a petrol station appears from out of the ground and the car cruises smoothly in. Tom fills up the tank and the girl smiles at him, all hidden wonder and enticement. "Let's go," she is saying. "Let's just go, leave this all behind us." A thrill crackles in the air and dust explodes from beneath the wheels of the car ... then, from above, we see the car in the middle of a black field, overturned and steaming. The girl is gone. In the distance, there is a light. Tom crawls from the wreckage and weaves his way across the field on skates ... and the light, the light just draws him on ... he is at work now, in the foyer. People wander around, talking in a language that he cannot comprehend. A man dressed as a butler taps him on the shoulder and he turns around. The man pins a number to Tom's shirt and smiles, a tooth falling from his crooked mouth as he does so, twisting to the carpet in slow motion ... the lift doors open and a hundred people enter the lift. Tom looks on. Two long arms encircle his waist and fingernails dig into him. In the mirror on the wall opposite, he sees the receptionist clinging to his body. And as he watches, helpless, unable to move, the make-up and the skin falls from her face and her clothes drop to the floor, leaving just a clattering pile of dry bones ... the lift pulls Tom upwards now and he is standing by his desk. His co-workers are all around him but they see him not. Tom looks up to the ceiling and sees a map of the world suspended from a thick wire. A piece of the map is missing and Tom knows instinctively that he must search for it. He puts his hand in his pocket and his fingers close around a perfect cardboard heart ... the lift doors open and there stands Michael. Tom feels at once reassured. He feels safe. The two men smile at one another. Tom moves out of the lift and into the next office. Michael remains in the lift and rises to a higher level ... now, now Tom is at home, at the top of the stairs. He opens the door to the bathroom and sees a hundred washbasins. A silver watch is wrapped around the hot tap. He takes it and turns it over in his palm expecting to see a name but there is no inscription ... the door to his parents' room is open and they are making love, his mother smiling from below the aching body of his father who in turn is gazing at the wooden headboard in raptures ... Tom opens the door to Little Norman's room and finds himself back in the lift. On the floor is a foil star on a stick. He looks at it and a tear slips from his eye ... the huge walkway on which he now finds himself is covered in a red carpet. It forms a square all around the edge of the large room. And across the deep gap, from one side to the other, is a glass bridge. You don't know how deep is the drop below until you fall. Michael is on the bridge now, walking to the other side. In the wall to which he is heading, there are two doors, one to the left and one to the right. As he approaches the end of the bridge, a voice booms out from above "Left! Left!" So Michael walks to the door on the left and the man dressed as a butler steps from the shadows and shoots him dead between the eyes ... Tom is on the glass bridge now. He feels sick. But he knows what to do. If the voice instructs him to go to the door on the left, he will choose the door on the right. If the voice tells him to go to the door on the right, he will enter the door on the left. And the voice roars "Right! Left! Right! Left!" leaving him just to stand there in terror as the glass bridge shatters beneath his feet....

And that was when he awoke from the dream. He was cold and damp and he shivered in that alleyway until morning.

Ron arrived later in the afternoon at the restaurant where he had arranged to meet Roger Peacock. Roger had been unable to cut short his working day and met with Ron just after six o'clock He had been at the table for almost ten minutes before Ron arrived. His genial nature, however, ensured that his guest and long-term associate was greeted with a cordial smile.

"Ronald," he said, standing, "you're looking great."

"You too, Roger," replied Ron, as they shook hands firmly and sat down.

The two men ordered their meals and sipped red wine as they waited for the arrival of the first course.

Roger was a lean man with a tanned face and a wiry frame. His dark hair was flecked with grey and white though his eyes still managed to achieve a boyish brightness at times. He had a passion for boats and the considerable ability to differentiate work from play.

"You look like you had a good holiday, Roger," said Ron, replenishing their swiftly drained glasses. "Where did you go?"

"Italy. Joan and I have been nipping back and forth there for the last couple of years. Wonderful place. The Italians may have their faults, and God knows they have, but when it comes to wine, women and song, there's none better."

"How is Joan? Still doing her painting? It was painting, wasn't it?"

Roger laughed.

"Yes, yes, Joan and her paintings. Our house has turned into a bloody canvass warehouse. You can't move for paintings. Don't get me wrong, though," he added, pausing to sip from his glass, "they really are very good."

Each man looked at the other when the other one was looking down or away. They did not have that beautiful feminine trait of being able to look directly into the eyes of another of the same gender.

Ron and Roger had met at a training course many years ago and had developed a friendship almost at once. Although different in character, and their interactions being predominantly superficial, each was still, in some way, fond of the other. They had inevitably lost contact in the previous two years since Ron had been given, and accepted, the opportunity to work from home. But through chance meetings and the odd business call, they had kept in some form of contact with one another.

"Those chaps at the office, Ronald," confided Roger, leaning across the table; "they seem to be getting younger by the day. I'm thinking seriously about imposing a minimum age limit. Forget all this nonsense about the minimum wage. It's the minimum age we need to look at! What do you think?"

"Wouldn't go down too well with the Unions, Roger, now would it?" replied Ron, smiling. He enjoyed Roger's company, even if he did insist on calling him Ronald.

The first course arrived and was quickly despatched amidst a thoughtful silence.

In between the first course and the second, there was a distinct lull in the conversation as so often happens when two people have too much to impart. Each tries to sum up the intervening period since last they met in such a way as to imply consolidation, excitement, progress even. And each is equally unsure as to how to suitably embellish the tedium of time.

As he sat there, finishing his food, Ron prepared himself to bring up the subject of Michael. His meal had been satisfying, as had the wine. The time was right.

"Roger," he said finally, looking up from his empty plate, "how has Michael seemed to you lately?"

Roger looked momentarily puzzled. The wine was slowing him down a little.

"Oh, Michael, Michael Parrish?" he said, as if a photograph of Michael had just been placed before him. "To be honest with you, Ronald, I haven't seen him for a little while. Why do you ask?"

"It's just that, well, Roger, the situation as it stands is that his wife, Chris, is frankly, well, she's getting rather worried. I just wondered whether he'd been okay at work recently. Any problems, that kind of thing?"

Roger was fiddling with what was left of his lasagne. He really didn't fancy it now.

"So has he booked time off, Roger, a couple of weeks maybe? When is he due back?"

Roger continued to move his lasagne around the plate in a manner that was beginning to irritate his dining partner.

"Roger?" repeated Ron, who was not used to being ignored.

"I've been away, Ronald, on holiday. I'm not fully up to speed with things yet."

"How long did he book off?"

Roger put his fork down carefully on the plate and looked up to face Ron across the table.

"I know that he was on sick leave for at least a week before I went away and that was almost a month ago now. I assume from what you say that he's not yet back at work, although obviously I can check that one out for you tomorrow."

"Sick leave?"

"Well, yes. Sick leave. Off sick."

"I know what it means," said Ron, just managing to stop short of being terse. He poured himself another glass of wine, draining the bottle.

"Shall I order another?" asked Roger, picking up the empty bottle.

"Not for me," replied Ron.

Roger ordered one anyway—for himself.

"Look, Roger, I know none of this is your concern, but up until he went away a couple of weeks ago...."

"A couple of weeks?"

"Yes. Up until a couple of weeks ago, Michael was fine. There was nothing wrong with him. I mean, it's not exactly been the weather for pneumonia has it? What I'm getting at is, from the week before you went away on holiday until the time Michael left for who knows where, there was nothing wrong with him. He was perfectly fine."

"Physically, maybe."

Ron paused to take in this last remark.

"What do you mean 'physically, maybe'? What are you trying to say?"

The waiter brought over the bottle of wine, uncorked it, and poured into Roger's glass. Ron declined the waiter's offer and the bottle was left on Roger's side of the table.

Roger sipped his wine before rejoining the conversation.

"Exactly what I say, Ron. Physically, Michael seemed fine to me too, although neither of us are doctors are we? He wasn't ill, well, not in that way."

Ron was beginning to see now where this was heading. His emotions started to take shape, forming from a mixture of confusion, fear and anger. He was on the back foot now. He was thinking already of all sorts of consequences and none of them were good.

"Ronald," said Roger, sensing now that he had the opportunity to take hold of the conversation, "I know you've known Michael for a long time and I truly admire your loyalty. It's just one of the many things I do admire about you, your loyalty. And I, myself, have always found Michael to be a pleasant, affable chap, a little off the wall at times, perhaps, but then aren't we all in our own little way?" He paused to gulp some wine, allowing it to fortify him before continuing. "But it had been coming long before I went on holiday. He was changing, you see, becoming very quiet, so to speak. I know he's not the most outgoing of people, but it was as if, well, as if he was on a different planet if you know what I mean. Of course, his work was suffering, suffering badly. He's always been something of a dreamer, I know, but this was different somehow."

Ron dabbed his lips with a serviette. He was calmer now, though there was still a primitive, quaking quality to his voice.

"Roger, tell me. What reason did he give for going off sick? What was on the certificate?"

"There was nothing on the certificate, not really, just stress or something. I could barely read it from what I remember."

"Was he under pressure at work?"

"His workload was no different. If anything, it was probably lighter, what with all those bright young things around. So, no, I wouldn't say he was under pressure at work."

"Didn't you talk with him, ask him what the problem was?" asked Ron, still feeling uneasy. Was it better or worse that Michael was ill again? He hadn't decided yet.

"I did. Yes, of course. The day before I went away," replied Roger in a sombre tone.

"What did he say?"

Both men were quieter now, subdued. The meal was drawing to a close. Soon they would go again there separate ways.

"He told me some very odd things. He was very strange, so easily distracted. I suppose he didn't look well, but I couldn't put my finger on it, but like I said, I'm no doctor. There was some other stuff as well, but as you can imagine, this is all very strange to me. I don't know if he's got some sort of illness, whether it's some elaborate joke or whether he's gone round the twist. All I do know is that he needed time off work and he took it and 'stress' probably sums it all up as good as anything else. And I went to Italy, thankfully."

Ron was silent, completely silent. He knew he had to put the question to Roger.

"Did he mention my name at all?" he asked, not making eye contact.

"I'm sorry, Ronald, what was that?"

"Did he mention me at all?"

Roger thought for a moment.

"No," he said, "I don't believe he did."

And the meal ended in silence.

Ron managed to thank Roger for his company before they parted. As he left the restaurant, his mind was reeling and rocking with all sorts of thoughts. Why now? Why did it all have to happen now? As he walked, he tried to clear his head by breathing deeply the evening air. He dared not acknowledge his deepest fear, He reassured himself that there was no way Michael could know. But if he had known at that moment just how much Michael did know, he may well have stayed in Big Town indefinitely until he had found him, instead of looking for a telephone box from which to call his wife.

The railway station that opened out into the main street was noisy and packed with sweaty people. There was a row of telephone kiosks just inside the entrance that were party to all manner of conversations and the minutiae of people's lives. In one of them stood Ron. He was having difficulty dialling his own telephone number; such was the state of his mind and perhaps the residual effects of the wine. Twice he dialled wrongly before finally having some success.

The telephone rang in the hall and Diane answered it. She was hoping it would be her husband. He had been gone all day. And his dinner was almost ready.

"Hello?"

"Love, it's me. I can't talk long. I don't have much change. I'm just calling to say that I'll be back in about an hour, hopefully. I'm just leaving now."

"No luck then?"

"No. Look, I've got to go."

"Christine got another note from him this morning," said Diane, "the same as before apparently—written in a crossword. She brought it over for you to see, but you'd just left."

"What did it say?" asked Ron tentatively. It had been a long day.

"It was very odd. Christine didn't understand a word of it. She seemed to think it would mean more to you than it did to her. She really is in a terrible state, Ron."

"What did it say?"

"Hang on, dear, I'll go and get it."

And all the while, Ron watched the numbers count down on the display in the kiosk, mesmerised.

"I'll read it out to you, dear. I copied it out. It was so difficult to read with all those grubby black squares everywhere. Anyway, it says:

'ALL MY LIFE IT HAS BEEN BOTH WITHIN ME AND ABOUT ME
YOU KNEW JENNIFER
YOU DID
YOU DO
JENNIFER IS SEVEN YEARS OLD AGAIN
SHE WAS TAKEN FROM ME ONCE
YOU HAVE TAKEN HER FROM ME AGAIN
BUT I FLOAT ABOVE EVERYTHING NOW
I SEE EVERYTHING
I KNOW EVERYTHING
JENNIFER TOLD ME SHE TOLD ME RON
WITH HER EYES
I KNOW
I CLEANSED HER SOUL.'

And that's it," said Diane, finally. "A bit odd, isn't it? Christine is very upset. Who is Jennifer, anyway?"

There was no reply.

For back in the station, the numbers had counted down to zero. And the receiver hung limp, dangling like a hanged man, swaying silently in perfect, deathly motion.

Chapter Eight

The music almost swept George back into the street as he pulled open the door of the pub. He had decided to look for Tom locally first, reasoning that even if he didn't find him straight away, he may meet somebody who knew his son, a friend, a work colleague, somebody. He was unaware that Tom had neither friends nor colleagues.

He squeezed by the huge bouncer at the door and was immediately overwhelmed by a feeling telling him to just leave this place, to go back out of the door and into the street. Bright lights pulsed and glared red, gold and green. Sweat dripped from the walls and smoke fused with the lights to render everyone transparent, fading in and out of vision like true spectres of youth. The bass seemed ready to blow a hole through the wall and it shook the very floor upon which George now stood.

These people were alien to George. They were not of his kind. As he attempted to walk around the pub, he felt pounded by stares, glances and contortions of features that left him shaking. He saw young girls with make-up applied so vigorously and laboriously that it served only to mask their inherent beauty. They became grotesque caricatures, tottering on high heels, wobbling vaguely and uncomfortably in time with the incessant beat of the plastic drums. There were children, surely just children, in a tangled mess in the corner. Their faces were red and their eyes large. And they tried with all their burgeoning adolescent strength to keep from slipping out of sight beneath the table of their own destruction.

Tom had often called back as he was leaving the house to let his mum and dad know that he was just going out for a drink or that he was just off to the pub. These thoughts were with George now. He found it so hard to imagine that his boy was able to survive in an atmosphere of such raucous intensity. From where did he acquire the skills to merge in with this reckless crowd?

He tried two more pubs, without success, before making his way back home. It had been a doomed and fruitless effort.

The night was clear and the moon was full, giving light to the darkening streets. None of the street lamps seemed to work, except one, and that just flickered on and off, blinking shyly through the day and the night.

So George's eyes were on the ground now, following a path of despair. He emerged onto the main street again of this small town, flanked both sides by Banks and Building Societies. These were the only institutions able to maintain a fluorescent presence, providing a blue green glow with which even the moon itself dare not compete.

There were several short side streets off the main road, leading to deserted car parks or small alleys containing large, metal vats of rubbish. At the head of all the side streets and the alleys, on the pavement and on the forecourts of closed down shops, there were parked cars. And sprawled on, in and around these cars, there were children, some older than others, some looking like young adults, but children all the same.

So deep was George in his thoughts that he was no more than a yard away from one such group when he became aware of its presence. A car horn blared three times. George looked up quickly, though he had learned in the previous few hours not to look anywhere for too long. It didn't do to stare.

The car horn blared again, punctuating the music that now screamed from the car radio.

The children that stood around the car were of all ages. Some drank cheap lager from cans, almost all had cigarettes either dangling from their hands like an extra digit or stuck between their lips.

Though the night was warm, George felt cold now. He felt the eyes of the children upon him as he stood there and in those eyes, he saw only malice. There was no humour at all. He contrived to walk warily past the group and just as he thought he was through, a small girl stepped out in front of him. He almost knocked her over. She just stood there looking up at him. She was no more than ten years old and George had an urge to take her hand and lead her away from all this. It was when he took a hurried step sideways to avoid her that she took a drag from a smouldering cigarette and spat like a snake on the ground in front of his feet. Her face then cracked in half to reveal a huge, satisfying grin, exposing bright white teeth that sparkled like the thick gold chain around her neck.

And George hurried on, trembling.

When he finally arrived home, he sat in the dark in his armchair. Closing his eyes in the silence, images whirled before him. The flashing lights of the pubs were tattooed upon his retina. He thought of those people he had seen and the children with their drink and their cigarettes and their rings and their chains. Who were they? How did they connect with him? He was an alien in his own town—and Tom, what of Tom? The father then realised in an instant that he did not know his own son, had not known him for years, probably not since Little Norman. In truth, they did not know one another. Each was surely waiting for a miracle.

When Tom had been small, George had played with him until both gave in to exhaustion and utter contentment. They had played football in the kitchen, had chased each other up and down the stairs, and had charged into the garden in the summer evenings, throwing water at each other and everybody else. He had read to Tom of Peter Pan, of Robin Hood, of Dick Turpin and of Robinson Crusoe. He had taken him to football matches, both wearing the lurid scarves and hats Elaine had knitted them, and wearing them proudly too. And they had both leapt into the air together in ecstasy when their team scored. George had made Tom toys from wood—cars and trucks, plaques for his wall and a nameplate for his door. And he had stood over him while he dreamed, just watching the quilt cover rise and fall, wishing so vehemently to be inside that boy's head, in his thoughts and in his dreams.

And now that boy was gone. His boy, Tom, had run away from him.

The radiators hummed and droned. The fridge in the kitchen whined. The moon slipped behind a cloud and George fell apart in his chair.

"Tom," said Michael, "how do you find your life?"

Tom did not reply. He had become used to Michael speaking an almost constant stream of words, half of which he would listen to, the other half he would just allow to pass him by. It had been as if there was a radio playing in the background of his sufferings. But this question would not let him go.

"What do you mean?"

"Well, life, life is miraculous in itself. All those events and people and experiences that come together to make up your life, the things you look back on and the things you look forward to, your dreams, your fears. That is life. That is your life. And you are young, Tom, so young." Michael paused and continued in a more subdued tone. "When I was your age, I remember just trembling with life, with the fear of it and the longing for it. And I tremble still, Tom. Not with fear, or even longing, but because I know I am over the worst of it."

"And that's why you spend all day in this bloody park?" replied Tom. He was thinking of his mum and his dad and of Little Norman, of his reasons for coming to Big Town and of the forlorn hopes that he was trying so desperately to cling to.

"This place, this beautiful place, is not just any park. Just look around you."

Tom shrugged his shoulders and looked away.

"It is more than that," said Michael.

Tom was losing his way a little here. He had noticed over the past few days that his companion was becoming increasingly obtuse. A sense of urgency close to impatience would sometimes overwhelm Michael. He would become irritable and then somehow reach into himself and return to the placid, gentle man whom Tom had first met. Tom would waken sometimes and catch Michael's voice rising and falling beside him, talking, conversing with himself. And then he would stop and look at Tom, a bewildered, sad expression on his face, before falling into a protracted silence.

Tom decided to agree.

"Yes," he said, "I suppose it is."

After a moment of reflection, Michael began again, his voice calm and soft.

"So, Tom. How do you find your life?"

Tom knew that the moment had come. He had been unable to sit down and think of his problems, of his past or of his future. The days had drifted one into the other and he had just been drifting along with them. It had taken a stranger to bring him down from up there, to turn him around and begin to put him back together again.

"I suppose I'm still looking for it," he replied eventually.

Michael pondered this answer, trying to fit it into his own thoughts and experiences of being lonely upon this earth.

"You are your life, Tom. Your life is within you."

"Then perhaps I'm looking for myself."

Michael nodded.

Tom sighed deeply and shook a little for tears were surely not far from his young eyes.

"There are times, Tom, times in our lives when all we see is darkness, when nothing is clear to us at all. We are brought up to see with our eyes, but it is our eyes that betray us. True sight and true vision lay within us, Tom, within our souls. And that is where you will find yourself, within your soul."

"But how is that real life? How does that help me here, now? I need to get rid of this thing in me; this fucking feeling that stops me from being like everyone else. And I don't know where to start. I've left home. I still feel the same. I need to change something. I can't explain it. I can't even explain what it is I need to change."

Those tears were so close now.

Michael was looking at Tom as if he were looking at himself. He wanted to hold him, to bring him into his world, to show him the glory that was waiting for him. He tried to keep telling himself that it was too early yet, that the time was not right, but as the days had passed, Michael's hold on what society expects and respects, was gradually being devoured by that which had been within him for so long, an illness that had lain dormant, an illness that had been awoken by his love for a little girl.

"There is nothing to explain, Tom. Words just get in the way sometimes. Look into your heart, close your eyes and you will see your soul. Your body, the physical world, is all irrelevance."

"But I live and breathe in this world. You can't just forget it and pretend it's not there. Fine if you've got loads of money and a big house in the middle of nowhere, you can do all that philosophy stuff. But I've got nothing. Fuck all."

"Your soul, Tom. You have your soul."

Tom breathed a little harder now.

"Anyway," he said, "where has it got you? You're in the same position as me."

Michael smiled knowingly. He saw him and Tom as two extremities, one at each end of the journey.

"What are you laughing at?"

"I'm not laughing at all, Tom. I just know how you feel for I was like you once. Lost. Confused. I was just like you, Tom."

"So then why are you smiling? Anyway, you don't know anything about me."

"I know everything about you, Tom."

"Bollocks."

Silence.

Birds singing.

That's all.

Tom was becoming irritated now. One more person telling him that he knew what he was going through knew him better than he did himself. He was desperate to get himself together, to get a hold on things.

"Look," he said, "I mean, all that seems to happen is I tell you things, you spend hours going on about some crap, and then the day's over and it starts all over again."

Michael looked at the young man beside him, a sad and sorrowful look.

"If I were to tell you of my life, Tom, it would break the both of us. And I shall not burden you with it."

The two men sat there now on that bench beneath the sun, quiet for a moment, contemplative, each thinking his own thoughts, experiencing his own dread. How tenuous is our grip upon reality when the strings that bind us to the machinery of society are severed. A cloud wavered across the sun and shadows danced within the trees. But soon the sun was bright again and the air warm with foreboding.

Michael looked at Tom, at this self-conscious young man so lost in life. And he knew he could help him.

"Tom," he said, "would it help you to know more about me?"

Tom paused. "It's up to you," he said. "I suppose. I mean I don't really know anything about you, do I?"

"Ask away, Tom. Ask away."

Tom thought for a moment.

"Is Michael your real name then?" he asked with little enthusiasm.

"Yes it is. Michael Parrish."

"And what are you, fifty, fifty-five?"

"Forty-eight."

"Sorry."

"That's okay."

"So are you from round here then?"

"No, no I'm not. Not really."

Tom felt, for some reason, a little foolish. "Look," he said, "this is stupid. Let's just forget about it. It's not important."

Michael thought for a moment. This boy was so young. Jennifer had been young. She still is, he thought to himself. How the past is connected to the present. You are never free, never entirely free. For it is the passing of time, that very abstract of creations, that deceives us all.

In the absence of a response, Tom plodded on with one more question. "So what do you do then?" he asked.

Michael then stood up and took off his jacket, laying it gently on the bench beside him as if anticipating the question. He then rolled up the sleeves of his stained white shirt. It was then that Tom realised that through these days of unbearable heat, Michael had remained attired in his suit. And then he looked at Michael's bare forearms, suppressing an appalled look as he did so. For up the entire length, from the wrist to the elbow, there were deep scars, perhaps every quarter of an inch. The scars were white and tight, standing out clearly as if they had been painted on. Tom could not help but stare.

"You ask me what I do, Tom," said Michael. "And I will tell you. I save souls."

Tom did not speak. No words came to his mind. He just kept staring at those scars.

"I save souls, Tom. I cleanse them. I suffer pain so that others may not."

All Tom could do was to repeat what Michael had said.

"You save souls?" he said almost mechanically.

"I cleanse them."

And Tom had to ask the inevitable question, just had to, as you or I would have had to.

"How do you do that?" he asked, as a child talking to a conjurer.

The sky above began to darken a little and it seemed now as if this small corner of the park was now on its own, floating in the universe. Seclusion. Desolation. You could feel it in the air. Michael felt in the inside pocket of his jacket and withdrew a small penknife, its blade glinting in the waning sun.

Tom moved, as if to stand.

"Do not fear, Tom," said Michael. "It is I that will feel your pain."

Tom stood now and backed away a little.

"Listen to me, Tom. And trust me. I can save your soul. I bear the scars of a nation, of a world. My world. Each mark on my arm is a soul saved."

He then held the penknife against the skin of his outer right forearm and dragged it slowly across, reopening one of the scars. Blood oozed from it. Tom was unable to look away.

"That is my mother," said Michael.

He did it again, a little further up.

"That is my father whom I never knew."

And he did it again.

"That is my childhood."

Blood was now dripping down his arm, the cuts filling each other with blood, overflowing like some child's painting.

"You see, Tom, the pain is mine."

Michael then swapped the penknife into his right hand as the first drops of rain began to fall. It was then that Tom noticed one long, snaking scar on Michael's left arm, from the base of the wrist, like a long vein up to the elbow and possibly even passed that.

"And this," said Michael, "this is Jennifer."

He then followed the scar with the penknife, his eyes closed, feeling the rain and the pain. Tom just stood there, a carousel of changing images spinning in his mind, bright and reckless. The sounds of Little Norman as his breath was taken from him, sorrow, pain, anger, colours flashing as the images raged on, racing on wild horses of adolescent fury. It was such an assault upon the senses that he thought he would vomit.

"Your pain, Tom. Give it to me. Let me cleanse your soul," said Michael, his arms outstretched.

But Tom heard him not. When all clarity of thought is gone, when the eyes are the eyes of the desperate and the frightened, there is just for a second a means of expression that stands out above all others, begging to be used.

Tom gazed at the figure before him.

Little Norman.

Little Norman.

You can't touch Little Norman. You just can't.

This was the moment for Tom to release his anger and his sorrow and his pain. He had no choice.

So he sighed an imperceptible sigh before crashing his bony fist into Michael's face, meeting it with a sickening crunch. He did it again. And he just kept doing it. He couldn't make himself stop. Over and over he punched the unresponsive face until, at last, he staggered back, almost falling with exhaustion. And there before him lay the wreck of a human form.

Blood streamed from Michael's skin and ran in tears down his face. The crevices that his life had forged with so little mercy carried the blood as if they had been created for that purpose alone. His legs and arms were those of a puppet whose strings were no longer held, lacking in tension and in spirit. Tom just looked on, unable to move. And then suddenly, without warning, Michael's body slipped off the bench upon which it had fallen, and thudded onto the gravel whereupon his wide eyes met the thunderous sky.

And Tom stood over Michael; his eyes drawn to the now upturned hands, those smooth white doves of hands that had touched the Beautiful Guitar with such gentleness, that had woven patterns in the air, speaking such words as the tongue could not. Those white, white hands so tinged now with red for in the centre of each palm, there issued forth small drops of blood.

Tom felt now unable to control his own breathing. He tried to inhale deeply but found he could not remember how. So hard was his heart pounding, he thought it would burst through his chest. He ached all over, just ached in agony. And as a symphony does change its mood within a single bar, so the sky cracked open, just tore in half like a sheet of paper. The rain thrashed down upon this scene, creeping now down Tom's neck, scratching the skin of his back as if the drops of rain themselves were the broken slithers of a shattered decanter sky.

The young man lurched sideways and scrambled over to where his bag was and where the Beautiful Guitar lay weeping in its case. He grabbed them and tried so hard to keep his eyes from closing, to keep himself upright, as he staggered out of the park. The gravel sprang up from beneath his feet and the black and flashing sky pursued him into the street.

"Tom? Tom Spanner?" came a voice in the darkness.

Tom whirled around, terrified.

And there before him, her hair dripping and her eyes bright, stood a light amidst the storm.

It was Sandy.

She had saved him.

Back in the Country, a man tries to get hold of a situation.

Jennifer. Laura. Laura. Jennifer.

These names shot around Ron's head. The message from Michael had read that Jennifer was seven years old but Jennifer had died almost a quarter of a century ago. Jennifer had been where it had all started. Laura. Laura was seven years old. Ron could not understand it. All he knew was this sense of terror. He knew not what to do next. All he had wanted to find out from Michael was why he had left. He dared not submit to his worse fears. If Michael was ill again, fair enough. Perhaps it was just the illness. But this talk of Jennifer perturbed him. Laura was only seven. Seven year old girls are good little girls. They always do as they are told. Always. Good little girls. Ron smiled.

Laura is seven years old, beautiful, gentle and perfect. She sits in front of the television, her legs crossed, in the lounge, alone. You could draw her and you could paint her. And if you did, you would surely make millions. She has the grace and the surety of one who is years older, yet bares so faithfully the fundamental wonder of the child. She does not move. She just sits there in front of the television. But the television is not even switched on. It is her reflection in the dark screen at which she gazes. The face that was once so bright and so vibrant is now old upon her shoulders. The tears scrape her skin as they fall, so bitter are they. She neither wipes them away nor pays them heed. She just sits there, in front of the television, her legs crossed, thinking about her Dad. And all the while the smell of after-shave lingers in the air.

Chapter Nine

Sandy's flat was small, clean and tidy. Leading off from the square entrance hall were four white doors which led in turn to a compact peach coloured bathroom, a lounge, the main bedroom and, lastly, to a second bedroom that was home to all assorted bags and boxes. Sandy had not long moved into the flat and was still in the process of decanting her belongings. She had not envisaged the second bedroom as anything other than a place to store her belongings.

Tom sat on the settee in the lounge, shivering. Raindrops trickled from his hair to his forehead then on down his nose where they lingered for a tantalising moment before dropping softly onto the carpet. He was cold and he was tired. As the heat of the room began to warm him, he started to feel sticky and uncomfortable, irritated by the sodden clothes that clung to his skin as they dried. The hard black case of the Beautiful Guitar lay before him and he stared at it as if expecting some form of explanation.

"Tea or coffee?" asked Sandy from the kitchen that adjoined the lounge. "It's all I've got I'm afraid," she added, peering at Tom from behind an arched alcove.

"Coffee please," replied Tom.

His mind had separated into a thousand pieces. He felt as if he was in the body of another and he could not make sense of it at all. He could not get a hold on what was happening to him, could not grasp anything that was in any way familiar. Earlier that month, he had been sitting at a desk, daydreaming, safe, warm and certain of what the next day would bring. And now he was, quaking, in a flat in Big Town with a girl he barely remembered from school offering him solace.

"White or black?" asked Sandy.

"Black, please."

"Sugar?"

"No thanks."

Black coffee. Black coffee.

When Tom was eleven years old, he had progressed from his school reading books about children and magic and animals, to those books his father read. It had been a great step for him, not just in terms of literary maturity, but also in terms of moving a step closer to his Dad. And he had no moderation in his views of these books. Each one he read was the greatest book ever, for they were grown up books. Real books.

He would scour the small bookcase in the front room and devour the books mercilessly. From the first page to the last, he had been hooked. Every page overflowed with agents, double-agents, spy masters, assassins and wizened old hands who were forever being called back into service for one more crack at their elusive, life-long adversary whom you never met but in the haunted moments of your dreams. They were glorious books, glorious, fantastic books.

Interrogations beneath the single, crackling bulb, midnight flights to dark Berlin, drop zones, safe houses, and 'dead' letterboxes. A gunshot was just a snap in the night, a dead body just a dead body. Travelling to the Antarctic on a desperate frozen mission, wasting away in the heat of the South American jungles. Everywhere, there were hidden secrets, hidden pasts and hidden lives. And during his early youth, more than anything else, Tom wanted to be a part of this incredible world of deception.

Irony gets us all in the end.

It kills the best of us.

Just walk away and smile.

That's all I do.

So black coffee had been Tom's way in. Every spy drank black coffee. Without exception, they lived on it. During long nights of code breaking and questioning, black coffee flowed through veins instead of blood.

Tom had been so innocent, as naïve as the child he surely still was, a young man alone in a world now whose truths no book could ever come close to recounting. A truth nobody would ever believe. There is no despair for the very young. There is no terror for the child. There is only shape and form and outline. It is when we grow that fear and terror creep into our lives.

"I don't know how you can have your coffee like that, no milk or sugar," said Sandy bringing in a steaming mug and a towel. "It smells so strong."

Tom took the mug from her and wrapped both his hands around it. Sandy put the towel beside him on the arm of the chair. She had intended for him to dry his hair with it and his face. He looked so forlorn, she thought, as she returned to the kitchen to begin preparing something to eat.

The clatter of the saucepans and the low whoosh of the grill as it was turned on were like a slap to Tom's face. Only a few weeks ago, he had possessed it all, a monthly income, a room of his own, privacy, and a mother who did everything for him. He missed these things now. Even trivial conversations, banal television programmes, boredom itself. He missed all of these. At the time, they had passed unnoticed like breath; so superfluous were they to the tortured meandering of his mind. But now he realised how secure was his existence then and he couldn't see what had led him to jeopardise that security.

We all see things from different angles, different sides.

And the cruelty of loneliness burst upon him.

He had dared to look below the surface. He had questioned the basis and the direction of his life. And then he had acted, acted upon some indefinable instinct, almost on his conscience, sought to be at one with his innate self. If there is such a thing as a crime against society, then Tom has surely committed it. He has breached the surface of the norm. He has crossed the tracks. And like all those wretched souls before him, he will surely go down.

"Have you got time to have something to eat, Tom, or have you got to be going soon?" asked Sandy from the kitchen. "I'm just having cheese on toast, but you can have something with chips if you like, or soup."

"I'm ok for a while," replied Tom, unable to lift his voice much above a mumble. "Soup will be fine," he added.

"I can't hear you. It's this grill."

"Soup. Soup will be fine. I like soup. Thanks."

It had been such an effort to talk.

Tom was very hungry and he would have ravenously eaten two, three, four plates of chips, but he was feeling the need to deny himself—a beautiful, instinctive reaction.

When it came, he ate the soup in silence, holding the bowl close to his chin and scooping the soup into his mouth with such a mechanised action, it were as if the spoon were controlling the hand.

Sandy just watched him from the other side of the room. She had only just recognised him when he flew out of the park yet she couldn't quite isolate what it was about him that had changed from the boy she had known at school just a few years previous. There was definitely something different about him, she decided, something almost primeval, basic, indiscernible. It did not detract though from the feelings that pulsed through her—more, it served to fuel them.

When Sandy returned to the kitchen to clear up, Tom took the chance to look around him. Remaining hunched forward as if he were still sitting on the bench, he just lifted his head, straining his neck a little, and tried to come to terms with his surroundings. It was a homely and uncluttered room. Posters of wild animals and drawings of flowers adorned the walls and a small shelf above the television harboured several miniature bears in various pseudo human guises. A bookcase rested beside the settee and Tom leaned over to look at the books, his wet jeans tight and hard as he shifted his legs.

The bookcase contained a mixture of popular novels, magazines and household instruction manuals, as well as a few videos and some old newspapers. He decided, after not recognising the majority of the titles that they were not worth reading anyway. His views on anything cultural or aesthetic had always been tinged with an ardent snobbery and a stubborn disdain for everything other than that which satiated him. As people, we are so diverse, our component parts so magically discordant.

Tom was still looking at the spines of the books when Sandy came back in and sat down on the settee, careful to avoid any dampness. She picked up the towel and placed it, still folded, on her lap, stroking it, smoothing it. Tom did not acknowledge her presence.

"I haven't got many books," she offered apologetically, "I think there's a few more in the back room that I haven't unpacked yet. I've not really had much time for reading since we left school. There's some old school books down there actually, I think, on the bottom shelf."

"I chucked all mine," said Tom, still with his back to her. It was easier to talk that way.

At last, he drew himself from the bookcase and sat back on the settee, beside Sandy. It was only a small settee and she was closer to him than he had thought. He could almost smell the perfume she had put on that morning before going to work. It meant nothing to him though. The scent of fear and confusion still filled his nostrils and clung to his every breath. There was little time for beauty as yet.

"Was the soup all right?" asked Sandy.

"Yes. Thanks."

"Do you have to be back at any particular time, Tom? I don't want you to miss your train or anything."

"It's fine."

"That's good."

It had been so very long since Sandy had seen him. She had become a woman and he a man.

"So, how have you been? School seems so long ago, doesn't it? I suppose it is really. You were going to that bank, weren't you, or was it an insurance company?"

Sandy felt herself racing. She became suddenly aware of her speech being pressured but was somehow unable to intervene in order to slow it down. Perhaps it was a fear of silence for she was beginning to feel a little uncomfortable.

"Insurance," replied Tom, at last, his voice flat and indifferent. "I'm not there anymore."

"It does get boring, doesn't it? I've been at the same bank since school. It gets to me sometimes but, then again, I wouldn't have got this place without it. Everything has its good side, when you think about it."

Her voice was lively and alert, particularly in contrast to the dreary monotone of her guest.

Tom did not respond. He was barely listening at all, his mind drifting from one scene to the next, one world, and one vision after another. He was the shipwrecked cabin boy, all dripping clothes and pale skin, washed up bewildered.

"You should dry your hair really, Tom. You'll get a cold," said Sandy with genuine concern.

Tom did not answer.

A strand of Sandy's long dark hair fell across her face and she pushed it back gently. Tom saw this out of the corner of his vision and momentarily marvelled at the femininity in the act. It was the cue for him to look at her secretly as she brushed some minuscule piece of nothing from her shoulder. And he saw the innocence in her face and he began to feel the perceptible warmth of her near him. He had not been this close to anybody for so long, save Michael, not so physically close. An aura of gentility and acceptance floated about Sandy, emanating from every breath and every inconsequential movement.

"How long have you been here?" asked Tom, looking back now towards the floor, his voice still devoid of tone.

"About three months now. I've changed quite a few things. Still can't find room for all my stuff though. It's funny, I move out of a little room at my mother and father's, but I can't fit all my stuff into this big flat."

"I bet it cost you a few quid."

"Don't ask!" replied Sandy, her eyes dark, playful, gleaming. "My father helped me out quite a lot. I'm going to pay him back though. He says I don't have to, but I will."

"Worth it though, I reckon. Your own place."

"Yes. It makes you feel...." Sandy paused, searching for the words. "Grown up."

And then, as suddenly as it had sprung to life, the interaction thundered to a halt.

Sandy cursed her friends. They had ruined her conversation. All they seemed to talk about were soap operas, shoes, men and each other. They would sit in the bank stereotyping in an easy, unconscious way. She realised now that she had been sucked into the routine of it all, a routine whereby a conversation was merely the exercise of facial muscles. A routine where talking is no longer a source of learning, revelation, excitement, but just the exchange of already known and perceived views and observations. They all might as well just chew gum. And now she was struggling in her attempt to gauge mood, feeling, direction, looking for the words to regain the momentum, and to somehow keep Tom involved. He was her guest after all.

Tom felt the silence burning into him. He hated all this talk of all these mundane things he had left behind. Pleasantries, he supposed it was called, exchanging pleasantries. They weren't pleasant to him though. They were just precursors, crafty forerunners for what was inevitable. Then, at this moment, he would have talked about the price of curtains all day if it meant he didn't have to talk about himself. He had no pride. He was naked now, naked and vulnerable, just like the rest of us.

"Do you still live at home, Tom?"

See. Personal questions. Fucking personal questions.

Tom looked at Sandy from beneath his dark brow.

"Why?"

"I just wondered," she replied, aware of the change in atmosphere, feeling now that she had lost any ground she had previously gained.

This was not Tom, she thought to herself, not the Tom that had occupied her mind night after night, day after day, when they were both so much younger.

"Are you warm enough, Tom?"

He nodded his bowed head, his wet hair hanging down, tangled and formless.

"You still play your guitar then," continued Sandy, her eyes falling on the hard, black case. "You must be really good at it by now."

"Not bad."

"How come you've got it with you? Were you on your way somewhere? I haven't kept you, have I?"

"From what?"

Tom looked around at her sharply; rage lingering in his eyes for a second.

"From what?" he repeated, this time softly, almost pleadingly.

His mind throbbed. There was a torment within it. All the bitter experiences of his short life came together as one. He saw only failure and misfortune. There was no redemption. Only shame. Pain and longing scratched at the door to his heart, coming home to rest, creeping into his tired eyes. And sorrow floated out upon warm, warm tears. Once he had started to cry, he was unable to stop. His whole body shuddered in mute disappointment as anger and blighted innocence were wrenched from deep within him drop by drop by drop.

Sandy just sat there watching him. She made no motion towards him and she said not a word. She took in for the first time the ragged nature of his clothes, the dirt on his hands and the smell of decay that lingered about him. And she understood. He did not need her at that moment for this was a private agony of which she had no part.

So the intensity of the emotion under which Tom had gratefully bowed was lifted. His body stuttered as it broke free and his breath was returned to him once more.

"Tom," whispered Sandy, coming close to him now. "Tom, it's all right. You don't have to tell me anything. It's all right. I'm sorry."

He shook and shivered, tremulous. His clothes were still damp upon him, as if freshly saturated with his own tears. Sandy put her arm across the back of the settee and pulled him gently towards her, holding him so close. She laid his head upon her and gently stroked his sodden hair.

"Shh," she said softly, "shh...."

He mumbled something but the words meant nothing. She held him tighter now, closer. His aching limbs left him. They were no longer a part of him. And they stayed like that for almost an hour, entwined in one another, until Sandy felt upon her now damp breast the rhythmic breath of sleep.

"That's it," she whispered, "that's it. You sleep now. Shh.... shh...."

And the young man fell asleep in her arms.

When Tom awoke the next morning, Sandy was gone.

Compared to the alley where he had slept previously, the settee had been a silken heaven. He felt as if he had slept for years. He had not woken every ten minutes, heart pounding, intensely aware of every footstep, every noise and every silence. He had woken strangely content. When you're asleep, life still rolls on. Things are dealt with, put into order within us sometimes while we're asleep in a way that the conscious mind cannot even begin to contemplate. It was as if Tom had been lowered prostrate and shivering into dark waters and had emerged wrapped warm and tight in the clothes of another. Once again, the spectre of premature redemption peered its head into his wayward life and smiled seductively in his direction.

Tom lay quite still on the settee and gazed at the ceiling. It was so comfortable in this room. Everything seemed so soft. And he was high up, perhaps on the fourth or fifth floor, high above the streets. Thoughts ventured onto the cluttered stage of his mind, exiting shortly after making their unbidden entrance. His road had been rough, very rough. It was time now for a break, to think like everybody else, to just relax.

Relax mate.

There was a note on the coffee table. The handwriting was large and curly. Tom read it over twice. It read 'I've gone to work. I'll be back at about six. I'll leave earlier if I can. Make yourself at home. You can have a bath if you want to. Please don't leave before I get back. I'll make you something to eat when I get in. Help yourself to anything in the cupboards. See you later.' Sandy had signed her name and added her work number in case he needed it.

Tom sat back on the settee, not sure what to do. She had left him alone in her flat. She didn't know him, not really, hadn't seen him for years. At school, they hadn't even been friends, just classmates. Yet she had let him stay the night and now she was offering to cook him something to eat when she got home from work. It didn't seem quite believable to him that someone could have that much trust. He knew there was no way he could break that trust and perhaps she did too. There are some beautiful people out there.

So he wandered around the flat, quietly, feeling slightly uncomfortable. He found the bathroom and carefully used the toilet. It could have been made of crystal such was his experience with the walls and trees that had been the backdrop for his relief the previous few weeks. He ran himself a bath and removed his clothes. They smelt strongly of the rain from the previous night. It was only once he had got into the hot bath and smothered himself in soap that he realised how filthy he had become. The water turned a dull grey colour through which Tom couldn't even see his legs. He lay there for some time, just calm and silent. Eventually, he got out, rinsed the bath with the shower hose and wrapped a large peach towel about himself. As he was doing so, the gratifying silence was pulled apart by the ringing of the telephone. He walked through cautiously to Sandy's bedroom where the phone was, and picked it up.

"Hello?" he said, warily.

"Hello. It's me. Sandy."

"Oh. Right. Okay. Good," he said, much relieved. "You sound different on the phone."

"So do you. I was just seeing how you were."

"I'm sorry I wasn't awake when you left."

"Don't worry," replied Sandy, pausing now. "Are you okay with washing machines? You can wash your clothes if you like." He did not reply, thrown as he was by the question. "Or you can wait until I get in," she added.

Tom was thinking furiously now. Long term plans or minute by minute. Decisions were being made for him again. What to do? Dreams, freedom, warmth, security, loneliness, cold, backward step, any step, go, stay, find Michael, stay, stay, stay.... for the minute ...

"Tom, I don't know what's happening with you, and you don't have to tell me, but I want you to know that you can trust me. If there's any way I can help, I will. And don't think you're 'putting me out' or anything. To be honest, I'd like the company."

Stay, stay, stay....

"Thanks," replied Tom softly. "I'll see how it goes."

He thought of secret documents and of midnight meetings, of the stars, the trees and of cold, cold alleys.

"Well, I'd best be going. I'll see you about six."

Tom said goodbye and put the phone down. He wandered out of the bedroom, a towel still wrapped around him, and slumped down onto the settee, feeling weary again. From what he could remember, Sandy had been one of those girls at school whom he had despised, whom he had judged as short-sighted and narrow-minded. She had got top marks in every subject. When a volunteer was called for, hers had been the first hand in the air. And she had never got drunk with the others. She didn't know what real life was about. He vaguely remembered her as having very few friends and that she was picked on by some of the other girls. But now, now she seemed different.

She was old then, Tom.

She is younger now.

He got up, turned the television on and watched Sesame Street.

Whilst Tom was sprawled on the settee, Michael was in the park, battered and dazed. The bruises were showing now on his face though the blood had since dried and was intermittently flaking off. And as he sat there on the bench, an earnest young man in a dark suit approached him.

"You are in need of Love," said the earnest young man, looking down upon him.

"I am Love," replied Michael, looking up.

"There is one," continued the earnest young man, "one who can give you all the love that you need. He will love you for who you are. He will forgive you your sins and he will deliver you unto Heaven. He will look upon you as his own and he will cherish you. Your sins were washed away when Jesus was nailed to the cross. He suffered so that you may not suffer. He died and was resurrected so that you too may join your father. Jesus will save you."

Michael looked deep into the eyes of the earnest young man and held his upturned palms before him.

"I am Jesus," he said, tears in his eyes.

And the earnest young man left, affronted.

Sandy arrived back at the flat just before six that evening. She opened the door to the lounge and found Tom on the settee, his eyes closed, the towel still wrapped around him. He had slept all afternoon. She looked at him as he lay there. He seemed such a lonely figure, so frightened, even as he lay there perfectly still. It was as if he had just fallen down to earth.

Tom awoke to the sound of clanging and clattering in the kitchen. It nudged him awake, a fanfare as it was to the next stage of his reckless life. He was suddenly aware that the towel did little to fully cover him, so he began arranging it hastily, looking for his clothes.

"I'm just doing some tea," called Sandy, hearing the frantic rustling in the lounge. "Do you want coffee?"

"Cheers."

"Your clothes are in the washing machine," she called again. "Hope you don't mind."

And these thoughts, these thoughts streamed through his mind. He could be on the run or undercover. He could be a poet, an artist, an author, anything. Was this a final chance to re-invent, to begin again? Re-focus, re-adjust and succeed. Don't look inwards. Look outwards. Watch out. Be one step ahead. And in that moment, he felt he had finally worked out the rules of adulthood. He had become wise to the ways of the world and its ways. Michael was wrong.

The contamination of the child was complete.

And Little Norman was nowhere to be found.

Sandy took the TV magazine from the floor and placed it on the coffee table.

"Tom," she said, "you don't have to answer me if you don't want to, but, well, I've been thinking. You seemed so scared yesterday when I met you. Are you in danger?"

He felt an obligation to answer, so soft was her voice. Maybe it was his dwindling conscience.

"Kind of."

"Oh."

"I can't really say any more than that."

He looked at her coolly—as cool as you can look in a peach towel anyway.

"Where have you been staying?" asked Sandy, trembling a little, though she knew not why.

"Around. Just around."

An image of him crying the previous night jumped into Tom's mind now. What had been a necessary release, he judged now, in hindsight, a weakness. But it was now that he was truly weak, unable as he was to face up to the decisions he had made. Cry now, Tom. Just cry mate.

"What do you plan to do?" asked Sandy. She didn't want to press him too much. She just wanted to help him.

"I don't really plan. I just take things as they come."

"Are you going to go back to work?"

"Fuck them. I wouldn't go back there. I can't anyway."

Sandy flinched as he swore.

"Do your parents know where you are?" she continued, timid now.

The mention of his Mum and Dad brought him down and hurt him.

"Did they know where you were going?"

Tom did not answer. He just looked into his black coffee.

"Have you spoken to them, let them know where you are?"

Again, there was no answer.

"Do you still live with them?"

"What is this?" said Tom angrily, still looking at his coffee. "What am I, five years old or something?" He paused and took in the unpleasantness in the air. "Look, I appreciated how you helped me yesterday, but show me where my clothes or and I'll be out of your way."

Sandy didn't know what to say. She was just trying to help.

Tom looked at her. She looked straight back and sighed. She had the most beautiful eyes.

"If you want me to go, I'll go," he said with some consideration, some awareness of the effect his words were having. He was flitting from one branch of his personality to another like a bird with a broken wing.

It was the classic line, the classic test.

Sandy put a hand on his bare shoulder.

"Tom," she said, "I thought I'd made it clear you could stay here. Try and see it from my point of view. If you're staying here and you're in some kind of trouble, I think it's fair you let me help you with whatever's wrong. That's all. And you should let your parents know."

Tom coughed a couple of times.

"Are you all right?" continued Sandy. "Do you know what I'm trying to say?"

Her hand was still on his shoulder. He didn't want her to move it.

"I'll phone my Mum and Dad in a minute."

"Tell them you're staying with a friend," said Sandy, smiling and removing her hand from his shoulder.

"Okay."

"Only if you're sure. The phone is in my room."

"I know. I answered it earlier."

"Oh yes."

There was a short silence before Sandy spoke again.

"Pies and chips all right for dinner?" she asked.

"Cheers."

Tom dialled a number. Any number. He held the receiver face down on the bed for a minute or so before replacing it. He stayed in the bedroom for a further minute before going back into the lounge.

"Any luck?" asked Sandy at the kitchen doorway.

"No answer. They must've gone out."

"Oh."

"I'll try again tomorrow. They don't go out much, especially two nights running." He thought for a second. "Then again, who knows?" he added.

Sandy felt she had missed so much at school and bitterly regretted her scholarly diligence. Her textbooks had not prepared her for situations such as this. Things were happening that she didn't quite understand. Was she mad, stupid, naïve? She didn't know. Is this how people get into trouble, she thought, is this how it all starts?

And as she was thinking these things, Tom played lightly on the Beautiful Guitar, softly, tentatively, almost as if he were caressing a faithful pet that he had ignored for too long.

"That's nice," said Sandy. "What is it?"

"Nothing really. Just a tune."

Tom played a song by Mississippi John Hurt, improvising some of the lyrics and leaving out some of the more difficult runs. As he sang, his voice developed an American twang that Sandy initially found a little amusing. But maybe you had to sing it that way.

Without prompting, Tom played two more songs, though his one-woman audience was barely able to distinguish between the three. Perhaps it was just one long song with some very odd words.

After allowing the final note to hum meaningfully, Tom coughed and closed his eyes for a moment. He was tired now, and so was Sandy. She crawled off to bed and he slept on the settee, the Beautiful Guitar standing over him, still protecting him, though he knew it not.

In that wonderful limbo between consciousness and sleep, Sandy had convinced herself that she needed Tom. As she slipped from reality to dreams and back again, it all seemed so clear. She believed in fate. This surely was the work of fate. A chance meeting on a rainy night—it couldn't have been written better—DREAMLAND.

Chapter Ten

Childhood and adolescence bring with them mistakes and inconsistencies, errors of judgement and of perception. It is almost a physical affliction.

There are some people who glide across life's surface like a breeze. For them, there is no pain and there is no terror. For theirs is a path ordained, a path bereft of the fear and intensity that ferments within our very hearts.

And there are others.

We struggle within life's waters with hearts bursting. So hard we try, so hard. And we cry out as deeper we fall beneath the depths of our innate wonder. And as a seed, we sink and are embedded in the sands of our birth.

And we grow mighty within and gentle without, surely as was intended.

There are some people who glide across life's surface like a breeze.

And there are others.

Us, mate.

Us.

Shortly after his seventeenth birthday, Michael had found himself in a room that smelled of sweat and urine. A room with a single window high out of reach, a room whose door could only be opened from the outside. That room was all he could remember from his one-month stay. And, finally, he had emerged into the sunlight of a new day complete with a diagnosis, a supply of medication and a letter to his GP—truly a young man grown old.

Whilst in that hospital so long ago, the only world Michael had been able to understand was that which came from within. When the body is trapped, the mind is prone to roam. And when the spiritual transcends the physical, you cannot fence a man in.

Now he was alone once more. For a short while, he had enjoyed the company of another stranger that had happened by chance to wander across the plane of his world. But now, now he was alone. It seemed that fate had decreed that he be alone, that his life be one of enduring pain. There were so many areas of his life over which he had no control. He was forever being pulled into life and thrown out again. Only in his mind was he truly free. There in that blissful arena could he dream, invert, rearrange and distort. There alone could he pursue that spark that would one day ignite his soul and allow it to burn forever.

Sitting in the park, Michael closed his eyes and succumbed freely to glimpses of his past, a past that had never let him be, a past that had betrayed him, ensnared him, and tortured him. He saw in the void a young man face down on a bed screaming. He saw two pale hands seeping blood and he saw the metal fork on the table that oozed blood also. He saw darkness and light and emptiness. The scent of despair was in the air and the taste of hopelessness wavered upon his tongue. He thought of Jennifer and Laura of Laura and Jennifer. Ah, innocence, innocence, fetch me your soul, just your soul, and permit me to wrap myself in its beauty and its sweetness.

What do you do at times like this, what do you honestly do?

You just let yourself go, float above it all, and let the world take you in all its anger.

"Mr Parrish?"

"Yes."

The two Policemen exchanged glances.

"You look in a bit of trouble Mr Parrish."

"Yes."

"We've had some reports, Mr Parrish, that lead us to suggest that it would be beneficial for you if you were to come with us."

"Yes."

"We're going to take you to a hospital, Mr Parrish, and have you looked at. Is that okay with you? Some nasty bruises you've got there."

"Yes."

So, they had come for him at last, come to take him—in the Garden. They had come silently, leaving not a trace. No time to say farewell, or even to lop off an ear. They had come for him at last.

In the back of the car, Michael's mind turned to Heaven and the Firmament.

"Do you know how many stars there are in the sky?" he asked.

"Millions?" said one of the Policemen.

"Billions?" said the other.

Michael paused before answering.

"No," he said, "just one. One or two."

Tom woke early on Saturday morning and was looking out of the lounge window into the street when Sandy came in. He had been staying with her for three days now. She no longer asked him questions about his situation or about the night in the park. He was a new man now with a new start. He was surely in control now.

"How long have you been up?" she asked him.

"Not long."

"What do you want to do today?"

Sandy wanted to ease up behind him as he stared out of the window, ease up behind him and hug him, hold him close. She had never felt like this before. Perhaps this is what it's like to be young, she thought. Working and keeping the flat had drained her over the past few months. But she was happy now.

"I don't mind," replied Tom. He turned around and, as he did so, was surprised at how close to him she was, how close was her body. She stepped back slightly as if by instinct.

"Well, I usually go shopping on Saturdays. There are a few things I need to get anyway. Did you want to come with me?"

"All right."

Sandy went to the kitchen to make some coffee for them both. She was getting used to the taste now. Tom had not been out since coming to her flat. The thought of them walking down the street together excited her in a way she couldn't fully understand. And she loved it.

"Tom," she called out over the noise of the boiling kettle, "I think it would be an idea to get you some clothes or something. I understand if you don't want to collect any from home, but if you're going to stay here for a while, you'll need something. Don't be offended or anything, it's just that you could do with more than you've got." She found it so much easier to talk to him when they were in different rooms.

Tom smiled.

"Don't worry," he said as she brought their coffee in, "I'll sort something out."

"Are you going to go home and get some then?" asked Sandy, sitting down.

"I've got a few quid on me. I'll pick something up."

"Have you got enough?"

"Who has?"

"If it's a problem, I can lend you some. It's ok. I've just been paid. Perhaps I can treat you?"

She liked the idea. So did he. He drew her to him on the settee and put his arm around her, careful not to spill the coffee.

Sandy listened to the beating of Tom's heart. And so did he.

Tom tried to go over recent events in his mind as he walked along with Sandy, but he just couldn't focus his thoughts. There was something stopping him. All he could think was that things were going right for him at last. But he was no longer Tom Spanner. His confusion and despair had left him to be replaced by a void, nothing. He was just an actor improvising in his own farce, assuming the most suitable persona for each situation. The people that passed him by were merely extras. And the girl by his side was barely a prop, though she had managed to get him to write down his parents address for her to add to her little address book. He kept the phone number to himself though.

The streets were a mass of colour. It was a parade. At each side road, huge groups of people gathered, waiting to cross. And when a driver made the unfortunate mistake of stopping his car to let one or two people in front of him, the crowd would surge forward and overwhelm the car like some writhing tide of disparate limbs.

The shoppers wandered around without direction, lost in the glorious madness of it all. But if you look closely, very closely amidst the hustle and the fervour, you will see figures that do not move, bemused, ragged figures—at the station, on the steps of the museum, in the parks, in the churches, in the doorways of your shops and of your theatres—or maybe just there on the ground by your feet. You may pass them by. You have passed them by. As have I. You may turn away, dart out a quick smile perhaps and then head bowed and shoulders hunched, hurry away wondering grief-stricken at the torrid gaze you receive to your token act of kindness. Like the Statues, the Palaces, the Cathedrals and the Parliament, these people are this town. They will be here forever, long after you and I are gone. And you don't even have to pay to see them. Not if you don't want to.

They are the products of a society that congratulates itself on the just nature of its laws and its propensity for fair play, a society that stares in rabid disbelief at poverty and human violations across the world and sees not the scars upon its own skin.

Think about it. A man does not beg by choice. He does not willingly subject himself to the ignominious torment of procuring small change from strangers. Would you? Think about it.

Occasionally, there will be a documentary made about the homeless and the deprived. In kitchens all across the country, kettles will boil until the adverts come on.

Now and then, perhaps, a minor celebrity, famous for who knows what, will descend into the bowels of the town for a week, just to witness the pain of it all. But they will soon be back to their house and their city in the skies. Their conscience will win medals and they have one more chapter completed in an otherwise turgid autobiography.

A Member of Parliament may stand up before jeers and order papers to plead on behalf of the dispossessed. But his words will not be heard. He will have his answer even before he has finished asking his question. 'Does not the honourable member know that we are spending more in that area, in real terms, after inflation, than ever before? In fact, as he should be aware, we have actually set up a working party to address the real issues. The claims of the honourable member are purely scare mongering and political point scoring and will not be taken seriously by anyone. The public will not stand for it!'

And the public will not stand for it—for they are far too comfortable sitting down.

The play will go on and different actors will fill the roles. The script will remain the same. As will the final act.

This is real. It's you and it's me. If you were to touch with a trembling hand one of the people on the street, it would not pass through them. It would touch flesh. It would touch the same body that was once held so tightly by the mother on the day of its condemnation. The same body that sat next to you at school. And that face will be in a photograph album somewhere, smiling the smile of hope. Those feet may have played football with you in the playground with a tennis ball whilst the rain came down. And those lips may have once been kissed so softly.

There is no worse punishment than that of being ostracised, to be alone in a bedroom, on the stairs, in the street, anywhere, feeling that not a soul would care if you were alive or dead.

A man may make a mistake. He may be the victim of his own folly and head off down a road that can only end in failure, hounded by dream and desire. For how long must that man suffer?

Who is it that has the right to judge another and rule that he be severed from life? Let me tell you. It is the prerogative of the friend. Believe me.

Sandy was so tempted to hold Tom's hand as they walked. It would have been so easy, so natural. But she couldn't. He seemed somehow much bigger than her now.

Tom had forgotten all those lonely nights, lying awake, thinking what it would be like to have a woman love him, really love him. It was ridiculous to him now. He did not recall the heartache, the embarrassment and the agony. It had all been swept away by this newly acquired sense of maturity.

Tom was beginning to realise he was capable of being able, at will, to shut down various parts of his personality. Thoughts and visions, that one minute he would die for, would float away on the breeze of a restless night. It was as if he were finding himself daily, consciously searching for a way to be. He was able to swing violently from altruism through apathy and cynicism to amorality and back again. And sadly somehow he had convinced himself now that he was in control of the process.

That morning, Tom and Sandy went into nearly every shop in the main street. She bought him a pair of jeans and a shirt. He said he would pay her back. She told him not to worry. So he didn't.

As they walked back from the shops, they began to notice various groups of people gathered on the street corners and outside the pubs. They were different in character to the shoppers. They had a different aura. And then Tom realised. Saturday. It is the middle of August. It was the first day of the new football season, a day o f incredible anticipation for some, a day of dread for the uninitiated. Over the coming season, hearts and dreams would be broken, along with a few relationships—but mainly hearts and dreams.

Little Norman had loved football. Tom had used to play with him in the garden. He would be in goal whilst Little Norman took amazingly long run-ups before swinging his small foot at the ball. Tom would dive in slow motion as the ball rolled towards him and Little Norman would look on with eager eyes. I wish you could have seen those eyes. I will always remember them. And Tom would be sure that his dive looked authentic. It had to look real for Little Norman. The ball would roll just out of Tom's reach between the jumper and T-shirt their mother told them never to use for goalposts and before the beaten goalkeeper could get up, the demon striker would be wobbling towards him on those chubby legs to retrieve the ball, all set to score another stunner. And he would never tire, Little Norman. It was always Tom that became weary. He would force himself to save a few shots or feign an injury in an attempt to bring the game to a gentle end. But Little Norman would always look so concerned if he thought his big brother was hurt in some way. He would stand over him and pat him with his soft magic sponge of a hand until the pain was gone. And at the end of the game, the two brothers, fourteen years between them, would make their way back indoors, Little Norman nudging the ball before him as he went. Then their mother would inform the country's greatest number nine to take that thing outside young man and take those dirty shoes off before you even think about coming in here. So Little Norman would throw the ball out into the garden and stand there watching it rolling over and over again as it disappeared into the bushes.

Little Norman would have played for England.

Tom felt an intense atmosphere around him. As he walked, he recalled those precious Sundays when he was twelve or thirteen, when he played football for a local boys' team. But surely that was somebody else? He was looking in now on the life of another.

Each Sunday morning, he would get up early and clean his boots on the doorstep, chipping off the dried mud from the last game with his mother's best kitchen knife. Only the best would do. He loved his boots then. He would pack his gear into a carrier bag and travel on the bus to the car park where everybody sorted out lifts to get to the game.

Those were the days of innocence—those glorious days before shame and hate.

Tom hadn't possessed a great deal of skill on the football field, but he used to play with such heart. He would run about that pitch until he could barely stand. If he was fouled towards the end of the game, or just tumbled over in exhaustion, he would lay still on that churned up mixture of mud and grass, his eyes closed for a stolen moment in an ecstatic reverie. All he had wanted was to drift away. To go where the footballers go.

After the game, he would barely be aware of the score. It didn't matter at all. And the dinner that his mother would prepare on those Sundays, well that was fit for the greatest player that ever lived. It was the smell that Tom most cherished, the perfect aroma of it all, the roast chicken, the gravy, the roast potatoes, even the vegetables. If he tried hard, he could visualise it, but he could never conjure up that smell. He would tell his mother and father how bad the referee was and how the other team were so much bigger and how he almost scored. And they would nod and smile. But he never told them of the pure bliss he felt, laying there on that football pitch alive in an aching dream.

The further Tom and Sandy walked, the more the football supporters outnumbered everybody else. Tom felt a moment of affiliation with them. He had collected all those stickers, bought the magazines, gazed at the statistics. But he had been younger then. Sandy was wary and nervous. It was different for her. More than ever, she wanted to cling to Tom. She looked away from the scarves, the faces and the shirts, not out of contempt, but out of some kind of fear.

The kick off to the precious new season was still two hours away but even that was too long. The gap between the final whistle of one season to the first whistle of the next is an eternity. You scratch around for three months watching videos and flicking through old programmes, convincing yourself that this will be your year. You spend three months coming off a drug only to spend the next nine months taking as much of it as you possibly can.

Sandy hated it all, the singing, the chanting, and the stupidity. Just as she thought they had made it safely through the crowd, two men and a woman walked towards them. They wore scarves that looked like they had just been bought off a street vendor and they looked uncomfortable in their attire, not proud, but self-conscious.

The two men, instead of passing Tom, just continued forward until they were stood right before him. The woman stood in front of Sandy, her men by her side. Tom and Sandy had no choice but to stop. One of the men, the taller out of the two, spoke in a thin, refined voice that would certainly have been grey were it colour, so lacking in character and emotion was it.

"What are you doing with her?" the man asked Tom. "Your own kind not good enough for you?"

The woman smiled a white tooth smile. The other man just stared vacantly.

Tom did not know how to react for his instinct had left him. This was not in his script. His throat was dry and his tongue hung heavy in his mouth.

As each second passed, the more the events, the scenes about them, were ripped away, torn out as if they had been cut from a picture and pasted elsewhere, leaving behind just this surreal tableau.

Tom took Sandy's hand and tried to walk away, but the staring man just stepped a pace to his right and continued to stare.

"Excuse me," continued the tall man. "I asked you a question. Didn't your mother teach you any manners?"

Tom still could not speak. Sandy dare not.

The woman did not take her eyes off Sandy, who in turn was intent on not returning the gaze. The tall man whispered something to the white tooth woman and she laughed. Sandy smiled, hoping against hope that things weren't as bad as they seemed.

"What are you smiling at?" asked the woman, her voice more of a bark than anything else, so in contrast with her precise make-up and bright clothes. "Are you laughing at me?"

The woman stepped forward until Sandy could smell her perfume and almost taste her cigarette ash.

"Or do you fancy me?" she asked, sneering.

She then blew a kiss at the trembling woman before her and ran a course hand slowly down Sandy's cheek.

Tom looked across.

"Are you looking at my girl?" asked the tall man, moving forward.

"No," replied Tom, his voice, when he finally found, higher than he would have liked.

The other man just stared.

"Why not?" asked the tall man. "Don't you like the white girls?"

The situation was grotesque. There was nothing that could be done or said to stop it from progressing in the only way it could. It just had to unfold in its own agonising fashion. Tom was numb. He couldn't get hold of his mind. If only they would give him room to limp like old Charles Grandon, maybe then they would leave him alone. There was a silence that lasted forever in Tom's mind.

The tall man lifted his hand and stroked back his greased black hair.

"Is that why you're with this fucking packie?"

Before he could answer, Tom was aware of a sudden movement beside him. The woman had grabbed Sandy's arm and was trying to take the bag of clothes off her. Sandy resisted until the white tooth woman yanked at her dark hair, the pain causing her to release her grip on the bag and it fell to the floor. The woman picked it up, grinning. Sandy was on her knees, tears on her face.

"What you got in there?" asked the woman, very pleased. "Fucking bananas?"

The two men laughed.

And so did Tom. He hadn't been able to help it. It wasn't a conscious thing.

Within seconds and without warning, the tall man punched Tom in the stomach. He bent over on to the ground and tried to curl up in order to protect himself from the kicks that assailed him. Sandy just stayed on the ground petrified. She cried as the white tooth woman continuously jabbed at her with high heels, playing with her, teasing her. Fucking bananas.

The other man stared on.

As Tom lay there on the ground, receiving blow after blow, he tried to reach for Sandy, his eyes pleading with her. But then he felt his eyes just close, shut down.

At last, a siren was heard. The tall man, the staring man and the white tooth woman ran off, throwing off their scarves as they did so.

Sandy's vision began to clear and she tried to sit up. Her body was sore all over and she couldn't feel her face. She felt ill and dazed. And then she saw Tom's new jeans and his new shirt on the dirty ground and she tried in vain to reach out for them. But each time she stretched out her arm, they just slipped by her.

A policewoman helped Sandy gently to her feet and led her to the waiting car.

"It's all right," she said kindly. "Just sit there for a while. There's an ambulance coming for your boyfriend."

Sandy wept in the front of the car. She could not think. The pain in her body drew a cloud over reality, making it vague and indistinct. Her boyfriend. Tom was her boyfriend. That was good. That was what she wanted. And then she heard that laugh again. Tom's laugh. It had lasted no more than two seconds but it rang in her head now, over and over, that laugh—that obsequious laugh of ignorance.

She looks over now to where Tom is being carried to an ambulance. But he isn't there at all. Not really. He is lying peaceful and serene on a huge football pitch somewhere far away, just laying there lost in naked wonder.

Chapter Eleven

George awoke to the sound of a digging machine. He tried to drag himself back to sleep, but the low rumbling noise would not let up. During the night, the first rain had fallen for what seemed like months, breaking free from the sky and spattering the dark houses. George had stayed awake for a while just listening to it against the window, transfixed by its momentum and rhythm.

Drinking his morning coffee, the remnants of any routine he may once have had, he stared at the linoleum floor and thought of his wife and of his son. The stain on the floor had taunted him in recent days and he had taken to just looking at it, praying that one morning it would transform itself into some message of hope. But it never changed, not even for a tantalising second.

The noise outside grew before subsiding again for a brief moment, only to return again with greater ferocity. George moved to the window to see what was happening. It appeared that someone had ruptured a water pipe. A stream of water was being pumped along the side of the road, gushing over the broken tarmac. A van from the Water Board pulled up and a man attached to a clipboard stepped smartly out.

"When it rains, it pours," said the man to nobody in particular. "When it rains, it pours."

George watched the scene through the window. The workmen were an eclectic assembly of people, all sizes and all ages. Their clothes were befittingly besmirched and their hair was dishevelled beneath their protective hats. They wore strong boots more suited to climbing than walking and each of their faces hinted at untold hardships.

When the men became aware of the man with the clipboard, they made no effort to acknowledge him. They merely continued talking amongst themselves in a relaxed, easy fashion, taking time every now and then to stare into space, focussing on something indiscernible far off in the distance.

One of the men was sitting on the kerb looking at a newspaper, a curious grin scrawled upon his face as if he had only just that moment understood the punch line to a joke he had been told some years previous. He stopped short of laughing but clearly shook with joy.

Another man was leaning upon a spade, his heavy forearms crossed on the handle. Determination oozed from his craggy rock face features. *This was just one more road. I've seen worse than this. Back in sixty-seven when Tommy Halloran and me worked on that tunnel, now that was tough.* Any moment now, a photographer will arrive on the scene and take a picture of this man for a book that nobody will read. Or maybe a party of schoolchildren, led by a thoroughly disconsolate teacher, will gather round and take notes on stained paper. And the man just stood there, supported by his spade, doing absolutely nothing.

One of the older workmen was looking at the flowers in a front garden on the other side of the road. The summer had been unkind to the blooms and the overnight rain had done little as yet to revive them. He peered at them with expert eyes, leaning over a low wall, assessing them, appreciating them. Suddenly, a net curtain was jerked upwards to reveal cold grey eyes and a manicured hand. The workman turned silently away to rejoin his colleagues.

George saw all this through his window.

The man from the Water Board walked up and down the road, surveying the destruction, paying little heed to the men about him. He wrote something down on his clipboard, murmured to himself, and drove off again in his little white van.

George drew back from the window. He would have toiled sixteen hours a day to mend that road, to make it smooth and right again. He would not have needed any sort of break. He would have accepted minimal wages, or maybe even none at all. And he would have done the work of a hundred men. If he had died on that road, it would have been a graceful and a meaningful death; far removed from this ignominious death that daily stalked him. Just give me a chance. That is all I ask.

All across the country, my country, there are people hating, despising every minute of their working day. Moan. Complain. Gossip. Deceive. Pettiness. Pettiness. He doesn't like me, she doesn't like me, look at him late again, fume, steam, stagger beneath the weight of your one-eyed view. Oh how indispensable I am.

Bollocks.

To work is a luxury greater than gold.

George would have valued every second at work. For he knew what it was like to be without it. Familiarity with desolation and despair is the greatest incentive for dedication just as the man about to be executed has at that moment the greatest thirst for life's waters. But only the lonely and the deprived understand this, truly understand it. The man behind the huge desk with the pen in his hand understands only the huge desk and the pen in his hand. And that is the greatest sadness of all.

So the workmen faded away and George left for Big Town, thoughtful and determined.

Well, Ron, so Michael is safe now. He has been found, found not by you but by another. So where does that leave you?

We all have moments that we feel are pivotal, that we know will portend a change. So often, all we can do is to stand back and watch, await the outcome in fear and cold sweat. Control is beyond us yet it is our future that is at stake. Fear is strange, Ron, it comes and goes, bites us, slips back into the shadows of our foreboding, only to return again for more. I hope you are afraid, Ron. You should be.

Michael sat in a small room, an empty chair either side of him and a desk in front of him. The faded paint of the magnolia walls was cracked and peeling. A thin layer of transparent plastic covered each window. It was neither warm nor cold. It was almost like being in a void—a quiet room in the midst of perceived madness. Michael had time to think, though he knew it would do him no good. He was relaxed now, accepting and resigned. "I am yours now, father," he whispered to himself, smiling a salt-water smile that would have broken your heart.

A man and a woman entered the room. The man sat beside Michael on the left and the woman sat behind the desk. She arranged some papers before her, took a pen from her pocket and looked across at Michael. She seemed timid and nervous and Michael liked her at once.

"You are Michael Parrish?" she asked, her accent strongly Germanic. She had short blonde hair and a pale, pretty face.

Michael leaned forward in his chair and clasped both hands together before looking up at the woman with those eyes of his. "Yes," he said. "I am."

"I am Dr Muller. I work for Dr Chesney. This is a Psychiatric Hospital and this," she added, nodding towards the man seated beside Michael, "this is John. He is one of the nurses on the ward."

Michael turned and smiled at John and nodded. John the nurse and Dr Muller. He leaned forward again and sighed. Let it run, Michael. Just let it happen.

"I am going to ask you some questions, Mr Parrish, and John will be making notes."

Dr Muller looked at Michael for some sign that he understood. No such sign was forthcoming, so she continued anyway, as if trying to remember her lines from a play after her fellow performer had missed his cue.

"So, Mr Parrish, can you tell me what has been happening with you lately? What has brought you here to us?"

Michael paused before answering, reflecting upon the tone of the question, and the delicate features of this lovely Doctor. "It was meant to happen," he said at last. "I was waiting for them. They came. And here I am."

"When you say 'they', could you tell us who 'they' are?"

"The two Policemen who brought me here. I'm afraid I don't know their names."

Dr Muller sought out John with a quizzical look.

"Came in on a 136. ASW saw him an hour ago."

"He's not on a section?"

"No. He agreed to come apparently," replied John, shrugging.

Dr Muller nodded.

"Yes, fine. So, Mr Parrish, why were you brought here to us? Do you know?"

"I am just playing my humble part," replied Michael. He paused before continuing. "As are we all."

"Mr Parrish, if you'll forgive me, I have not met you before. I do not know your case. Perhaps we can start with some more basic information? How do you feel in your mood?"

"Very well thank you."

"Do you feel low at all, what may be termed as 'depressed'?"

"No, no I don't."

"How do you feel?"

"Relieved, I think. Yes, relieved."

"Do you know where you are now?"

"I am in hospital."

"Do you know which hospital?"

"I'm afraid I don't. I'm not from this area."

Dr Muller looked at John before looking back at Michael.

"John will talk to you about that when we've finished Mr Parrish, if you could just answer a few more questions for me? Do you sometimes see or hear things that other people can't, visions, voices, anything like that?"

Michael sat there serene. They had come for him. He looked into Dr Muller's eyes and allowed his own to sparkle, dance with them for a moment.

"Mr Parrish, have you ever heard voices, suffered from hallucinations?" repeated Dr Muller. She had been on duty for sixteen hours and now here comes this man, out of area, smiling at her as if it were she that was being questioned.

"I hear just one voice, that of my father. I see just one vision, that of my sister. And soon I will be back with them both."

"Fine," said the Doctor, writing as she listened, ready to conclude the interview now. She was getting tired. Dr Chesney could do some work for a change. "I just need to ask you, Mr Parrish, do you have any thoughts of harming yourself or anyone else?"

Michael closed his eyes. His life had been long and hard. When he finally spoke, his voice was jaded, weary and much quieter, barely audible. Dr Muller had to lean forward in order to fully hear what he said.

"I talk with souls. I listen to hearts. I have no body. Neither do you, nor does this fine young man beside me. We are all floating in this space people call life. It is not for us to hurt each other. We accept and we go on. That is the way to peace. Accept and go on."

Dr Muller and John exchanged knowing glances. He'll be fine. No problem.

"One last thing, Mr Parrish," said Dr Muller, looking up. "Those marks on your face, how did they happen?"

"They will be gone soon."

Dr Muller signed the assessment sheet. Michael was struck then by how young she looked. Ah, Jennifer, soon I will hold you again.

"Mr Parrish, I would like you to stay in hospital for a few days. It seems that you have been having a difficult time recently. You need a rest. You will be seen by Dr Chesney the day after tomorrow."

She stood up to shake his hand. He stood up also. And that was when she noticed the wound in the centre of his palm. "What happened to your hand, Mr Parrish? Is that recent? You may need a tetanus injection for that. I shall write you up for some medication anyway."

"That happened a long time ago," replied Michael, calmly. "It just bleeds when it needs to. Please don't worry about me. I am in good hands."

Dr Muller left the room, acutely aware that there were only another ten hours before she could lay in her lonely bed and think of nothing at all.

So, Ron, nothing has come out yet. But it will. Don't worry mate.

And Laura sits in her room with her toys and her dolls and her teddy bears, just gazing at them, willing them to come to life.

The summer is moving on now. From the hot, baking days and the slow, tortuous nights, we have rain every now and then and a mist that hangs low early in the morning before the afternoon sun breaks through for a brief period, only to slip into the cool of the evening. We pull away now from our people, our town, pull back and see a land, a country. Lives go on, situations, characters, twists of fate, miracles and disasters. We are all connected. I affect you and you effect me.

Life I will forever be in awe of you.

Big Town.

There was once a large building. It served a purpose. It stood solidly and clearly amidst the throbbing chaos of Big Town. It was an old building, neither beautiful to look at nor particularly clean. To tell you the truth, it wasn't even that big. It just felt big. Some of the windows were cracked and paint was flaking off the front door as if it were the dead skin of an ailing creature. But it was a home. It was a sanctuary.

Within the grey walls of the building, there was an indefinable sense of hope. It was, at the very least, an address. Lonely, battered people drifted inside and learned of companionship. Some were eighteen years old; others could have been a hundred or more. Age was nothing. Each accepted the other with the grace and the benevolence of the truly downtrodden.

Many people used the building as a base from which to continue their search for work. Each day, they may return forlorn. But it was a place in which hope could be revived.

Where would such a place exist? Build it for me tomorrow. Think of me. Help me. You are I. We are honest and kind, but show me a space and a time when we can just be; for the honest and the kind are the radicals now of our day.

It has been known for fear to take hold of the mind. The rejection of a man for the dirt on his hands and the holes in his clothes is a rejection borne of fear. We are all scared, in truth. I know I am.

So, for a while, the people who called this building their home stumbled along with their lives. They searched for desire and hope and life with every breath. It was a silent search, a quiet, steady, remorseless search for a feeling. To make it through another day with your integrity intact was to succeed. The people who actually helped out in the building suffered themselves from a permanent weariness. It was the fatigue of the long-distance runner who just has to keep moving, for were he to stop and rest even for just a short moment, his legs would surely give way and support him no further. Their heartbeat and their drive was the metronome by which so many people breathed. They were the beach upon which the desolate were washed by wave after wave of disdain and misfortune.

There were people who had suffered intensely yet were on the street, cast aside as if they were barely human. Suffering compounds suffering. You can't play with a man like you can play with money. You cannot place a monetary value on so rich a quantity as life. So do not try to tell me because you will always be inaccurate, false and unreal. But with your money and your calculations you can kill a man as surely as shooting him in the head.

So, as time passed, there came news that the building was to close down. Rumours eased their sly way into conversations, worries took hold and the seeds of condemnation were sewn. A council official hinted that the closure date would be within the next three years. A curious relief held everybody. Three years. For those who survive by the day, three years is a lifetime.

Some weeks after the initial news had broken, a larger, taller man from the council visited the volunteers that helped out at the building. Or perhaps it was the same man in a different suit. The man led them to the kitchen area, for that was the only place in which he felt at ease. And holding a thin, clear folder in his hand, he informed all present that the building would be closed within fourteen days and demolished within eighteen days. He cited health reasons. Health reasons.

"You see," he said, "this entire building is a risk to both yourselves and those people who stay here, a risk to life, as a matter of fact. There is nothing that can be done, no, nothing. It is out of my hands now. I can assure you that we have looked into all possibilities, every one. I am here to pass our decision onto you and I am leaving it in your capable hands to pass this information onto the people that come here. You will have a greater, well, familiarity, with them than I would. Oh, and before I forget," he looked through the folder and found a scrap of paper from which he read before continuing in a decidedly wooden tone, "I feel as bad about this as you do." He put the scrap of paper back in the folder and proceeded to complete his speech. "So, don't be downhearted. We can't let sentiment get in the way of people's lives, can we, in the way of progress? No, of course not. After all, we all want to help these people, but sometimes, they just have to learn to help themselves. Anyway, you will be kept informed of any further developments. Good day to you all. Keep up the good work."

And the man that nobody had ever seen before, left, never to be seen or heard of by anyone ever again.

The men and women who had at last found a place that accepted them had to be told that their home was to be hauled down for luxury flats. Limp assertions were passed on but they did little to lessen the blow. A home is an affirmation of ones credence as a human being.

During the days that followed, the volunteers made an effort to liaise with various other local charities, church groups and foundations to provide support in the short term.

Health reasons. They were closing it for health reasons.

The windows were boarded up and so was the door. The electricity was cut off, the water supply too. There was no light, no warmth, and no sustenance. All the furniture had been removed for either sale or dumping. All that was left after the demolition were cold stone floors and cracked walls. But it was still a home. You can take a man's job as quick as you can write his name, but you can't take his home as easily as that.

One night, a hand wrenched free one of the boards covering a broken window and a ragged body slipped through the gap—and then another and another. Seven worn souls sat on the cold stone floor that night, just staring into the blackness. Rain fell outside like splinters. But they were at home and felt it not. They sat there shivering in the morning, having remained awake throughout the long night.

The foreman of the demolition team sighed. The people did not move. He made a call on his mobile phone, of which incidentally, he was immensely proud, and took his men back with him until the next day.

Twenty-four hours later, there were nineteen people on the cold stone floor. None of them spoke. The warmth of human company seeped into their hearts.

On the third day, the weekend having passed, a police van arrived, the front door was kicked through, for no particular reason, and the people were led from the building, emerging in small and silent groups into the fierce light of the world, hungry and tired.

The foreman took a deep breath and instructed his men to begin work. The building was rubble in the click of a finger. And the people, the people were gone. They did not stay together, for they were not friends. They were just fellow sufferers, each with their own story, their own pain and their own dread.

Big Town.

George walked through the streets of Big Town, looking for his son. He wandered aimlessly, following no map, no plan, trusting now only to miracles. Tom could have walked right in front of his very path and George would not have seen him. It just felt right to keep walking, keep moving. His eyes scoured the ground before him as if that were the best place to start. His head was bowed as he walked, perplexed and grieving.

And as he looked upon the ground, he saw depravity. For the first time in his life, he was brought within touching distance of victims. He saw young boys cowering beneath cardboard, their faces blotched and marked, their hair greasy, lank, and itching. There were not just three or four of them, but hundreds and hundreds. Boys and girls, though he could barely tell the difference, Tom's age and younger, laying there, looking at the sky, feeling its distance.

Before becoming unemployed, George had known little of the outcasts of his country. He had believed in the ethos of work. Toil is rewarded, sloth rejected. This had been his philosophy. But now, he was beginning to perceive an extraneous influence, a force against which there is no answer—not hard work, not honesty, nor, perhaps, even innocence. No answer at all. And it made him quake. He walked through the children, the men, the women, young and old and the air was filled with smells, sounds and visions, filled with an atmosphere he had never known before and would surely never forget.

Don't talk to me of numbers and figures.

Show me your comfortable heart.

Show me your comfortable soul.

And let me sleep upon your conscience.

George returned home just before midnight and sat at the kitchen table. He made himself a drink, took a cloth, wet it, and wiped up the coffee stain from the floor.

Tom, I love you so much.

I will look for you tomorrow and forever.

There was courage within George now, just as there is courage within all of us. He slept for four hours before returning to the shattered streets of Big Town.

Chapter Twelve

Tom was discharged from hospital the day after the assault in the high street. They had kept him in overnight for observations. He had been slightly concussed and had suffered bruising to his ribs and his back. Sandy had stayed with him for as long as visiting hours had permitted and she was there to meet him the next morning when it was time for him to leave.

Sandy had spent the night alone and Tom's absence had burned into her. It is so easy to become accustomed to the presence of another. You are drawn in despite yourself. It is a trick of life; it is some kind of magic that controls you entirely. You see things differently. You begin to dream, compromise, justify and before you know it, that other person has become a part of you and you a part of them. But in her mind as she had tried to sleep that night, all Sandy heard was Tom's laugh, that momentary, instinctive laugh that made her shiver every time.

That laugh had cut her like a hefty blade, scything through her cocoon of emotions; that haven in which her love for Tom had been so secretly nurtured. Justify, compromise, and dream. She could not reconcile her view of him with the way he behaved. She realised that she did not understand him. Her father had always taught her not to pass criticism on that which she did not understand. So she would wait until she saw him again, until he was back in her flat.

"Do you want to lie down?" she asked him as they both sat together on the settee.

"I'll be all right, thank you. I feel like I've been lying down for a week."

His voice was quiet and detached, subdued in tone, strained.

Tom had been thinking too, reflecting. He was being thrown from one situation to another on some turbulent sea upon whose surface he had striven vainly to walk. He had allowed it to take him. He knew now that he was heading for the bottom, to the depths of his own ocean. Please teach me how to float. Give me time—time to learn. That is all I ask.

"Would you like a drink?"

"No, I'm fine."

They sat beside each other in silence. But it had to break. There was too much to be said for it to last.

"Tom," said Sandy, continuing to gaze at the opposite wall, "why did you laugh with those people yesterday?"

Tom breathed deeply. What could he say? He knew the question was coming. It had been on his mind from the moment he had awoken in that sharp, white hospital that morning. He couldn't even look at her.

"What do you mean?" he murmured.

"Yesterday. Those people when they said those things about me. And you laughed. Why did you laugh?"

It is time now for you to come down from the stage, Tom. Take your bow and return to yourself, your true self. Follow your heart again. Go to your soul. He turned to look at her. She did not acknowledge him. As she stared forward, he allowed his eyes to imbibe of her beauty for she was indeed beautiful. He saw that now. He was surely at her feet now, looking up. And she was beginning to shake a little.

"Look," he said, unable to take his eyes off her. "I don't know why I laughed. All I can think is that I was just scared and it just sort of came out. I was a fucking idiot. I know how it must have looked." He sighed now before continuing. "Last night, I was thinking what I've turned into, the things that have happened to me and the things I've done, not just recently, for a while now. Like I said, I'm just some fucking idiot, just some fucking idiot chasing something that isn't there and hurting good people along the way. Sandy, I'm lost, mate. Fucked. I'm sorry."

She turned to him now and he saw at last the tears upon her face. He felt stranded, naked and vulnerable. He was a child in a strange, strange world. So he reached for her. And she reached for him. They held one another and each accepted the tears of the other in silence.

They stayed sitting there, entwined for three hours. Neither spoke nor moved. The touch and the warmth of another human being can wash away pain and reconcile loss like nothing else. In that embrace, there was safety and dreams and fear and longing.

And the moon peered through the window, gazed in solemnity at the scene, and could not tear itself away.

Michael sat in his room, eyes deep in the past. There was no present and the future was only days away. They had given him some medication to help him sleep the night before and its effects clung to him still. He felt weary and listless. The room had in it just a bed and a locker. The floor was grey and the walls a pale yellow. Light filtered through the single window and reflected the outline of the frame onto the tile floor. A mirror of light was there before him.

It was a subtle, enticing gateway out of there, out of everywhere. But it was not the one for which he was waiting.

There was a knock on the door and John entered. He was around twenty-three years old, had dark hair and growth of stubble around his face that made him at first appear slightly older. He spoke with a soft Southern Irish accent and he had an easy, natural way about him.

"Michael," he said, "sorry to bother you. It's just that we need to have a chat. I'm going to be your named nurse while you're here and we need to work out what we can do to get you out." In the absence of a reply, he added, "I'm John, you remember, from yesterday. When you came in."

Michael looked at him and sighed. He liked John. He had liked him from the moment he had met him—just a few more days now.

The two men walked down the long ward corridor into a room at the end. John put his heavy key in the lock and turned it, allowing Michael to enter first. The room was well lit and contained four or five chairs. Michael looked about him before sitting down on a chair beneath one of the windows. John shut the door, pulled up a chair, and sat down also.

"How did you sleep last night, Michael?"

"As well as I need, thank you. I took your tablet."

John smiled.

"It wasn't my tablet. It's just what the doctor prescribed to help you sleep. If you don't want it tonight, don't worry. Its just there if you need it."

Michael enjoyed John's voice, his accent. He was identifying beauty now, concerning himself not with anger and despair. For his time was short. And there truly was beauty everywhere.

"Anyway," continued John, "what we need to talk about is what needs to happen for you to leave here and go back home. So, basically, I need to know a bit more about you, how you're feeling, what your plans are for when you get out of here, and if there's anything we can do for you here to make things more comfortable for you."

Michael looked into John's eyes. There was redness at the edges of them, sore veins creeping into the blue pupils in which Michael saw honesty and something indefinable—life, perhaps. Or death.

"Where would you like me to start, John?"

"Wherever you like. We've got a while, so don't worry about time."

Michael felt relaxed in John's company. The room was quiet and it seemed to be far away from the unpredictable suffering of the rest of the ward. Were the walls to crumble and fall, he imagined there would be meadows all around, buzzing green fields strolling into Heaven.

Don't worry about time.

Michael thought deeply.

"We all live in a story, John. Our lives are just tales that nobody hears or reads. But you are now in mine and I am now in yours. That is how beautiful life is. That is the beauty of life."

John just looked at Michael. He was listening also for key words. Any mention of medication that he had been on in the past, names of family members, previous diagnosis, names of other hospitals. Anything perhaps that would make this man fit into the parameters of the patient. But he was prepared to wait. The alcohol from the previous night had stalked him throughout the early morning and he was appreciating now the solitude of this isolated room. So he nodded, indicating to Michael that he should continue.

"I have always known that I was different from others. I have known that for a very long time. It's nobody's fault. It's just the way it was meant to be."

"Different in what way?" asked John.

"In the sense that, well, in the sense that, yes I live in this time, this place, but outside it too. I see what you see but also I see within it, around it and through it. I see lots of things, beautiful things."

"What sort of things?"

"I see life. That is all. I see life and goodness in everything. And where there is no life, I give life. Where there is no goodness, I dream and there is goodness. My life is a cleansing of souls."

Michael closed his eyes. Not long now. Not long.

"Are you okay?" asked John. "We can carry on later if you want."

Michael opened his eyes and breathed life back in before continuing.

"I had a sister. She left me a long time ago. That was when I first realised that not everybody was like me."

"Was she older than you, or younger?"

"She was young then, but she is younger still now, so much younger, so young. At least I thought she was. I thought I had her back. I thought that she had come back to me, but I was misled. So now I must go and find her. Maybe. Maybe."

"Do you see her much?"

"I see her every day now, every minute. She is with us now. She will be with me always."

"Right."

This man is great, thought John, really great.

"So you've got a sister. Do you see her when other people can't?"

"I see her with my soul. I cannot speak for others."

Fair enough, thought John.

"When she left me, they put me in a hospital like this. Not as nice as this, but the same kind of place. That was a difficult time for me. Without my sister, I had nothing. So I gave myself."

"Gave yourself?"

"Yes."

"To who?"

"To you, John."

Suddenly, there was some shouting and thudding from out in the corridor followed by the shriek of a panic alarm and John leapt from his seat, flying out of the room.

Michael stood up slowly and looked upwards. He looked past the ceiling, past the roof and past the sky. He saw only Heaven now.

On leaving the psychiatric hospital just before his eighteenth birthday, Michael had begun his life again with a vigor and a pleasure in the world, a world of natural beauty of which he was the creator. Nature was, for him, the perfect embodiment of the spirit, the true bridge from vision to reality. And he was never to leave that exalted plateau. He would never return to the hatred and the factories and the smoke. His country was not one of steel and rust and fog and grime, but one of brightness, possessing a profundity that could only be found in the essence of the human soul.

The office where Michael had begun work at the age of twenty-one had not been ideal for the pursuit of inner paradise. Though he acquired a reputation as a capable employee, he had been known more for his lapses in concentration and his distractibility. He was often intentionally induced into long orations about flowers or the sea or the sky, merely as a means of alleviating the boredom of his colleagues. They felt this strange young man humorous. And they would turn him on and switch him off at will.

It had been at an office party that Michael first met Christine. He had been talking to a small group of people about some subject or other and was as they gradually dispersed, one by one, both amused and bemused, that Christine stepped from the shadows full of joy and admiration. She worked at a branch on the South Coast and the party had been for all those in the Southern Area Division. Such parties were frequently lurid affairs. Inebriated characters, old and young alike, would weave through the night, staggering and crawling upon hands and knees, faces blotched and heads in shreds.

Christine had been at the company for six months and she had learned in that time that a smart suit and a bright tie do not necessarily guarantee a sharp mind and a gentle heart.

Michael was different.

During that party, he had excused himself, citing the need for fresh air—'clarity amidst the fervour'—and she had followed him outside, outside into the dark night where they talked together until the moon rose, shone, and slipped beneath the reddening sky of the morning. They had spoken of their loves and their follies, their feelings and their predicaments. But he had not told her everything. Not about his sister, Jennifer, nor about the hospital or the marks on his hands.

As the months and years had passed, Michael and Christine saw more of one another and they eventually married on one cold April afternoon in a registry office. He had been twenty-six, she twenty-three. Ron had been there at the wedding, as had his new girlfriend, Diane. The years following Michael's discharge from hospital had re-introduced Ron to security. He had visited Michael almost daily during his admission. From what he could gather, they had diagnosed Michael as having some form of thought disorder. And that was fine.

So as each day of Michael's life went by, events and details were clouded by dreams, wild ideas, illusions and delusions, but, wonderfully, he continued to what the consultant would say 'function'. As he sits there now though, in that room, alarms going off, waiting for the nurse, all he sees are the dry, broken sticks of a child's shattered vision.

Dry, broken sticks.

A spark will destroy a forest whose time has come, bring it all down.

All it takes is one flickering light and it's gone.

The married couple had moved to a pleasant house not too far from the town and Christine had been transferred, at her request, to the same office as her husband. They had lived thereafter, for the next ten years, an uneventful, enclosed life. Neither had made any real demands upon the other. There had been no real expectations, hence no real disappointments.

And then, almost overnight, Michael had begun to drift away. His communication with his wife and everybody else faltered. He would shut himself in his study, just staring into space only he could see, his eyes fixed, urgent, and aflame. Christine would check if he had been taking his medication—his 'stress' tablets. Married for ten years and then this. Meal times would be passed in a heavy silence. Foreboding had taken his seat at the table and made himself very comfortable.

Christine had dreaded their journeys to work for her husband had grown sombre and detached. Not a word would be spoken between them. It had become impossible for her. So she had turned to their new neighbour and long-time work colleague for advice. Ron. Strong, dependable Ron. She had not wanted her marriage to fall apart. Ron would listen to her, console her. She had always admired him.

And then Laura had come along. The pregnancy had broken the cloud surrounding Michael and joy had rained upon him. It had come as a shock for Christine. They had not made love for over a year. Michael hadn't questioned anything. Ron looked on.

So Christine had handed in her notice and prepared herself for the change in her life, experiencing all emotions to their fullest extent.

Michael would come home from work with flowers that he would hide in different parts of the house for her to find, to stumble upon. He did all the housework and all the shopping, the cooking and the ironing. The physical effort had been nothing to him, for love was his. And every now and then, he would whisper to himself, "she's coming back, she's coming back." And he would skip a little, whistle and be unable to keep himself from laughing. "She's coming back."

Michael had been there at the birth, looking on in wonder as his wife struggled in agony. Of all the sights he had ever seen, and they numbered many, none compared to the birth of this little girl. For he saw things differently to you and me. He saw it all.

When the tiny blood-spattered child had emerged, Michael had wept. He had taken the baby in a towel and held her to his heart, tight to his heart. A tear had dropped from his eye and splashed onto the fragile forehead of his baby.

Laura had grown as a flower in Michael's eyes. He would spend hours just looking at her as she lay in her cot, delicate, fragile, light and beautiful. When she cried, he would hold her and whisper to her, waiting for the moment when their heartbeats were as one. And as he spoke so quietly to her, she would drift back to sleep, drift back to the wonderful land he had created for her. Michael no longer had to search for beauty in all things. It was there before him—his baby, his own baby.

Ron had been named as Laura's godfather, a role that he had assumed with no discomfort at all. Michael had insisted. Christine had remained silent.

Laura would never weary of Michael's affections. As she grew older, she was neither embarrassed nor ashamed. Some of her young friends, even at five, six years old, would be so hostile to their parents, resenting physical contact, petulant and proud. Oh so young to be so old. And Laura would look on, confused. She loved her mother dearly, but her Dad was her special friend. He was the hero in all her fairy stories, the face she saw when people spoke of Jesus—that thin, pale face with the sad eyes.

The whole period of Laura's early years had been a tense and nervous time for Christine. She would barely speak to Ron. He would call over on some pretext and find Michael once again there, playing with Laura, having taken another day off work.

Ron and Christine.

Only the closest of friends and lovers can truly break a man's heart and leave it in pieces.

Laura. Last year at infant school just finished. Summer, the summer holidays. How do we make sense of it all? Two weeks after breaking up from school, she lies upon her bed, covered in another's sweat, sore and terrified. Her teddy bears and her dollies gaze on, impotent. And when she wakes in the middle of the night, having finally got to sleep, she wakes in total fear. Michael is there, crouched on her floor, staring at her, tears all over the place, shaking and shuddering. She puts her arms around him, just leans across instinctively and cuddles him. And she cries too. Seven years old. He whispers through his pain and she slumps back into dark sleep.

When I wake up, my Daddy is gone. And I am very old.

Whilst Michael sits in that room, alarms still shattering his silence, Christine rises slowly from her chair and pulls her dressing gown tightly about her. She walks slowly, deliberately, to the study as if being led by the hand. She pushes open the door and enters. It is so neat and so precise. She looks around the room and moves over to the large desk upon which is a heavy, garish paperweight. Easily, calmly, she picks it up, turns and crashes it into the glass-fronted bookcase. No sound can be heard. There is no sound. She wrenches open the desk drawers and empties the contents out onto the carpet. She smashes the small lamp against the corner of the desk until the clay base is cracked and shattered. She pulls down the curtains, rips them, and throws them to the floor—still not a sound. She wrenches the telephone cord from out of the wall and hurls the whole thing across the room. And the destruction continues in complete silence until Christine, beaten, staggers out into the hall, a thin trail of blood following her out, seeping from her foot.

And Laura, Laura is upstairs listening to the silence.

Look closely now, for on the floor, by the study window, amidst the broken glass and the debris, amidst the artefacts of a fool, there lays a photograph, a small photograph of a beautiful girl. The edges are a little curled and the background blurred, but the girl herself is bright and smiling. The photograph was taken by a man whose love for that girl was greater than anyone could understand.

And on the back of the photograph, if you look closer now, a name has been crossed through and replaced in ragged writing with another. Where once it had read 'Laura', it now reads 'Jennifer—my love.'

Surely she is an angel.

Chapter Thirteen

Sandy decided to organise a party at her flat. She just needed to be amongst friends, to re-affirm her stability. So she invited some people from work and the couple from the flat below. In some odd way, she knew that the trivial talk and the loud music would allow her time to think with more clarity about her situation. Each morning she rose, she was unable to get a grip on her feelings. The common sense that had been with her always had now left her, left her with barely a sense of anything at all.

Tom was enthusiastic when Sandy told him of her plans for the party. He looked forward to meeting others now, for he was a stranger to them. Pre-conceptions and previous meetings would not influence them against him. This was his new life now and these his new encounters.

So long ago now the dreamer had set out from his bedroom to tap the true source of his soul. It's still there for you, Tom. Just stop. Close your eyes. And look all around you.

Throughout the day of the party, Sandy tidied the flat until it looked like an artist had sketched everything into place. She vacuumed and polished, cleaned the windows, washed the kitchen floor and made sure there was a place for everything. She had sent Tom out early in the morning to the shops for food and drink and he had gone willingly. It seemed to her that he had been less tense than of late. Maybe he had at last understood how kind she had been to him. As she polished the low coffee table, she wandered into dreams, allowing her eyes to fall into visions amidst the deep, smooth grain of the dark mahogany. She loved him. But she had never been told that love can hurt this much.

After she had cleaned the flat and while she was waiting for Tom to return, Sandy took the time to decide what to wear that evening. She looked through her wardrobe, all clanging coat hangers and swishing dresses each compelling her to choose them. The feel of the material on her fingertips excited her. And as she stood there, her clothes gazing at her, anticipation began to grow within her. Perhaps Tom would realise when he saw her in one of these dresses, when she had done her hair, put on some make-up, perhaps he would realise she was a woman now.

She finally decided on a long, black skirt and a white blouse with frills around the neckline and lace around the sleeves. Small silver buttons fastened right the way up to the neck and the material was a beautiful silk. She slipped the skirt on over her jeans just to assure herself she could still fit into it and viewed herself in the mirror from every conceivable angle. As she was stepping out of it to hang it back up, satisfied, there was a knock on the front door. She tossed the skirt onto the bed and hurried out into the lobby.

She opened the door.

"I think I got it all," said Tom, standing in the doorway holding two bulging carrier bags. Sandy smiled and took the bags off him as he entered.

"These are heavy. Did you walk all the way, or did you get the bus?" she asked as he followed her into the kitchen.

"Walked. I wasn't sure where the buses stopped," he replied, looking at his knuckles, willing them to return to even a semblance of their former hue.

After packing away the shopping, Sandy came into the lounge to find Tom smoking a cigarette. The smell made her feel ill.

"I didn't know you smoked," she said testily.

"Yes. It's just that I didn't have any fags." He smiled brightly. "I just got four less cans of lager and these fags with what I would have spent on the lager. I just won't drink so much tonight."

"Well I haven't got any ashtrays."

"Don't worry. I'll use one of them plastic cups I just bought."

He went into the kitchen, cigarette in hand, took a plastic cup from the stack that Sandy had just put in the cupboard, poured a little water into it and returned to the living room. He then sat down and, as if to demonstrate, inhaled deeply, rotated his eyes in a comic fashion, exhaled, tapped the ash into the plastic cup and smiled.

"There. You see," he said. "Sorted."

That afternoon, Sandy made some cakes and some sausage rolls and organised the rest of the food. Throughout this time, perhaps for an hour, Tom lay in the bath listening to the football on the radio. He emerged as the final whistles blew all around the country, dressed in the jeans that Sandy had bought him and wearing the black sweatshirt he had brought from home that had been washed the night before. He walked into the kitchen where Sandy was doing her third round of washing up.

"They fit okay, don't they?" he asked her. It was the first time he had worn the new jeans.

Sandy turned and looked at him. He looked lovely—he smelled lovely, so fresh.

"They look really nice", she replied, her eyes shining.

"Nice?"

"Yes. Really nice," she repeated.

"Do you remember that English teacher we had at school who looked like Kevin Keegan, well a cross between Kevin Keegan and Russell Osman?" said Tom suddenly, with energy and some humour. "I forget his name, but he always used to say how 'nice' was the worst word in the English language, that it meant nothing at all. Do you remember him?"

"Mr Crane," said Sandy, quietly.

"That's him."

Tom smiled. Kevin Keegan. Russell Osman. Mr Crane.

"Do you want a hand?" he asked, reaching for the tea towel.

"No. I'll be finished in a minute."

"Okay."

"You could put the drinks on the table for me, if you want. Put the cloth on first though. It's in the top drawer, behind the settee."

"Sure."

Tom arranged the cans and the bottles neatly on the table, the tallest at the back and the shorter ones at the front. And when he stepped back to view his work, he realised he'd forgotten to put the tablecloth on. Ah, well. He could start again; start again with small, ineffectual tasks. There was no such thing as time anymore—the next few minutes—that was all that mattered. And then there would be another few minutes. Such was the easy flow of his life now.

Sandy finished the cakes and covered them over with a net. Everything would be ready in time. The guests would be arriving in a couple of hours and all she had to do now was to get ready.

Sitting at her little dressing table, she sought in vain to accentuate the beauty of her eyes. She could not—for they were already as beautiful as the eyes of a child. She put deep red lipstick onto her soft lips and when she smiled, she emblazoned the room. But, come on, back to her eyes. They were indeed beautiful, but there was nothing she could do about the tiny red vein in the corner of each one—the sole reminder of where the tears had broken through.

After having made up her face, Sandy put on the white blouse. It was cool against her warm skin and it caressed her spine as it shimmered down her smooth back. She stood up and tucked it into her long, black skirt. And stepping into her shiny, black high heel shoes, she stood before the full-length mirror. She brushed her dark hair gently and let it bounce and swirl about her. But all she saw, all she saw in the mirror was the pain in her eyes. Turning, she walked into the lounge, closing the bedroom door behind her.

"You look nice," said Tom.

"Thanks," she replied, picking up an empty can of lager and putting it in the bin in the kitchen.

It had barely crossed Tom's mind to think of Sandy as anything more than a friend, somebody that was helping him out, being kind to him. Just a girl he used to know from school that he had bumped into. That was all. He neglected to see all those sideways glances, the way she looked at him, stared at him, the hurt she felt when he dismissed her or failed to respond as anything more than a young man who has fallen on his feet. He missed it all.

And who can say why?

Love, you conquer and you kill, you maim the innocent and you destroy the naïve. You break me apart with your lies and your deceptions. Were it not for you, Love, I may understand my life a little better.

Sandy stood in the kitchen, her eyes closed for a moment.
And she grew strong.

The first guests started to arrive at around eight o'clock and Sandy led each of them in turn into the lounge. There were thirteen or fourteen in total and in the small flat that was plenty. Tom felt at first a terrible loneliness as each person came in, one stranger after another. The regard everybody had for Sandy was obvious. He just sat uncomfortably at one end of the settee, peering over a magazine, like a teenager awaiting a circumcision.

The party meandered along, polite conversations punctuated now and then by lewd comments from two young men who had attached themselves tenuously to the table of drinks. One of them worked with Sandy, the other was his friend, the two of them replete with shiny hair, earrings and painted on stubble. By ten o'clock, they both felt ill. An hour later, one was asleep in the armchair, the other vomiting into the bath. Sandy ordered them a taxi and they left in tatters like two survivors from a bomb blast. 'Well, another great Saturday night lads. Another success. Well done'.

Tom had begun to enjoy the conversations that permeated the air around him. He was a little disappointed to see the two young men leave. They were in fact a similar age to him though he viewed them as being much younger. On their departure, he became acutely aware that he was the only male left at the party and the huddle of women who stood before him continued to talk boisterously, competing with the music from the stereo. He looked at them, leaning back, nodding at the required moments and smiling when he had to, pulling himself into their group. The alcohol was beginning to lend him confidence.

After two or three more of the guests had pleaded early mornings, Sandy came over to join the group of women who had edged perceptibly closer to the settee where Tom sat. Up until that point, for most of the duration of the party in fact, she had actually been in her bedroom consoling a middle-aged middle manager from the bank whose love was a love unrequited. This particular man had discovered her huge desire the previous night and she didn't know how she could face him on the Monday morning. Sandy had nursed her with kind words and a gentleness of touch until the woman fell asleep on the bed, cradling a diminishing bottle of vodka and wondering at the cruelty of life.

Sandy ushered one of the women to one side of the room and spoke to her briefly—moments later, the two of them sat down beside Tom on the settee. The woman who was now wedged between Tom and Sandy was tall and bright and she exuded wonderful vitality that immediately contrasted with the soft, quiet demeanour of her friend. From what Tom could see, through the veil of smoke before his eyes, she was definitely worth getting to know.

"This is Karen," said Sandy, introducing her friend to Tom. "She works at the bank, don't you Kay?"

"I show my face," replied Karen from beneath her painted eyelids. She took Tom's hand and shook it limply. "And you must be Tom?" she said, still holding his hand.

"Yes."

Karen withdrew her hand before continuing. "You're a lucky man," she said, in her seductive, cigarette-damaged voice. "This woman here can't stop talking about you. Isn't that right, Sand?"

Karen grinned the grin of an idiot. Sandy smiled, embarrassed. She remained strong.

"Do you want another drink, Tom?" she asked.

"No, I'm fine. Thanks. I've still got one," he replied, motioning to the can in his hand.

"Kay?"

"Vodka and tonic please, Sand."

"Vodka?"

"Yes. Vodka and tonic. The water of life. My life, anyway."

"I'll do my best," said Sandy, drifting back towards the bedroom, wondering how she was going to wrest baby from mother.

As soon as Sandy was gone, Karen shuffled still closer to Tom until their hips touched. She was wearing a short, black leather skirt and a tight, low-cut top. And when she spoke to him, he could almost feel her lipstick upon his ear.

"So are you and Sandy together then?" she asked, her voice luscious and gorgeous.

"How do you mean?" replied Tom.

Karen smiled. Those teeth cannot have been real, so white so perfect were they.

"Don't play with me, Tom," she said, coyly, putting a manicured hand upon his thigh and leaning over. "Does she steal the covers, or do you?"

Tom didn't know what to say. He could have listened to her voice all night. But as he looked up from the hand upon his knee, looked at that face that was now so close to his own, he saw that she could have been fifty years old. Through the smoke and the gloom and the hazy vision of the drinker, she had been stunning. Her voice remained alluring and her tight top, well, it might as well not have been there at all.

As the evening progressed, there were periods where the music stopped and each guest waited for another to restart it. The room grew darker and limbs grew less and less loyal to their source. Half empty cans winged themselves on to table ledges and windowsills, perching there like colourful tin birds, only to be nudged into premature flight by some unseen, mischievous force. Crisps and peanuts were crushed into the carpet until you couldn't walk anywhere without feeling a crunching sensation beneath your feet.

The party was all very amiable, if a little disjointed. Occasionally, two or three women would break off into a group to talk about one of the others, who was perhaps in the bathroom or elsewhere, smiling wanly as their victim returned.

Fuelled by alcohol and gossip, the party continued until long after midnight. For some, the time went too fast, for others, too slow. For Sandy, it was definitely the latter. Each time she looked across the dark room at Tom, there he was, next to Karen, so close to her. But she didn't notice that each time she looked away, he sought her out with pleading, longing eyes of redemption.

There is a moment when you recognise your love to be a love alone. And you know deep inside that moment will never leave you.

At last, the revellers faded away. One by one, as shadows, they slipped into the night.

Sandy had to call a taxi for Karen. She was, by the end of the party, barely able to stand even with assistance—too much water of life. Tom held her upright and guided her to the door. The following morning, she wouldn't remember his name. Within twenty-four hours, she would have forgotten they had even met—just one more night out, one more extension of youth. Carefree. Beautiful. Lonely.

Sandy turned the lights on in the hall and the lounge. She had not been so cruel as to do it whilst Karen was still there. She looked disconsolately at the mess before her. The light seemed so bright. She felt a little sick. Her mother would have said that it was all just a part of life's learning.

Tom went to the kitchen and started to put all the empty cans into the sagging bin bag. Sandy watched him in silence for a moment and before he could notice her, wandered to her bedroom, fell out of her clothes and slipped in between the cool sheets. The soft pillow soothed her dazed head immediately. And she just slept. She didn't dream. Just slept.

Tom had not drunk excessively during the party. The first three cans had made him feel full. He was never a lager drinker anyway and Sandy hadn't any whisky. A solitary fourth can of warm lager had steered him through the final three hours of the night. Karen had bored him senseless with her painted smile, her inane remarks and the way she kept touching him. It was like spending the evening with some irritating mechanical doll.

But Karen had at least given him a chance to reflect. In her make up and her facile ways. He had seen in human form a part of himself. Shallow. Laughable. He saw his frailty in her eyes and his deception in her smile. And he saw how he had let himself down. With each word from those traffic light lips and each touch from those traffic light fingers, he had taken one more painful step closer to the man he truly was. He had seen himself naked. And standing now over a bin bag full of crisp packets, broken cans and empty bottles, he attempted once again to clothe himself in the raiment of dignity, gentleness and wonder. He felt shame and confusion. He felt guilt and he felt terror. In essence, he felt like Tom again.

The night fell about Big Town, a warm, tight night. The darkness would not let the sun break through. It held out, dim and stagnant. Beneath the blanket of night, people slept and thought and paced and laughed and cried. They loved and they fought and they ran and they hid. They lived and died in the night for the night is the shoulder upon which the tears of the day are bound to fall.

Let me fly above your town, just float above it and I will come into your homes and your houses, into your streets and your dreams and your lives. I will drift in and out. I will see you as you truly are. I will see it all in a single night—for I am nothing without you.

The following morning, Tom made Sandy a cup of tea. He took it into her bedroom and placed it on her bedside cabinet. He looked at her for a moment and felt his heart within him. He then left her to wake with her radio and her tea whilst he tidied the lounge. And then he tidied the kitchen. In the course of a rambling, confused evening, clarity had sought him out and possessed him once more. It all seemed so obvious now. Where once there was bitterness and cynicism, now there was humility. Where once shadows, now light. But he still didn't think of Michael.

The eye can reflect feelings in a way that no tongue could tell. When Sandy shuffled, bewildered, into the lounge and saw Tom looking at her, she felt a warmth and a power that was overwhelming. So this is it. This is what it feels like. He moved towards her and hugged her close. He whispered into her ear, through her long dark hair, words that you and I need not know, should not know. And though she barely heard them herself, she felt their intensity.

Their feet moved in time with one another as if dancing to a slow waltz only they could hear, holding each other up. They stepped back and around until they found themselves in the bedroom. They stood a pace from one another and looked deep into eyes into souls. Sandy reached forward and slipped off his shirt, running her long fingers down his thin, pale chest. She allowed her teddy bear dressing gown to fall from her shoulders and stood there quite still, naked before him. She was in control now. She took his trembling hands in her own and laid him down upon the bed. She closed her eyes. He closed his too.

And they wrapped themselves about and within one another, wrapped themselves in a wonderful physical embrace to which there was no end.

Little Norman could have saved the world. There was something about him that nobody could fathom. He drew you in, left you feeling intoxicated. He would look at you with those wide blue eyes of his and he would move you inside, touch your heart, your soul, your very being. He would pad around the house in his bare feet, peering into corners and books and magazines. And he would gaze through his bedroom window, standing on his bed on tiptoes, filled with rapture by all that passed before him, dreaming, dreaming, dreaming. Everyone knew that Little Norman was special. That was the funny thing.

He could have saved the world.

George's trips to Big Town had almost broken him. Each day, he took the train to find his son. He had no proof that he was there. It was just something he felt. He had lost weight and at times found breathing laborious, unnatural. When he spoke to his wife on the phone, for she was still with her sister, he sounded strange to her, old and weary. And she would put the phone down after a terrible goodbye, only to fall once more into the arms of her sister, distraught and shattered.

Tom, mate. What have you done?

Still George could not find his son. At times, he thought his courage would fail him, that he would one day travel to Big Town never to return, just travel there and curl up beside the road. He had not thought of God since that first time he prayed. There were greater things to occupy his mind now.

The deprived and the despairing of Big Town through whom George walked in awe sat about fires in the night and stared into the flames, flames that they themselves had created. Amidst the crackling light, they saw life and survival, movement and spontaneity, the orange and yellow and red and blue flames wavering. Dancing their way through the dark heat. Smoke swirled away into the blackness of the night unheeded. The flames were where the magic lay.

George saw hundreds of battered shapes. He saw battered shoes and feet poking out beneath cardboard sheets, shoes that had been bought so long ago. Those feet had maybe skipped down the aisle in those new shoes to be married to a sweetheart in white, had danced on that wedding night until exhaustion overtook them, twirling around and around ecstatic and burning. And now those feet can but stumble from one dirt alcove to another.

Some people had dirty sleeping bags into which they would slide without even a sound. They would just lie there, shivering beneath the hot moon. People swarmed by but they saw them not. They saw before them just the flames of their intense pain, flames that illuminate the tragic and the forlorn.

All this happens.
All this goes on.
This is your town.
This is my town.
Big Town.

Chapter Fourteen

Christine sat on the edge of Laura's bed, watching her daughter sleep. It was so quiet in the bedroom, the only sound being the feint breath of the little girl beneath the soft and colourful quilt. Christine moved down to the floor and knelt beside her daughter's head, stroking the hair gently, rhythmically, keeping it from dangling across her face, away from her sore eyes.

All around the room there were dolls on shelves and cuddly toys slumped against one another, sweet, simple and innocent; there were posters on the wall of babies in funny situations, of animals all dressed up, and of the latest pop sensation—four boys in vests. It was a child's room. And on the low table beside Laura's bed, there was a grinning frog; it's grin so wide and so happy that you almost had to laugh yourself. Held firmly between its shiny green hands there was a sign bearing the advice—'SMILE: GOD LOVES YOU!'

Laura had always believed in the grinning frog. He had always cheered her up and given her hope. Sometimes, she would talk to him and she would feel better. Other times, all she needed to do was to look at him and things would not seem so bad after all. She knew with a certainty derived from innocence and faith that God did indeed love her. But if ever there was a time that she felt he didn't, she knew the grinning frog would be there for her.

So Laura's bedroom was bright and warm and cosy. It was the bedroom of a little girl. A child's own room is the sanctuary to which they are able to retreat when they have been chastised and demeaned by the adult world. It is their most secret of gardens, a place of dreams.

When you lay upon her in this room, your body so absurdly large upon hers, did you drag the colourful quilt across you in a moment of shame? Did you whisper any words into her small ears or did you just go ahead and do it? Afterwards, did you dress in front of her or did you scuttle out half naked, dripping, burning? And did she scream or just lay there silent, waiting for the grinning frog to save her?

Christine picked her daughter up in her arms and held her to her heart. She just had to hold her. She kissed her forehead and she smoothed her hair. And Laura, eyes closed though still awake, shivered. She just shivered.

One Sunday every month, Sandy visited her parents for dinner. This particular Sunday, the day after the party, she asked Tom if he would like to come with her. He assented without hesitation.

Sandy's parents lived on the north side of town, about three miles from the flat. Being a Sunday, or indeed being a day of the week, buses were scarce, so they made the short journey by underground. And for once, the Beautiful Guitar, Tom's very essence and innocence, stayed behind. It stood there in the corner of the room, in the middle of his heart.

The entrance to the underground station was dull and grimy. It was more like the entrance to a mine. There were bottles and empty cans amidst strewn pages from strange newspapers and pornographic magazines. And where a fruit and vegetable stall had stood the day before, just outside the entrance, there now lay a rotting collection of soiled and unwanted products. Tom took a kick at a sad cabbage on their way in and it just fell apart on impact.

The escalator was not working, so Tom and Sandy had to walk down the steep spiral steps. It wasn't too difficult for Tom, but Sandy had some problems in her dainty shoes. By the time he had reached the bottom, she was only half way down. As he waited for her, he looked about him at the posters and the placards on the walls, walls that had been stripped back to reveal damaged plaster, blackened brick and shadows of shadows. Then, he felt a sudden urge to look up towards the steps, to see Sandy from a distance, to see her as a stranger. To see her how others saw her. But by the time he turned around, she was with him once more.

As they walked together through the myriad of complex curved corridors to the platform, they became aware of a tune bouncing and skipping off the walls. And the tune became clearer and louder the further they walked, a joyful, happy tune.

The source of the music was a man on the ground. He was old and grey, as if he had emanated from the broken wall behind him, just eased his way through the crumbling plaster. He sat there, legs crossed, playing a battered mandolin. His fingers raced along the fret board as if they were madly bridging gaps, thereby holding the whole instrument together. You knew the mandolin would surely fall apart were the man to stop playing even for a moment.

Beside the mandolin man, there was a small dog. It was predominately white though it had a sizeable black inkblot of a mark on its back. The red collar around the neck was fastened to a silver chain that was in turn wrapped around the right wrist of the mandolin man. Each time the man changed chords or ran his fingers up and down the mandolin, the small dog would be jerked into the air. It would just sit there waiting for the next chord change and then it would jump at the slightest twitch of the chain, landing ready to participate the next chord.

The man was motionless as Tom and Sandy passed, motionless except for those manic fingers which seemed to possess a spirit all of their own, dancing and writhing so nimble and so strong. Tom and Sandy heard the sound of the train approaching and rushed around the corner to the platform. And they didn't see the creased cardboard sign propped up against the wall beside the mandolin man upon which was written in blue chalk—'PLEASE HELP ME FEED MY DOG'. From an A7 to a D to a G, the small dog hurled himself into the air in joyous glee, dancing to that one, sweet, sweet tune of resignation that plays on forever.

The train screeched and crawled, wounded and bitter, into the station. There was only one other passenger in the carriage that Tom and Sandy entered. He was a young man with a rucksack that clung to his back like a dishevelled, sullen child. This man was leaning forward, gazing at an unfurled map. The stifled music from his personal stereo seeped out in squeals of pain in a strange way that made it seem as if the noise came from between the man's teeth as he looked disconsolately on.

Conversation on the train was impossible; such was the incredible lurching and jolting of the carriage and the deafening clattering of the wheels upon the track. There were times when Tom felt the whole train would just topple over into one smouldering heap of iron. The windows shuddered and the door at the end of the carriage slammed against its frame over and over again.

Accompanied by this orchestra of modern machinery, Tom looked at the advertisements along the top of the carriage. He read with disbelief the inane, senseless words printed alongside faded photographs. There were adverts for cosmetics, newspapers and travel agents, all offering some form of vicarious respite to the sweaty commuter, the tedium of which they were an integral part.

The journey lasted ten minutes and with three stops. At the top of the escalator, on the way out, Tom and Sandy were greeted by a blinding flash of sunlight that filled the exit to the station like some huge torch shining down upon them, picking them out as they rose from the deep bowels of the earth.

Outside, the street was deserted. All the shops were fronted by iron grilles, padlocks on and alarms set. A slight breeze picked up dust and dirt and other debris, nudging it into the corners. There was a smell in the air, a Sunday morning smell of stagnation, which lingered above everything.

"So where is it, then?" asked Tom.

"Just down here. Up near the end."

They continued walking down the street and all Tom could see were shops. There were no houses or flats, just all these petrified shops.

"Here we are," said Sandy, smiling, stopping outside a small general store. "I'll just go around the side and ring the bell. Wait here for a second," she added, as she disappeared into a small alley beside the shop.

While Tom waited for Sandy, he looked at the slogans that had been daubed upon the iron grille that was pulled down over the front of the shop and locked tight to the ground. He stood there alone in the quiet street, just looking at the slogans. Moments later, Sandy reappeared and beckoned him to come around to the side door.

Sandy's father stood there in the doorway and smiled broadly. He was a tiny man in terms of both height and physique. His dark eyes were kind, gentle and full of charming energy akin with the vivacity and humour embodied by his persona. He kissed his daughter on both cheeks and shook Toms' hand firmly.

"Dad, this is my friend, Tom. I told you on the phone."

"Yes, yes," said her father. "That's right, you did. Tom, Tom, Tom."

He grinned a wide, satisfying grin and led Tom and Sandy through the door and up the narrow stairs to the flat above.

The flat, as Tom quickly discovered following a brief but enthusiastic tour, contained just three rooms. There was a bathroom, a kitchen, and a lounge that doubled as a bedroom.

Tom was introduced to Sandy's mother who was knitting in a low armchair in the corner of the room as they entered. She was a large woman and she rose unsteadily to greet them, shaking Tom's hand gently and looking deep into his eyes. She sat back down and put her knitting away carefully into a carrier bag beside her chair.

Sandy sat down on the floor near her mother's chair and the two of them spoke in a language Tom did not understand. But though he did not understand any of the words, he still marvelled at the fluency and proficiency of Sandy's speech, how it flowed, how it sounded. He was soon enticed away though into a conversation with Sandy's father whose diction was completely at odds with his swift, frenetic movements. He spoke slowly, almost painfully so, thinking long before each word. Tom found himself staring at the deep eyes and the crevices in that bony face. There was so much there, such energy and life and personality. If his face were a novel, it would surely be a classic of its genre.

"You work with my Sandjreka, Tom?"

"No. Out of town."

"Ah. You have known Sandjreka long?"

"We went to the same school."

"Ah."

There was a lengthy pause as Tom trawled his mind for something meaningful to say, something entirely sensible. Other than perhaps 'what letter comes after Q in the alphabet?' But he could think of nothing. Nothing came. The silence between the two of them seemed to last forever, until, finally, Sandy called across to him.

"Tom," she said, "come and look at this."

He got up gratefully from his chair and went over to join her at the bookcase that leaned precariously against the wall. She held in her hands a long, framed photograph, a wide-angled shot of all the children at Palmer's Secondary School, taken when Tom and Sandy were in their fourth year there. Tom gazed at it, transfixed. All those children were now a million miles away, in another world, another time. All that was left from those days now were mixed up names, faded memories and an incredible, deep feeling of longing for something that you know was never there in the first place.

As he scoured the faces, names sprung back into his memory. Those children were all so young, so perilously young. There was Darren Elliot, the boy who limped grotesquely and was always excused from rugby. And there was Graham Parkinson, the boy who would eat a hamburger in a single bite. It was great. He would creep up behind an unsuspecting group of girls and jump out in front of them, cramming the burger and bun into his open mouth before running away like a madman. And in the back row, partially obscured, at the furthest end, Tom saw Paul Regis. They had called Paul 'Thumper' at school because he was just like a rabbit—timid, nervous, and wide-eyed. Tom had never spoken to him though had probably laughed at him, ridiculed him with the others. But all that stopped the day Paul had been run over outside the school gates, on his way home after another day of being teased by everyone. Run over by a car—rabbit to the very end. He was gone. Tom momentarily recalled the bewildering feeling of shock when it was announced in assembly the following day that Paul had died. That had been his first dealings with death. That was about the time that Little Norman was due to arrive on this earth.

They stood looking at the photograph, Tom and Sandy, reflecting silently on the faces before them and wondering where those faces were now. Were they in work? Were they mothers and fathers themselves? Were they in prison?

Were they lost, lonely, confused, satisfied, broken, content? Each child has a story, the story of its life. And I want to read them all.

There are some things too huge to comprehend, too massive to come to terms with. For me it is the passing of lost years.

And then Tom saw his own face staring back at him from the photograph, a serious, weary face—the face of a boy with the troubles of a generation in his heart. In that face, Tom saw grief and bitterness. And that was before Paul Regis, before Little Norman. Perhaps he had always had those feelings. Perhaps he would never lose them, but just go through events to justify them. Perhaps they had just found a new means of expression. Music and words are beautiful.

"You look happy there!" laughed Sandy, pointing out the young Tom in the photograph.

Tom said nothing. They both stood there looking at the children, each seeing different things. Sandy's father crept up behind them and, reaching up, put a thin hand on each shoulder. He was so very small.

"Time for something to eat, now," he said softly.

The food was wonderful. There were more textures, aromas, sights and varieties of food than Tom had ever seen before. There were relishes and spices that painted masterpieces in the air above the collapsible table, lingering long after the tongue had first delighted at the taste. Tom had felt a little reluctant to serve himself too much food, but encouraged by Sandy's father who ate with a speed only equalled to his enjoyment, he emptied his plate, filled it, and emptied it again. Ah, gorgeous, gorgeous food.

After having eaten all his stomach could take, Tom sat back in his chair and suddenly found himself in an intense battle to contain a monstrous belch he felt building up within him. Just as he felt he had conquered the worst of it, a resonant bellow leapt from the small man beside him who grinned a toothy grin. This emission broke Tom's own resistance and he too belched gloriously just seconds later.

"Ah, you enjoy your food, Tom?" said Sandy's father, smiling.

"I'm sorry," mumbled Tom, embarrassed, shaken by the volume and timing of his own testament as to the extent of his enjoyment.

During the rest of the evening, they all watched television. There was a nature programme followed by a quiz show and then a drama. Tom watched the latter with tired eyes. He felt so content and relaxed after the meal that all he wanted to do was sleep. The warmth of the room combined with the continuing spicy aroma that permeated it teased him, tried to lure him into somnolence.

Towards the end of the film, there were some erotic scenes that caused Sandy to glance nervously at her mother to ensure she was still knitting and not watching. Every time Sandy looked back at the screen, her mother and father smiled tenderly at one another. Tom viewed all this through half-closed eyes, on the outside now, looking in on this family.

When the time came to leave, Sandy's mother stood up and shook Tom by the hand once more. He thanked her for the tea and she smiled, nodding her head slowly.

"It has been a pleasure to meet you, Tom," said Sandy's father as they stood outside in the fading light. He laboured over the words but meant every one of them.

"Yes, you too," replied Tom, shaking the small man's bony hand.

After a kiss goodnight for her father and a wave to her mother, Sandy led Tom back to the station and to the train that would take them both back home.

When Tom and Sandy arrived back at the flat, they were both very tired. Tom had a headache, due in part to a mixture of the heady smell of the spices and having to concentrate so hard when listening to Sandy's father. He sat down on the settee whilst Sandy went into the kitchen to make hot chocolate for them both. Before she could return with the drinks, Tom had closed his eyes. The flat was so quiet. Everything was still. Just as he was about to slip into sleep, Sandy handed him his hot chocolate.

"That was all right, wasn't it?" said Tom, sipping the hot drink, feeling it burning his lips. "Your Dad's a good bloke."

"Yes, he is," replied Sandy.

Tom noticed some hesitation in her voice. He was in tune with her now, closer to her. He could sense her in a way that he had been unable to before.

"What's the matter?" he asked. "Did I do something wrong? Except for the burp, I mean. I'm sorry about that. It just sort of came out."

"Dad does that all the time," she said. "He always has done."

"Well, what then? Was it something I said?"

Sandy put her drink down on the floor, turned and looked at him. She was nervous, shy and self-conscious.

"What is it? What's wrong?" Tom was becoming unsure now. Thoughts would not come clear in his head. He did not know how all this was going to unfold. Hold on, Tom. Hold on.

Sandy took a deep breath and continued to look into his eyes as she spoke.

"This morning," she said, "what happened this morning was, look, I don't know how to say this, but, what you did, what we did, it's just that, did you mean it?" She let go her breath now in pure relief.

Tom put down his hot chocolate and watched the steam weave towards him like some spirit rising, He leaned across, closed his eyes and kissed her softly on the cheek. It was the most sensitive thing he had ever done. And he hadn't even had to think about it. Tears came to her eyes and she cried, sobbed. All day she had been wondering. It had meant so much to her. He held her to him and she continued to weep. Joy. Love. Cry it all out. Hold me like this every day, every morning, every night. May your embrace be my embrace and may I never be without you.

That night, Tom and Sandy slept in each other's arms like two wanderers in a strange land, clinging onto the only thing they knew. Their thoughts and dreams were far apart that night though their bodies were so close. They were in the same place at the same time and that is all. But who can tell what tomorrow brings?

This is a moment. All we have are moments. Just live them.

So Sandy was in love.

And Tom, well Tom just slept in that soft bed, held in the arms of another, praying that the yellow moon would hold off the morning forever.

Chapter Fifteen

Who can say what leads a person to suicide? No man can pass judgement on the feelings and thoughts that must consume the mind in those final moments. They are beyond our understanding—for death to be preferable to life, to be the answer, the end. You are gone from our world and our conscience and move briefly into our memories to disappear forever as you were. I would have spent an hour with you, a day, a lifetime even. Just one word from me, and you would be with us still.

Jennifer. You are gone and I am almost alone.

It had been so long ago.

It had been barely a second.

Fourteen years old, young, fresh, vibrant—so full of life and love.

Jennifer.

At fourteen, she had fallen in love with a boy seven years older than herself. He had just started work and, with the money he earned, would take her to all kinds of marvellous places she had never known existed. She would hang off his arm as they walked down the street, full of pride and bursting with an eagerness just to enjoy every moment with this man.

Such was her pretty, elfin face; she could have passed for eighteen, twelve or thirty-five. There had been a maturity about her features, a worldliness that had made her all that more fascinating. She was a young girl, but oh so old in so many ways.

She had loved the way he put his arm around her waist, squeezing it every now and then with his strong hand. And she had absolutely adored it when he would meet her outside school and pick her up in his car and his suit, hair slicked back and shoes as shiny as ebony.

The young man with whom she was in love was generous and kind. He would look after her brother too. He cared for them both in a way. And that made him even more special. But if she needed love, she knew her brother was in even greater need. They had been so close, the brother and the sister. She would look up at her brother, he being older, but she knew how he cherished her. He had once told her that she was an angel, pure and clean and untouched, soft and beautiful. And she had laughed. He had just looked down.

During the summer, just before her fifteenth year, Jennifer and her man grew closer together. Ah, Michael, it was so hard for you, wasn't it? To see your angel float away from you to another, to touch humanity in so base a fashion.

I love him, Michael.

I love him.
Michael leaves.
Jennifer's man arrives.

They are in the woods now, walking with one another. Thatched branches mottle the air into an intricate, woven roof of nature. It is strangely warm here beneath this canopy of dry trees. The ground is hard, dusty and unforgiving.

I have been waiting for you. Did you have a good morning at work? That's good. When have you got to be back? An hour with you is eternity. I do love you, Ron. Yes, we can go over there if you want. Aren't those trees beautiful? Those tiny twigs and how old that bark is. This is an amazing place, isn't it? Have you been here before? I'm not surprised you came back to it. It's like a little corner of Heaven.

Your hands feel cold. Are you cold? Do you want me to warm them for you? Of course I will. There, that's better. Are you sure you don't want to sit down somewhere softer? This ground is quite hard. If I'd have known we were going to rest, we could have brought that blanket from out of your car. Then now I'm sitting down, it doesn't feel so hard after all. When you pull me into your chest like this, Ron, I feel so safe. I feel that nobody can hurt me. Especially when you wear your suit. It's strange, but when you wear your suit, I feel so grown up.

I can hear the birds up there. Do you think they are watching us? They sing so sweet, don't they? You're very quiet, Ron. Are you feeling okay? I can hear your heartbeat with my head on your chest when we lay down like this. I could stay here all day. If we closed our eyes, I wonder if we could wish ourselves somewhere, anywhere, and just be in that place together, just the two of us forever. What would it look like, that place? Would it be fields and meadows or a desert island somewhere or a small boat adrift on a bright blue sea? I wouldn't care where it was, I don't think, for as long as I was with you, Ron.

When you hold me to you and kiss me, I feel weak and light. You control me with your arms and your strength. You seem so much bigger than me as I lay here on my back, looking up at you. I don't think of the earth beneath me, nor the trees or the sky above me. I just look at you and you are all I really see. Angels could come flying down from Heaven. A thousand people could walk by and I would not see them. You don't know what you do to me, Ron.

This is like a fairy tale for me. I suppose you would be my hero. You are my hero. If I were to tell you all I thought of you, night would fall before I was even half way through. And as I look up at you, knowing that your lips will soon meet mine, I have to close my eyes, for then I can hear your breath, your heartbeat, smell you and sense you. When I close my eyes in these moments, just before you kiss me, I experience all of you with all senses other than sight. For with my eyes closed, I see you still. You don't notice the way I stare at you sometimes when you're not looking. I could draw you exactly; paint a picture of you from my memory tomorrow or a hundred years from now.

And I, lying there, eyes closed, wait for you.

I love these moments. When we are married, we can make love and I cannot wait for that time. Oh to be your wife, your lover. Just to kiss you and have you embrace me satisfies me like nothing else. It satisfies me more than I could imagine, for it does not destroy my dreams. You are so strong. I love these moments. Waiting for your touch. Waiting for your kiss.

I lay here still.

I wait for you still.

And I open my eyes now, unsure.

And then I see you.

You stand over me; stand over me, looking down. Your face is strange, dark. Maybe it's a shadow, a passing shadow. There is some sort of darkness about you. I can't really see your eyes at the moment. And you have such lovely eyes. And I realise now, in my naïve way, as I take my eyes from your face, that you are naked. You stand above me, naked.

I hear the birds a little now. I see some of the sky too. A picture is forming around you, a picture of beauty, natural beauty as you come down to me now. Your legs are astride me now. You are sitting upon my stomach. You feel heavy and I struggle for breath for a moment. You don't seem to notice this. You don't look right at all.

I try to say something but your lips are on mine before I get the chance. They feel rough and hard. Not like usual. And then I realise you haven't shaved. You always shave, Ron. And you're moving your body around as if you are trying to escape from it—your naked body. I feel the sharpness of small stones and sticks jabbing at me through the back of my dress. You bought me this dress. It was the first thing you ever bought me, Ron. I still can't talk. I think my lip is bleeding. My breath does not seem to be my own. You control even that.

I think I am scared now. Things are becoming blurred. This is either going really fast or really slow. I don't know. Time seems to mean nothing. There are movements and none of them are mine. My eyes are closed tight. Whether I open them or close them, it makes no difference.

You've ripped my dress down the front. I could not hear the tear though above this strange noise you are making. I can just feel that it is torn. You're grunting like an animal. Your nails are scratching me. I don't know if you mean it or not. Your hands are rough. I think the skin on my back is touching the dirt now. And I think it's bleeding. This is hurting me now. And still I cannot make a sound. The birds are singing. I think I can hear them singing.

My body is on the ground. You are on top of me. You put your hand down my knickers. Your fingers are inside me. I feel like I am being stabbed. I have gone numb. And then for a moment you stop, stop only to pull down my knickers.

You are fucking me now. You are fucking me. So that's it. You are fucking me now. Fucked by you. I am letting you do this to me.

That is my body down there. My dress is torn. There are scratches and bruises all over me. I ache already.

I think you are finished now. I still cannot open my eyes.

Yes, you are finished. I cannot hear you breathing anymore.

At last, my eyes are open. You are standing there, leaning against a tree, dressed, and smoking a cigarette. I didn't know you smoked.

Fourteen years old.

Jennifer had lain in those woods, not moving. In truth, though, she was not there at all. Was she in a field, a meadow, on a raft, or washed up on a desert island? Who knows? Ron had looked at his watch, walked over to her, helped her up and led her back to his car. Intent on not being late for work, he had dropped her off at the bus stop outside his office and sauntered back in to sit behind his ever-expanding desk.

And what of Jennifer? What had she done? She had gone home, changed, checked her purse and bought a packet of headache tablets and a can of drink. That evening, she had sat in her room, the room that Ron had rented for her and Michael, just sat there and took one tablet after another, the drink breaking up the chalky taste in her mouth and allowing her to swallow them all. It had taken her almost half an hour to swallow all the tablets and each minute of that time, she thought of the mother she barely remembered, of bright places and of when she was a small child, playing and dancing and singing and living. As each tablet sunk to her stomach, so her courage grew. It had seemed so straightforward, so easy. Living is not everything, not to the person who wants to die. Shatter me and break me. But let me kill myself.

And Michael had come in late that evening, after meeting his friend, Ron, and going to the pictures with him. He had come in to find his angel dead on the bed. She had changed into her pyjamas and had still been ever so slightly warm when he had touched her. His little sister was dead. His angel was gone, away and free to float above in his sky and in his dreams, to sail through his veins, to dance to the beating of his heart. His angel was dead.

Time passes. Trees grow old and seasons change. We are years on now.

"I've left Michael Parrish's old notes in the drawer for you, John," said the ward clerk, motioning at the bottom drawer of the filing cabinet. John was in the middle of another long day and his reactions were slowing. Before he could indicate his thanks to her, she had retreated from the madness back into her computer and her telephone.

Several hours later, long after the ward clerk had gone home, John looked at the clock on the wall and willed the seconds on. The ward had settled down a little, he had drunk as much coffee as he could and his body craved a real drink. He had done all the writing he needed to do, it was just a matter now of waiting for the night staff to come in and hoping nothing else happened on the ward in which he needed to get involved. So he decided to look at Michael's old notes, the file from the hospital that had looked after Michael at the age of seventeen.

The file was of a light blue colour with black writing on the front indicating the name of the patient, the date of admission and the date of discharge. Michael had been there for almost a month. Not bad for a seventeen year old, thought John. He looked through to try and find some information about that previous admission. The writing in the notes was akin to that found on some fifteenth century pamphlet, ancient, scrawled, faded and intriguing. However he looked at it, John could not decipher the writing with any consistency. So he looked at the back of the notes for any typed letters or a summary of the admission, a discharge letter perhaps. And then he found, in rounded schoolgirl writing, the admission notes, those written by the nurse the day the patient arrived on the ward.

John read the admission notes, looked at the clock and continued reading. During this time, Michael slept in his side room. He slept most of the time now.

My angel. You are asleep now, asleep in my arms. I will hold you until you awake. And you will awake. The night is upon us now. Look at those stars in the sky. Look at that moon. Yes. I will hold you until you awake. My angel.

The night staff came in and John put Michael's file back in the drawer. He greeted the staff wearily and began informing them of the events of the day. Michael, being the latest patient to be admitted, was last on the list.

"Michael Parrish—new admission. He's pretty settled, isolating himself for most of the day though, spending long periods in his room. He seems quite low actually. We got his old notes up. His only other admission was about thirty years ago, when he was seventeen. Apparently, he was admitted back then after he was found at home with his sister who had been dead for about four days. It turned out she'd taken an overdose. Anyway, he was in hospital for about a month back then. Self-harmed a couple of times then—that's where the scars on his hands come from—diagnosis of schizoaffective disorder. He doesn't seem any problem. I phoned his wife today and told her he was here and that we'll be looking to transfer him to a hospital closer to where he lives within the next few days."

"Why is he in?" asked one of the night staff.

"Looks like he had the shit beaten out of him," said John. "He's a bit bizarre. No problem though. Nice bloke, actually. He won't be here too long, I wouldn't have thought."

Handover finished, John went home, drunk half a bottle of whisky and slept on the floor of his rented room.

So, at seventeen years of age, Michael had held his dead sister in his arms for nearly four days. During that time, he had neither cried nor moaned. He had just held her and gazed at her. And her eyes had been wide open, staring into his—innocence into innocence. He had spoken not a word to her, but she had understood him. He had touched her mind and her soul, her very being. He hadn't noticed how she had grown cold and stiff and odorous in his arms for he had seen only the light surrounding her.

Four days of death. And from it, he had brought forth life. Things that had been strange to him up until that point, incongruous and abstract, now took on a calm clarity. Life came into focus for him during those four days. And as his mind had tried to make sense of it all, his soul just gloried in the freedom, reigning over consciousness and form.

And during that time, as he had held his angel to him, his body, his primitive, wretched body had betrayed him. It had inflamed him with a sexual arousal that would always come back to taunt him—her body next to his. He had fought it with his mind and overcome it with his tears. It was from that moment that he chose to follow the path of angels.

When he was found with his dead sister by the landlady, a smile had been scrawled across his face, a cheek little boy's smile that would haunt that woman forever. The ambulance and the police had come to the scene and Michael, still smiling, was taken to the nearest psychiatric hospital for assessment. And all he had said to the doctor on admission was 'I have cleansed a soul. I have cleansed a soul.'

We find Michael now lying on his bed, staring at the high ceiling of his room, thinking of Jennifer. Why had they taken her? She had come back and they had taken her, but no more. A life of pain and torment is drawing to a close. That is all we have here.

That is truly all we have.

When Christine was informed that Michael was safe and that he was in hospital, she cried. Relief, fear and anger all merged into one and the tears just fell. It had been five weeks of frustration and bitter moments. And now it was over. He had been found. She didn't know whether she wanted to hug him or kill him, so swung the poles of her emotion at this time. It had been his absence that made her realise how much she really loved him.

On calming a little, she went upstairs to tell Laura.

Laura was lying on her bed looking at the patterns on the ceiling. Her wide eyes stared at the brightness of the light above, losing themselves in the molten glow of the bulb. When she heard the door open, she curled herself up and faced the wall, closing her eyes tight.

Christine sat down gently on the bed and leaned across to whisper into her daughter's ear.

"Daddy's okay. I've just had a phone call. He's okay. He's in hospital because he isn't very well. He's very tired."

Laura was silent. Her heart pounded fast. Daddy I need you, I need you now.

"Tomorrow afternoon, I'm going to try to speak to him and maybe go up and see him. And then we can get back to how things used to be."

Laura thought this over in her head. 'Mummy's going to see Daddy'.

"Can I see Daddy too?" she asked, her voice cracked and straining. She had barely spoken a word since he had left.

"I think it's best if I go on my own first, just to see how he is, and then after that I'm sure it'll be fine."

Laura thought some more.

"Who will be looking after me when you're with Daddy?"

"Uncle Ron will look after you, Laura. I haven't asked him yet, but I'm sure he will."

Uncle Ron. Laura sighed so deep. Seven years old. Uncle Ron. She knew there were so many different worlds. She found new ones every day. But now, right now, words didn't interest her. Life didn't interest her—to be so old so young. Uncle Ron.

Michael lay in his bed that night knowing that the time was near. He had almost worked everything out. He was acting only on instruction now. He played no part other than that which a puppet might play. He was just waiting for the next move, the final move. The medication was easy to conceal. He hadn't really taken any since he had been in apart from the sleeping tablet that was foisted upon him on his first night on the ward. The medication they wanted to give him would have done him no good. It would merely have served to blur the one voice that led him on his way through those last few days.

Michael thought of that photograph in his study drawer. So often he had looked at it, gazed at it as the face merged from Jennifer to Laura and back again—from beautiful child to beautiful child. He saw that photograph now. The image was there before him and he smiled to himself as the night staff shone the torch into his room to check on him. In the morning they would say he had been 'smiling inappropriately.' Had he heard that, he would have smiled even more.

He thought of Laura and of the last time he saw her, would ever see her. He remembered how he and Christine had been to the park that summer evening to watch an outdoor version of Othello whilst Ron looked after Laura. He remembered how when they got back home he heard Ron and Christine talking in the kitchen. They had thought he was upstairs. He could remember the very words, the whole conversation, that spark that had set him on fire.

"Do you think he knows?"

"He can't know. There's no way he could."

"Ron. He's not stupid."

"He would have said something before now. We mustn't let it come between us."

"There is no 'us' Ron. Not any more."

"As you wish. As you wish."

A pause.

"Laura will always be a reminder of what we once had, Chris. Laura will always be mine."

Silence.

And he remembered how he had gone up to Laura's room and just sat on the floor, looking at her laying there, trying in vain to see Jennifer in her. And he had cried then, silently, cried tears of pain for his sister and for this little girl that he loved so much and whom he knew from that moment he would never see again—and those two in the kitchen talking still and Michael up there in his Heaven.

The night falls upon Big Town and Michael watches the moon. He sees it rise and sees it sink. And the sun rises into the red of the morning sky and sets him on fire. It blazes into him, burning him, cleansing him, filling him with the fiercest heat you ever felt.

And he drops to the floor.

And he weeps.

It is a forest fire, a forest fire....

Chapter Sixteen

Sandy and Tom woke late on Monday morning. She had booked two weeks off from work and was looking forward to spending every minute of that time with Tom. She still felt sometimes though as if she barely knew him. He would sit quietly for long moments, just staring at the Beautiful Guitar or he would stand at the window gazing into the light and into the darkness. But two weeks together would bring them closer, would bring her closer to him.

The telephone broke the peace of the morning. Sandy reached over to answer it, brushing Tom's chest slightly with her arm as she did so.

"Hello?" she said, and then "Dad? What is it?"

After a few moments, she told him she'd come round to the shop as soon as she could and hung up the receiver.

"What's wrong?" asked Tom, sleepily, tuning his eyes to the day.

"It's Dad. I've got to go over there. I'll see you later."

"Hang on. I'll come with you," said Tom. "What's happened anyway? What's the problem?"

But Sandy wasn't listening. She was trying to do her boots up and thinking frantically of what she was going to find at her parents' shop.

"Come on, Tom. We've got to go now."

There was a sense of urgency in her voice that Tom did not question. He dutifully dressed and within minutes they were both rushing down the stone steps of the underground station.

The train was packed with commuters and the air was thick with mistrust. A stale, putrid smell lingered in the air emerging from no identifiable source. People squeezed into one another, their bodies touching in mute disgust as the train rocked and rolled its way across Big Town.

Once off the train, Tom and Sandy breathed again and ran down the street to the shop. As they neared it, Sandy in front now, they saw a Police car parked outside in the road. Tom was some yards behind Sandy, his lungs finally avenging themselves. He eventually came to a halt beside her, taking in huge gulps of air, stooping over, his hands on his knees. Meanwhile, she was in the process of explaining to the policeman who she and Tom were and they were then allowed to enter the shop via the gap where the glass front door had been.

The shop was a complete shambles. Tins rolled on the floor and newspapers had been torn into pieces and thrown about like so much confetti. Cereal packets had been burst open and their contents sprayed about in erratic circles. The display cabinet beneath the counter had been smashed, broken glass flashing and gleaming between sweets, stamps and packets of football stickers. The tall fridge had been pulled over and milk poured from the milk bottles like pale, creamy blood, oozing around the cans and the cartons and the debris. The top of the floor freezer containing lollies and ice creams had been shattered so that slithers of glass mingled sly and unnoticed with the ice. Everything from the shelves had been swept onto the floor by clawing hands. Even the faded, knee high statuette of the little blind girl and her dog, even that had been kicked to the ground, revealing just a few old coins and a used condom.

Tom looked around at the destruction, the noise of car engines passing by slowly outside the only sound to be heard. When he saw the broken statuette of the blind girl, he felt strangely satisfied. He had always hated those things but had never really been able to explain why. And the condom had been a surreal touch that he momentarily appreciated. That feeling of appreciation left him though when he looked around at the walls.

On every wall, there were the words, long, straggly letters in red paint forming expressions of hatred, dripping and flowing as if the very wall itself had bled them into form. We have all seen the words, the words of ignorance and cowardice and fear. We have seen them on subways, on bus shelters, in lifts, in schoolbooks, newspapers and on the gravestones of the dead. Hatred we look upon you. And we grieve for you.

As Tom and Sandy looked about them, alone and separate, she in shock and he no more than curious, Sandy's father appeared in the doorway behind the broken counter. He seemed so small and so frail and so very far away. Sandy moved slowly towards him, stepping through the chaos at her feet. She eased her way around the back of the counter and, reaching out for her father, held him to her chest. She looked down upon his head and wondered at him as he shook there in her arms. He was so very small yet larger than you or I.

"Are you all right, Dad?" she asked him.

He looked up at her, his eyes pulsing and twitching. He smiled sadly and nodded.

"Did they hurt you?"

"No," he replied, continuing to hold his wavering smile.

He saw Tom at the front of the shop and lifted a thin arm in acknowledgement.

"Tom," he called, so quietly that not even Sandy heard him. "You like my shop?"

Tom saw his lips move but that was all. And he could sense the tears that were about to fall from those large and soulful eyes.

"Is Mum okay?" asked Sandy, though she knew deep down that her mother would always be all right. From an early age she had formed the impression that her mother would live forever.

Her father frowned. It was as if a sudden pain had taken hold of him from within.

"Your mother is upstairs. I have not wanted to disturb her. Maybe you can be able to see her. I think she would like for you to."

He put his hand on her shoulder and moved away from the door to let her go by him and up the stairs.

Sandy found her mother sitting on the floor in the lounge. As far as she could tell, after a cursory glance, the flat itself seemed to have been undamaged. She felt her heart beat faster and she shivered a little as she imagined her mother and father up here, listening to the sounds of destruction as it happened, listening to the laughter and the anger and the hatred, wondering if it would lead up the stairs to where they lay shaking.

Her mother was murmuring words that appeared somewhat incoherent and strange to Sandy, eyes closed, arms held in peace upon her lap. A passive strength pervaded her. She had been in this position for an hour, praying. And Sandy knew that her mother would have been praying not for her own safety, nor even for the safety of her husband. She would be praying for the souls of the people that had wrecked the shop, the people that had left her husband terrified that morning. She would be praying for them.

Sandy went into the small kitchen and made a cup of tea. She brought it in and placed it on the floor by the peaceful figure of her mother who was in such a holy state of grace, she barely noticed the presence of her daughter.

Downstairs in the shop, Tom had begun helping to clear things up. Sandy's father had taken some bin bags from the storeroom and together they filled them with the soggy newspapers and the broken cartons.

The policeman left. There was nothing further to be done. They would log it. These things happen, unfortunately, Sir. These things happen.

When Sandy returned back down to join Tom and her father, she was subdued and thoughtful. Her father looked at her.

"She's fine," said Sandy, meeting his gaze with the eyes of her mother, before moving over to Tom.

"Tom," she said, "I'm going to stay with Mum and Dad tonight. I need to be with them. I'm worried about Dad."

Tom glanced over at the small man who was struggling to tie up one of the full bin bags. "No problem," he said, continuing to fill his own bag.

"I'd just be wondering how they were all the time if I was at home and they were here. It would just be for tonight."

Tom laid the heaving bin bag to rest for a moment and spoke to her.

"You don't have to justify it," he said gently. "I'd be the same."

And for a brief moment, he saw his mother and father before him and guilt assailed him with a sickening rush of vengeance. And he felt shame. Just for a moment, shame.

"Could you do me a favour, Tom? Could you just pop back to the flat and get my nightdress and a few blankets. Dad sold my bed when I moved out. Do you mind? I'll give you the train fare. I've got some money on me."

"That's fine," said Tom, "but what about all this?" he added, eyeing the still shaken interior of the shop. "Don't you want a hand with it?"

"Tom, you go," interjected Sandy's father, who had moved unseen to stand beside them. "Come back when it is nice again." He smiled and looked up at Tom. "You are a good man, Tom. A good man."

Tom filled the rest of the bin bag and put it outside the front door before saying goodbye to Sandy and her father. He stepped out into the light feeling a terrible loneliness. His heart beat fast and hard and he had a horrible feeling of foreboding within him now. Something was happening. Something out of his control was happening. It was as if things were moving again now, moving on as if the real world had caught up with him at last, followed him and tracked him down. And now it was surely ready to snare its prey.

Fate gets you in the end. Through the powers of coincidence, timing and cynicism it gets you.

When Tom arrived back at the flat, he found the door to be slightly open. He thought nothing of it at first and just went in. It was only when he opened the door to the lounge that he froze. He was just going to get a quick drink before gathering together Sandy's things. The stereo was gone. There was just a gap where it ought to have been. He walked over to the corner of the room and stared at the four small indentations in the carpet.

And as he stood there, it became clear to him what had happened. An overwhelming feeling of coldness consumed him. His throat tightened and it was a struggle even to breathe. He dare not turn. His heart beat now not within his chest, but within his mind. He tried in vain to concentrate, to rise above the beat of his own heart, but that thumping sound filled the entire room now. At last, after a minute or an hour, he turned, still dizzy on his feet.

It is fear, just fear.

And then comes a moment of relaxation. So the television and video were gone as well. Ah well. He breathed slower now, regaining control of his senses. He went into each room of the flat, fear coming and going, relief following sharp upon its heels. Finally, he came back to the lounge and stood there. Nobody else was in the flat. They had been and gone. He was alone.

And then it struck him in the stomach as if a demolition ball had crashed through the window taking him with it.

The chink of light was gone; that one unique candle of hope and aspiration that had always burned within him, that indefinable, inexplicable object of hope.

That escape route from a turgid life, the one, single element that kept him from thinking of Little Norman twenty-four hours a day. It was gone.

The Beautiful Guitar.

The Beautiful Guitar.

He tore from room to room, under the bed, in the wardrobe, behind everything, above everything, inside everything. He slammed his fist against the wall of each room as he left it with a force that shook it to its roots. He had murder within him now, a rage that propelled him like a tornado. By the time he stopped, he was exhausted.

When the crutch is removed, the body will fall.

And the body fell.

The Beautiful Guitar was still the key to his dreams. It had lain beside him in the torment of his youth and it had stayed with him on his arduous foray into adulthood. It was the receptacle of his essence, the mirror of his being and the last refuge of the child within him.

And now it was gone.

If he had found the Beautiful Guitar broken and shattered in the street outside, at least then he could have touched it, held, kept it still. But for it to just vanish like that, well that was more than he could take.

So he did what he always did, what he had always done and perhaps always would do.

He ran.

He just ran.

He runs now out into the streets of a thousand faces. His chest aches and his mind burns as if the fire that had once burned in his heart had now risen until it could rise no more. He has to keep moving to prevent himself from thinking. He just runs and runs, wayward and relentless. And as he runs, the people about him begin to change, to develop strange forms, inconsistencies and deformities. He becomes acutely conscious of their strangeness. They move in incongruous ways. Their faces are contorted, eyes so deep and black they could be lumps of coal. Their mouths are huge and wet, their teeth crunching and grating like some broken contraption of days past.

Children lie on the ground, trembling with a huge fear as the shadow of man soars above them. A young man plunges a knife deep into the heart of his lover and they can't put her back together again. Old men and women lean against one another as holes open up in the ground around them, enticing them, cracking the floor beneath their weary feet.

There's a rumbling in the sky and it cracks open, erupting, spitting out its fury onto the world, onto Tom.

The people cower beneath the rain and beneath the shattering light that crashes down upon them, pure arrows of fire. Tom's eyes are closed now as he runs and his legs take him through the rain and the hail, through the bodies and the blood.

He saw all of this.

He saw it all.

Finally, he burst out into a clearing and staggered to a halt. He opened his eyes and looked about him. At first, he thought he was on some kind of waste ground, rubbish and debris everywhere. But as he strained for breath and clarity of vision, he realized that what he had taken for rubbish, were actually people. They were ragged and torn, prostrate against the earth, some asleep, none dreaming.

Is this where the abandoned fall? Is this where it all ends? Is this my destiny?

He managed, after some moments, to pick out a blurred figure advancing unsteadily towards him. It was the thin frame of a boy wearing a dirty grey anorak and jeans that were so crusted with dirt; they could have been fashioned purely from mud alone. He was perhaps sixteen years old. His face was streaked raw and his hands were deep in his stiff, cold pockets. Tom stood watching him, mesmerized as the rain fell, unable to move. The boy halted a yard from him and looked up at him with huge brown eyes, beautiful, pleading eyes. And the boy spoke in a voice pitiful and plaintive.

"Can I sleep with you?" he asked.

"Yes," said Tom. "Yes."

And at that moment of relief, he sensed a movement behind him. It was a large man, tears upon his face, a man broken with emotion.

So Tom turned and saw his father.

They moved slowly towards each other beneath the blackening sky.
And the father held the son to his chest.
And the father kissed the son.

Chapter Seventeen

The early morning of late summer gazed down upon John as he walked through the quiet, serene hospital grounds on his way to the ward. As he approached the ward door, he consciously cleared his mind, listening to a song in his head. He did this every time he came to work. It was as if he were preparing to cross some barrier between the real and the surreal, though as days passed and his experience increased, he found it more and more difficult to return to reality. The surreal was simple. It had become natural for him to accept it. Returning to the world after fifteen hours on the ward helping people at the most crucial times of their life, well that was where the alcohol helped.

He turned the key in the lock and let himself onto the ward. The corridor was dark as the semi-recumbent night staff had yet to open the curtains. John heard movement towards the area of the office, some ten yards away, and slowed down his pace. It didn't pay to catch staff sleeping. He would just give them time to smooth their rumpled clothes and prepare their wide-awake countenance.

On going into the office, John acknowledged the nurse that had been in charge that night, but the nurse did not respond, so frantically was he looking for his spectacles. So John picked up the patient list clipboard and began his tour of the ward, checking that all patients were accounted for. It was a routine job that was done at the start of every shift—a nice easy way to start the day.

Female dormitory. Eight patients. All present. All breathing.

Male dormitory. John held his breath. You could bottle that smell and destroy armies with it. Nine patients. All present. All breathing.

First side room—fine. Second side room—fine. Third side room—fine.

Michael's room.

John saw that Michael's curtains must have been opened for the window in the door was filled with light. He opened the door as quietly as he could and let the light warm him. And Michael's body hung before him.

There was a smell in the room that John would never forget. It was a sour, acrid smell, a mixture of sweat and urine and death that would taunt his senses for months afterwards. He called calmly for help and two of the night staff stumbled into the room. One turned away immediately, the other entered. John stood on Michael's bed and tried in some way to support the limp body. It was so heavy and damp. He almost toppled forward. He moved his hands up to the tie that Michael had used to hang himself and tried to tear it, rip it in half to bring the body down. The two night staff just stood there, unable to speak or move.

John turned on them in anger.

"Just get me some fucking scissors!" he shouted and they both went off together, relieved, leaving him to stand on the bed alone with Michael's body floating beside him. John tried to breathe deeply and as he did so, everything slowed a little, just dropped down a gear. And it all seemed all right.

The night staff returned with some scissors and one of the other morning staff that had just arrived in. John got off the bed and, with aid of the morning staff, pulled the mattress onto the floor beneath the hanging body. He then took the scissors and climbed onto the metal frame of the bed. The morning staff held onto Michael's legs as the tie was cut and bravely helped lower Michael to the mattress. The body dropped down with a thud. John immediately jumped down and knelt beside Michael's head, instructing the morning staff to feel for a pulse. There was none. Neither was there a heartbeat.

John instructed the night staff to make the necessary calls. Then he looked down upon Michael. The face was almost yellow. There were grey lines upon it. He looked thirty years older. The neck was raw, bearing the marks of the tie. It was like some wax model from a horror film. John was not shaking yet. That would come later. As would the tears. But for now, he was in control. He turned to the morning staff, who was standing over the body unable to take his eyes off it, and told him that they should try CPR. Finally understanding, the morning staff knelt beside Michael's chest.

John looked at Michael's lips, those lips that had been so rarely kissed yet from which had come such eloquence and kindness. He tilted the head back slightly, checked for obstructions and pinched the nose. As he did so, mucus oozed out and onto his fingers. He breathed deeply to prevent himself from vomiting. Again, he breathed deeply, slowly, before bowing his head until his mouth was upon Michael's cold, moist lips. And he breathed his air into the hollow body. The morning staff performed the necessary amount of compressions but as John was about to breathe into Michael once more, his mouth so close to the hole in the face of the body, another compression followed, initiating a burst of stale air from deep within Michael's body that passed into John through his parted lips. For a second John was filled with death. He felt he would collapse, vomit or scream. But he did none of these. Everyone is a hero.

In time, the ambulance and the doctor arrived along with the rest of the morning staff. Michael was dead. It transpired he had been dead for over an hour before John had found him. It was just the sun that had kept him warm.

John went home that afternoon having written statements, reports, talking to other staff and managing the shift. He went home and cried. It would take a long time to free himself of the image of Michael hanging there before him, surrounded by so much light. The smell of the scene would come at all sorts of times, bringing with it sensations and emotions he thought were long gone. But the most lasting memory was the taste of death upon his lips, having that putrid air pumped into him for that single second. That would change him; haunt him, in so many different ways.

That evening, as Michael's room was being cleared, a newspaper was found at the bottom of the locker, just a regular daily newspaper from the previous day. It was folded neatly, and almost intact. The only thing missing was the crossword that had been carefully removed the previous evening, removed by the slender, beautiful fingers of a tragic man.

He was a friend of mine.

England

1989

Winter

THE CLEANSING

Chapter Eighteen

So the summer waned and died in the arms of autumn. The cool breezes became icy winds and the branches of the trees began to crack. Autumn is the cruellest season. It seems there are but a few short weeks between the hazy sunshine of the falling summer and the bitter gales of winter. The birds abscond to warmer places whilst the animals hide themselves away in the earth of their design. Leaves tumble to the ground and conkers thud into the soil to be collected by frantic children.

The curses uttered during those hot and sticky July nights are quickly forgotten. It hardly seems credible that, just a few weeks ago, you were writhing on your quilt a burning wreck. Now two hot water bottles are still not enough. All the windows are closed firm and you hear their mournful tears throughout the night.

Winter brings with it a sense of relief. It is callous but clear. There are no tempting bursts of sunshine, no momentary glimpses of an all too perfect sky. Where autumn is deceit, winter is stone cold truth.

Christmas becomes the focus again, the beacon of light in a vicious sea of survival. As November nears its malicious finale, colours begin to flicker in the shops, blinking innocently in the face of gloom. Bright toys replace the lapsed Summer stock and the vision of some new beginning peers craftily through the bleak mists of the morning.

It is week before Christmas day.

Only two weeks before the New Year.

Just a fortnight before this one is over and forgotten.

George awoke early and stumbled downstairs in his pyjamas. His bare feet almost froze upon the cold linoleum of the kitchen floor. He tiptoed over to the cupboard in bearable pain, took out three mugs and made a pot of tea. As he was pouring the hot tea into the mugs, the letterbox cracked shut in the hallway.

On the doormat lay three envelopes. All bore George's name. The first letter that he opened was a glossy affair informing him that he had won a two-week holiday in Brazil for himself and his family. The second told him he had won the pick of any of three top of the range cars. He did not even concern himself with reading the small print. He had learned during his term of unemployment that nobody gives anything away, not really, particularly to those who need it most. To the man bereft of both money and opportunity, the word 'free' is little more than a cruel misnomer. The third letter remained unopened.

The mornings of tearing open letters with enthusiasm had long since passed for George. The bills, the rejections and the false hopes had seen to that. A letter was no longer a potential source of interest, more a daily reminder of circumstance and a test of tolerance. They weren't real letters anyway. The ones he had written to Elaine whilst she was with her sister in the summer—they were real.

He took the two largest mugs upstairs and placed one carefully on the chest of drawers beside Tom's bed. The other, he took to his own bedroom. Elaine was sitting up in bed, her back resting against her propped up pillows. She smiled at her husband as he entered, whispering 'thank you' to him when he handed her the hot mug of tea. She grasped it in both hands and let its warmth numb her fingers. It had been a cold night, but she had slept deeply.

After having gone back downstairs to drink his tea at the table, George sat down on the chair and opened the third letter. It was from a local timber company asking him to come and see them the following morning. He looked at it again. He read the letter for a third time, his hands clammy. His heart was beating so fast. And then he slipped the letter back into the envelope almost as if it would disintegrate into nothing were it to be exposed to the air for too long.

Six months earlier, he had written to all the timber firms in the local telephone directory asking them if there were any positions available to which he might be suited. He had included with each letter his employment history and relevant qualifications. That was all he could do. In truth, it had been an effort made in desperation. He hadn't really expected anything to come of it. But now it seemed it had paid off. G.Allman's Timber wanted to see him. They wanted him.

George thought about all of this as he got dressed, ready to go to the Department of Social Security office to sign on. He kissed his wife goodbye and made sure that the letter was safely in his pocket before he left the house. He didn't want anybody to find it. He would surprise them. At last he thought, all my trials Lord.

The pavement crackled beneath a layer of frost. There had not been any snow yet, just sharp, chilly reminders that worse was to come. As George walked, he could not quell the growing excitement within him. The interview tomorrow would be his first for more than a year. And they had written to him. He had not phoned them, pestered them. They could have just phoned him.

But they hadn't. They had taken the time to write to him. Someone had read his letter and then written back to him.

So George's excitement stepped into the precarious realms of anticipation.

Standing outside the DSS at the far end of town, there was a little girl. Her hair was a dirty blonde, her cheeks cold and pale. And on her forehead were two pink blemishes that the bitter wind delighted in teasing until they resembled smouldering eyes of pain. She wore jeans and a thick brown jumper through which she shivered.

"Got two ones?" asked the little girl as George approached. Her voice was harsh and sharp.

George stopped and looked at her closely.

"Have you got two ones, mate?" she asked again.

He stared at her face. She couldn't be more than eight or nine years old, he thought. He felt in his pocket and found a ten pence piece.

"Will this be all right?" he asked, handing it to her. "It's all I've got."

The little girl took the coin from him and placed it gently into a small red purse that she gripped between white fingers. George looked at her again but she just turned away, an expression of deep thought upon her aching face. So he continued on into the DSS, leaving the little girl outside, wondering at the two red marks on her forehead.

Inside the DSS, the usual queue had formed. The interior was like a doctor's surgery. The walls were a pale yellow and the ceiling a foreboding grey. There were posters on every wall depicting unfortunately shaped characters doing various jobs. And each poster contained a slogan at which the line of people would either stare at with failing bitterness or to which they would avert their eyes altogether.

'Show Employers What You Can Do!'

'Take A Step Forward—Join A Training Scheme!'

'We Are Here To Help You—We Care!'

'It's Your Life—Shape It!'

There were about forty people in the queue when George joined it. Each time he signed on, he always seemed to see different people. What becomes of them all?

There are so many lives and so many sufferings of which we know nothing. They are all around us.

Not a sound could be heard within the walls of the DSS. Nobody wanted to talk. Nobody wanted to look at anyone else. Each was in his or her own private agony, getting through as best they could. It was an internal struggle. There were no complaints about the length of time spent waiting and there were no angry glances. There was just a sense of betrayal so acute as to not require an explanation. There were no words that could be said, no gesture that could accurately depict the pain of it all. It was just too vast a feeling.

The area at the end of the room was reserved for Fresh Claimants. The recently unemployed would enter the silent sanctum with an air of nervous confidence, bravado almost, striding by the stationary queue with loud, steady steps. And what followed was always a marvel to see. The further they progress towards the back of the room, the slower becomes their pace. Unseen hands and eyes strip their clothes from them until they sit naked and grateful upon that hard chair, in full view of everyone. But no one is watching. After five or ten minutes, grasping a handful of forms to ensure respectability, they leave, adopting a funereal tread that has suddenly become so natural. They are clothed now in a dull cloak of indignity, sliding out of that ever-open door like a shadow.

Just as George found himself before the wire mesh of Box 2, the shutter was dragged down without explanation. The same young woman who had previously occupied Box 2 then hauled up the shutter covering Box 1. The queue shuffled silently to the left without question, as if they were all bound together with real manacles rather than these chains of pain that truly held them fast.

A man behind George spoke.

"It must be really difficult working here," he announced to nobody in particular. "Really depressing."

George didn't look around. What the man had said was just too much for the people there to comprehend. If they started to think about it, analyze it, it would surely have dragged them down further. Or else, they would have dragged him down. That was why there was always silence. Words had hurt so much in the past. Words said, words written, words thought. Nobody can handle words. Not really.

The young woman on the other side of the wire mesh picked up George's UB40 when he passed it to her and slid back a form in return. She had blue eyes and long blonde hair that she continuously played with, twirling it about her fingers. Around her neck, she wore a gold chain. Her blouse was as taut and abrasive as her manner. The mat in front of her was covered in graffiti. There were scribbles, drawings of dogs and men and the names of various football teams. Ah football. The young woman thrust a pen under the mesh and George signed his name before passing it back to her along with the form.

"You need to fill in this other form," she said. "It's a new one." Her voice was sharp and shrill. She may as well have said 'pretty boy, pretty boy.'

George took the green form that had been handed to him and walked over to a white table near the door. He looked through the form and saw that most of it didn't apply to his situation at all. He wasn't sure why he had been given it to fill, but he had learned not to question at moments like these. It could send the whole system into chaos. He was about to sign it anyway, when he realized there was no pen on the table. So he walked back to the wire mesh window and the people silently let him through.

"I'm sorry," he said to the young woman, "but could I borrow a pen to fill this form in please?"

The rouged cheeks of the young woman lost their fake colour. Her blue eyes tinted grey. In her hand she held a pen. Her eyes locked upon it as if she had just been caught with the murder weapon in the billiard room. If only she could somehow conceal it. With no alternative at hand, she turned and disappeared for more than ten minutes. Meanwhile, the queue increased by another twenty people and was now out of the door and into the street.

Can you imagine the ignominy?

Can you feel it?

You're in the street now. You're waiting in the street.

In place of the young woman, a man around George's age came to the meshed window holding between thumb and forefinger, almost at arms length, a chewed black pen. He passed it to George without a flicker of his banal countenance.

"Please bring it back," he muttered.

George turned his back upon him, feeling a great urge to walk off with it, just to fulfil the equation of the ignorant and the blind. But he couldn't. They would never take his dignity. That was for him alone to lose.

That evening, George searched through the wardrobe for his suit. He still hadn't told Tom or Elaine about the interview. And he barely dared to whisper the words to himself, those words that brought with them such fear and unknowing. "I might have a job." He had to sit on the edge of his bed when he had finished the sentence, so powerful was it. It took so much out of him.

For the first time in years, he would be able to buy his wife and his son something special for Christmas. He felt a shiver rush through him as he recalled the winter evenings when he would arrive home from work, his beige duffel coat warm about him, with a small present for Tom, maybe a book or a tape or a game, or most wonderful of all a new Subbuteo team. He would be more excited than his son walking up the road to the house, unable to stop himself imagining the look of joy on that little boy's face.

This year, he would not be reduced to skulking around the market and the bargain stores on Christmas Eve, searching in desperation for things he could afford. No more, George. No more.

For the man who is poor will be forever reminded of his own complete poverty. He will watch his children as they sit before the naked tree and feel like cold slaps the smiles on their faces and the disappointment in their eyes. They will open their meagre gifts and they will say 'thank you Mummy, thank you Daddy' in a voice that shakes. And you will want them to scream at you in full anger and to hurl at you the gifts, wrapped alone with such foreboding. But they will just sit there before the silver tree, quite, quite still.

And tomorrow will not be another day—for there are no other days but these.

As he looked through the wardrobe, his hands touched the material of some of Elaine's dresses. He smelled them and ran the tips of his fingers lightly through them. She looked so elegant in this one and that other one was the one she wore on her thirtieth birthday. The first thing he would do when he got paid would be to take her out to dinner. And he would buy her a new dress. They hadn't done that sort of thing for ages. Not since Little Norman.

His suit, when he eventually found it, appeared at first glance to be in reasonable condition, better than he had expected anyway. There were no great marks or faded areas that he could see. He took it into the bathroom and tried it on. The thin material brushed against his legs in a strange fashion. He had grown so used to wearing jeans. He put on the jacket over a pale green shirt and then put on his tie, the only tie he had. Stepping furtively out of the bathroom, he returned to the bedroom.

He looked at himself in the full-length mirror. The trousers were a little tight and he wasn't quite sure whether the brown tie went with the shirt. But overall, he was satisfied. Dressed in his suit and with something to actually look forward to, he felt a bigger man already. And in that instant, he realized just how small he had become.

George rose early the following morning. He was a child beginning that first day at school after the longest of summers. He had his morning tea and left the house an hour before he was due at G.Allman's Timber. He didn't want to be late.

The sky was like a sheet of ice. There was not a slither of light. The wind cut George's face and burnt his eyes. He walked with his head bent low now, though his spirits were high. He hoped the slippery ground wouldn't claim him. Not today. Not in his suit. Grey clouds began to break free from the white of the sky and drift slowly across town. The wind picked up loose debris from the street and wafted it carelessly into the path of any who dared confront it.

George quickened his pace lest it snowed or rained. The sign for G.Allman's Timber reared up before him. He stopped short of his destination and turning to face himself in the dark window of the Electricity Showroom, he pulled a metal comb through his thin hair. Satisfied, he took a deep breath and walked on into the foyer of his prospective employer.

After waiting for twenty minutes in the small reception area, George took the letter out of its envelope and read it again. Maybe he had made a mistake? But no, he was right. He had arrived on the correct day at the correct time.

"Mr Spainer?" asked a woman who entered through an unseen door.

George put the letter hastily back in the envelope and rose to meet the woman. 'This is it' he thought to himself. At this point, his stomach began to leave him.

"Mr Dawson will be with you in five minutes, Mr Spainer," said the woman, curtly as if he had been unconsciously harassing her throughout the morning, "so if you really wouldn't mind taking a seat, I would be most grateful." Her eyes were magnets. He was of metal. And she lowered him back down to the chair.

The unseen door closed and, once again, George was alone. Just five more minutes and it would begin.

Ten minutes later, the woman reappeared and beckoned George to her.

"Follow me, Mr Spainer."

She led him to a large office and withdrew from sight.

"Mr Spanker. Do take a seat," said the man behind the desk. He had a very large voice and was at least fifteen years younger than George. He had a thin, brown moustache that seemed to have been pencilled on overnight by some errant child. And his eyes, his eyes never blinked.

"Mr Spanker, you wrote to us some time ago, did you not, inquiring as to whether or not we at G.Allman's Timber had any vacancies?"

"Yes."

"Well, we had no vacancies at that moment in time, but I'm pleased to say that we do now have a vacancy in our Sales Department. I have studied your curriculum vitae, Mr Spanker, and I see that you do seem to have had a good deal of experience with timber."

"Yes."

Mr Dawson paused and swivelled round on his swivel chair, all the way around, before facing George again. "Do you have transport, Mr Spanker?"

"I'm sorry?"

"Transport. Do you own a vehicle? Do you drive? Do you have transport?"

"No."

George was becoming a little uncomfortable. Sales Department. Vehicles. Transport. Surely this was a timber company. It was wood. And he was the person they wanted. They had written to him.

There are times when all we can do is sit and watch ourselves fall apart. We sit and stare as it all just slips away. We observe the fading of our dreams and the destruction of our hopes as if it is all happening to another. And we wonder at the injustice of it all.

"Mr Spanker. Let me make our position clear. It is not our way at G.Allman's Timber to pre-judge. We are a forward-looking company and we like to give everyone a chance to work for us. That is why we asked you here today, to give you a chance. We know what it must feel like in these times, writing to people, never getting a reply. We are not like that. We appreciate, we all appreciate, that you may indeed be very good with timber. I myself do not know one end of a piece of wood from another. We admire a craftsman as much as anybody. In these hard times, however, a company such as ours, all companies in fact, need to expand their respective markets. It's all in the selling, the advertising and in the marketing. We need people who can do this for us. Dynamism is the watchword of our times. And we're afraid, Mr Spanker, that you don't quite fit the bill. As it were."

George looked at the man with the large voice. What was he talking about? What did he mean by adverts and markets? And what did he know about hard times?

With each word that Mr Dawson spoke, George felt himself leave his body and float higher and higher above the scene, a prisoner staring down in awe upon his own trial. By the time Mr Dawson had finished speaking, George was barely in the room at all.

"Well," said Mr Dawson, coming out from behind his desk, "it has been very pleasant talking to you and we wish you the best of luck in your search for gainful employment."

But George was nowhere to be seen for he was above it all now, high above it all. He came back to reality briefly and allowed himself to be led out to the foyer in shock. He pulled at the door but it would not open. He then pushed it hard and found himself stumbling back out into the street.

And there she was again, the little girl from the day before.

"Got two ones?" she asked.

She held out her left hand. In the other, she gripped her small red purse.

"What do you mean?" asked George, tentatively.

"Two ones," she repeated. "Have you got two ones?"

He looked at her as he felt in the pockets of his suit, just stared at her. Then his fingers closed around a small metal object. It was a silver broach. He withdrew it and inadvertently scratched his finger on the pin. The broach was in the shape of a teddy bear and he gazed upon it, just a small silver bear. He had bought it for Little Norman to wear at the Christening and had pinned it to the tiny cardigan Elaine had knitted but the pin had kept coming loose and the broach kept falling off. So he had put it in his pocket all those years ago. It had been there during the Christening and during the funeral. Little Norman.

"Here you are," said George, softly, holding out the silver bear to the little girl.

The little girl took the broach carefully from the palm of this stranger. She turned it over and over, flipping it in her left hand. She then held it to her frozen cheek. "Two ones," she murmured. "Two ones."

And George gazed in profundity at the wonder in her eyes.

Chapter Nineteen

Tom's mother and father were both out in town when he heard a knock on the front door. He was lying on his bed half asleep and was reluctant to rouse himself. At the second knock, he trudged downstairs, pulling his T-shirt over his head as he did so, and opened the door. And there in the doorway stood two young women, one close to his own age, the other possibly four or five years older.

"Good morning," said the older of the two women.

"Hello," said Tom, trying desperately to think whether he knew them or not. They seemed so welcoming, so familiar and easy in their acknowledgement of him. "Can I help you?" he asked after some moments. "Mum and Dad are both out."

"I'm Sister Bonner," said the first woman again, pointing to a small metal badge to verify the fact. "And this is Sister Welch."

Sister Welch uttered an incomprehensible form of greeting and Tom looked at her quizzically. She was shorter and younger than her companion and wore thick, brown-rimmed spectacles that almost obscured her entire face. Her eyes looked wide and unnatural behind them as if they were actually painted onto the lenses themselves.

"I wonder," said Sister Bonner, "whether you would be able to spare us a few moments of your time. We're from the Church of the Latter Day Saints and at this time of year, we like to take the opportunity to talk with people about our beliefs and about our church."

Sister Bonner had large blue eyes and dark hair that hung to her shoulders. She sounded to Tom as if she came from the Midlands. He hadn't the faintest idea where Sister Welch hailed from. And then, to his surprise, he found himself trying to identify the form of Sister Bonner's breasts beneath her very masculine coat.

Since he had returned home, Tom had found plenty of time to think and to reflect upon his life. No matter how much he thought though, he could not reconcile what he had been through with what he had set out to achieve. He couldn't see that anything had been gained by his actions. His soul was still in turmoil, raging and ragged. He had lost his job and there was now an even more precarious countenance to his survival, his connection to his fellow man.

Through his life, he had never considered himself a religious man. He had believed at times in something akin to predestination, in fate perhaps. But since he had been back home, he had been unable to see any justification for the things that had happened to him. And this very fact was beginning to make him feel that there was perhaps another force in control of things, watching over him, leading him on. The two women on the doorstep had arrived at the right moment. Fate? Who knows? Tom was curious. But it has to be said that the big blue eyes and indeterminate breasts of Sister Bonner played their part in his decision to allow the women into the house.

Sister Bonner and Sister Welch entered and sat beside one another on the settee.

"Do you want a drink or anything?" asked Tom.

"No. We're fine," replied Sister Bonner.

Tom sat down in the armchair opposite the two women, the initial silence rising, only to fall and settle comfortably above the three young people in the room; three young people trying to find their way through life.

"This is a nice home," said Sister Bonner. "I can feel peace here."

"It's okay," replied Tom, casually. He felt quite secure at this time, in control. He could also sense something happening, or about to happen. There was a feeling in the air. His loneliness had left him receptive to experiences. It had left him vulnerable.

"That's a nice picture," said Sister Bonner, indicating the painting above the fireplace. "Who is it by?"

"I don't know. Dad bought it for Mum in a boot sale a few years ago."

Sister Bonner turned towards him. Sister Welch continued to stare at the picture.

"You live with your parents, then?"

"Yes. They're out," he replied, somewhat meekly.

Sister Welch turned and said something unintelligible to Tom. He thought for a moment that she might be American, or maybe Scottish. Wherever she came from, he could still not follow the words she spoke. He just smiled at her and she smiled back broadly, her huge white teeth all but swallowing up her pale, thin lips as she did so.

"Well," began Sister Bonner. And then she stopped. "I'm sorry," she said, "I don't think we know your name, do we?"

"Tom."

"As in Thomas?"

"As in Joad."

"Oh. Right. Well, Tom. Have you ever had a belief in God?"

"I believe in something, I suppose," said Tom, a little taken aback by the gravity in his own voice. "I think there probably is something else, but as for what you call it, God or whatever, I couldn't tell you."

"Do you know of Jesus Christ?"

"All the stories you mean?"

Suddenly, a picture flashed before Tom's eyes. It was an image of Michael, sprawled on the ground, stained and wet and covered in blood. And then it was gone, gone as quickly as it had appeared. This had been happening lately.

"You've read the Bible, Tom?"

"Not really."

He began at once to feel that tempting urge to manipulate, to take control, to shut out the child. He could not resist. He felt ashamed, though impotent, consciously allowing his mind to proceed whilst his heart and his soul gazed mournfully on.

The two women were polite and they were safe. They were women and they were interested in him. And that was all he needed right now—somebody to show him an interest, to listen to him and to validate his existence.

Sister Welch leaned over and whispered something to Sister Bonner. Tom looked at them both and waited. He looked closely at their hair and at their skin, wondering if it had ever been touched in the midst of passion. He became analytical. He observed, as much as he could around the spectacles of Sister Welch, that her complexion was smooth and tanned. A thought came into his mind that without the spectacles and with her hair down, she might be quite pretty. This thought soon passed. Sister Bonner was different. She was strong and powerful and pretty was a word that could not readily be applied to her. Handsome was closer. Yes, thought Tom, handsome.

"Do you mind, Tom," said Sister Bonner, "if we start by saying a short prayer together?"

"No. Fine."

"Would you like to say it, Tom, or would you rather one of us began?"

"You can do it," said Tom, hoping in a way that the incomprehensible and potentially pretty Sister Welch would be given the task.

Sister Bonner bowed her head and closed her big blue eyes. Sister Welch did the same. Tom bowed his head too, but kept a curious eye slightly open.

Personalities come and go. You change and you return and you perform. And in the quietness of the night, you ponder the susceptibility of your very existence. Things happen to you. They just happen. We are above it and we are within it all at once, above it and within it.

"Our Father in Heaven," began Sister Bonner, "we thank thee for giving us the opportunity to speak with Tom and for allowing us the chance to share with him the glory of your Kingdom. We ask thee to look after Tom and to reveal to him the truth of your majesty and your word. In the name of Jesus Christ, Amen."

The prayer affected Tom in a way he was unable to explain. His flippancy departed and was replaced by a respect for these two young women. Change. Change.

"Do you have a Bible, Tom?" asked Sister Bonner.

"No. I don't think so."

"You can borrow one of ours."

Sister Welch dove into her handbag and retrieved a small Bible that she handed across to Tom.

"Have you lived here long?" asked Sister Bonner as she flicked through the thin, almost translucent, pages of her own Bible.

"A few years."

"Good, right. Now Tom, I'm going to read to you a passage from the Bible and I would like you to tell me your thoughts about it when I've finished."

Tom nodded in acknowledgement.

Sister Bonner read slowly and clearly and without expression. Her voice was soft and smooth, the words appearing as blips amidst a low drone.

"Have you heard that before, Tom?" she asked, when she had finished reading.

"Something like it at school, I think. It might not have been exact, but I've heard the story."

"How did it make you feel?"

Tom thought for a moment. "Sad," he said at last. "Nobody helped him. They just let him die."

"Remember, Tom, He was God's son. He knew what He had to do and He was given the courage by God to do it. But, of course, He rose again and his body and soul were reunited. And that is why we're all here, Tom, because of Jesus Christ, because he gave up his life on earth for our sins."

Tom began to think he was elsewhere. He was sure that were he to look out of the window, he would see neither cars nor houses. It was so quiet in here, so perfectly serene.

Thus far, Tom had found nothing to argue with. Sister Bonner's voice invoked within him something spiritual, passive. Innately, he needed and desired direction. When he had opened the door to the two women and sensed the meaning of their visit, he thought he would remain in control, maybe toy with them, test them and show them how a man of the world feels about their textbook beliefs. He had wanted to disturb them with rational questions. But now, when it came to it, the security and the beauty of somebody else saying his own name left him overwhelmed.

"Do you have any questions, Tom?" asked Sister Welch.

He looked at her and realized he was beginning to understand even her diction.

"There's one thing I get confused about. If there was only one Jesus and only one God, how come there are so many different religions?"

"We were just coming to that," said Sister Bonner, glancing quickly at her colleague. This time, it was her turn to search through her bag. She brought out a book and placed it beside her on the arm of the settee. Tom couldn't see what it was called, just that it had a dark cover with small gold lettering upon it. He waited in silence.

"If you were to read the Bible on your own, Tom, from start to finish, you may find some of it confusing. It is as complex as it is simple. People tend to interpret those things that they don't understand and it is these interpretations, or should I say, misinterpretations, that give rise to different religions." She could have been reading it off a card. But it made perfect sense to Tom, there, at that moment.

"So who's right then?" he asked, just as Sister Bonner was about to speak again. Whether she had heard his question or not, he was unsure. She just continued on in the same, steady voice.

"The Bible is God's word, Tom. He spoke to his prophets here on earth and they wrote down what they saw and what they heard. And those things they wrote were put together and became what we know today as the Bible. Therefore, everything written in the Bible is what God wants us to know. In that sense, all religions are right. However, God only let a very few people know the correct interpretations of the translation from the original."

Sister Bonner paused and lifted her head. She smiled at Tom, a full, comforting smile. And she looked into his eyes. "I will tell you a story, Tom," she said softly.

The story Tom heard was set in the 1820's and it concerned a man named Joseph Smith. It told how an angel appeared before him one day and guided him to a hill wherein he found some gold plates. Upon these plates had been etched the words of God. Joseph Smith had then, under the guidance of God, translated the words on the plates and transcribed them onto paper.

"And here, Tom," said Sister Bonner, passing him the book that rested beside her, "here are the words of Joseph Smith. The words of God."

Tom leafed solemnly through the book. It was not a large volume but the print was small. The pages were very thin, so thin that he thought he might accidentally tear them with a crooked fingernail.

"Does that make sense to you Tom?" asked Sister Welch.

He looked at her. She seemed to have reverted a little to her previous incoherence, no more clear than the fading in and out of a far away radio station.

"It's clever. I suppose this Joseph Smith character could be anybody, could he? Just to show how God speaks to normal people and all that?"

Sister Welch looked at Sister Bonner. Sister Bonner looked at Sister Welch.

"Tom," said Sister Bonner, leaning towards him. "It is a true story. Joseph Smith was a real man. All that I told you really happened."

"Oh," said Tom, resisting the temptation to lean closer to her. Now, he was somewhat confused. He had heard most of the Bible stories at school, but never this one.

"God says, Tom, that the Bible is just one way to understand his word. He says that there will be other means of learning. And that book in your hand is one of those other ways, *the* way."

Tom turned the book around and looked at the cover to see if it really was by someone called Joseph Smith, but he found no mention of that name. There was just the title 'The Book of Mormon—Another Testament of Jesus Christ.' And at once, he felt he had been the victim of a spell, a magically impressive trick, an illusion of words and gestures. It was brilliant. And he had fallen for it. The words on the cover brought with them not visions of God, but of Donny and the beautiful Marie. He looked up from the cover of the book and, in his ignorance, half expected the pupils of Sisters Bonner and Welch to have gone from their respective eyes.

"We're going to let you have that book, Tom," said Sister Bonner. "And these too." She handed him some leaflets and then rose to kneel down beside his chair. "Would you like to say a prayer, Tom, before we finish. Until next time?" She gave him a blue card. "This tells you how to pray. Say each line on the card and, when you've finished, thank God for something in your life."

Tom took the blue card and read it to himself. He turned it over and looked upon the bowed heads of the two young women before him.

"What would you like to thank God for, Tom," asked Sister Bonner, her head still bowed.

Tom thought. His cynicism was rapidly returning. He considered the question hurtful and vindictive. He leaned slowly forward in the direction of Sister Bonner. Looking down towards the front of her chest, he saw only darkness. Mildly disappointed, he just murmured, "For being here, I suppose."

"Yes. That's good, Tom. And what would you like to ask God for?"

His heart became suddenly heavy with grief. What to ask God for? He had to say it. It was as if he were being made to say it. He was before God now, at his feet, or maybe standing next to him in a pub and all he said was "I want my brother back, please. I need my brother back." Tears came to his eyes now. His heart came to the surface. He felt cold and weak and vulnerable. But it made sense. It all made sense now.

Without prompting, Tom prayed. He didn't follow the hints and tips on the blue card. He just prayed as best as he could. It came naturally. When he had finished, he was reluctant to open his eyes, for in his mind, he held an image of Little Norman with a paper hat upon his head and chocolate sauce upon his face.

"Thank you, Tom," said Sister Bonner, her voice snapping open the shutters of his eyes. "That was very nice." Nice. Nice. "I've marked certain passages in The Book that may help you. Thank you again for your time. Here is our card."

Tom looked at the two women as they stood up, Sister Welch with her bottle thick glasses and Sister Bonner with her eyes and her seductively wandering breasts. Two young people so far away from him. He opened the door for them and as they found themselves back on the doorstep once more, Sister Bonner spoke in a strident voice. "The Bible," she said, "and the Book of Mormon are the first two steps on the stairway to Heaven. It's up to you, Tom, to climb them."

"Led Zeppelin," he said.

And the two women wavered a little. They glanced at each other and then back at Tom who took one last look into Sister Bonner's wide eyes before shutting the door to the bitter wind.

He was beginning to work things out now.

Little Norman.

Chapter Twenty

It was three days before Christmas and Tom was yet to buy a present for his mother and father. On previous occasions, he had merely withdrawn some money from the Bank and purchased the first thing he saw that appeared remotely suitable. When he thought about it now, he felt embarrassed at his past efforts—a Frank Sinatra calendar for Mum, gardening gloves for Dad, an ornament for Mum, a book for Dad—and so it went on, one more shoddy effort after another.

But this Christmas, things would be different. He needed to show his parents how much he really loved them. Telling them was out of the question. To his eternal shame, he knew he couldn't tell them. There was something indefinable stopping him. And when he sat there and pondered the depth of his love for those two people who had been through even more than he, a shiver of fear burst through him.

Tom no longer held a Bank or Building Society account. The money he received from the DSS he split between himself and his mother. The cut was roughly equal, though he would give her any change. It was as if he were subconsciously replenishing something he had taken. And this humble state of being came naturally to him now, this feeling of poverty.

The air was cold as Tom walked to the shops. It slapped his face and pulled at him. His hands clung to the insides of his pockets, gripping his money. The turned up collar of his denim jacket did little to stop the wind biting his neck. It was so cold out there.

Christmas had come fast. As a child, Tom had looked forward to it with eagerness and joy. From the end of October, he would wait in an excited state of anxiety, counting the long days and the even longer nights. It had all seemed so large then, so magnificent. And Little Norman had been right there with it.

As each day passed, he was beginning to remember something new about his baby brother, something beautiful, funny, something pure and innocent. Memories never let you go. They just don't leave you alone until you free them from the cage of your burdens, put them in perspective, and let them fly delighted into the skies of your experience.

The town centre was swathed in decorations. Tinsel hung from the shop signs and a large Christmas tree had been erected in the square, lights dangling from it, blinking wildly. People scurried from shop to shop and back again, crashing through doors and squeezing by one another. The benches in the square were empty. They just remained there unused, cracked and battered by the wind. Nobody could afford to rest. There just wasn't the time.

Tom stepped towards the seething mass and let it drag him forlornly in. After having been swept breathlessly in and out of six shops, he slumped onto one of the benches, still holding his ten-pound note furiously in his hand. He had almost bought his mother a large box of chocolates but had resisted at the final moment. He tried hard to think of things his parents might like. But he knew it wouldn't be enough. Whatever he bought would not fully explain his love for them.

So he trudged away, disconsolate.

When he arrived home and opened the front door, he could hear the dull, rhythmic thud of a hammer. The rhythm seemed odd to him now, yet it had been one of the main beats of his childhood. This sound of creativity had not been heard in the house for years. It seemed to be coming from the shed at the back of the garden, but he had not the interest to investigate. So he went upstairs to the softness of his bedroom.

The book given to him by the two young women lay face down on the floor where he had discarded it. He sat on his bed now and, leaning forward, picked the book up. Though there were many pages in it, it felt flimsy and weak in his hands. He lay back upon the bed and held it aloft as he looked at it. A feeling of uneasiness came over him, a sense of distaste. You don't know me, he thought. Nobody knows me. He began to scratch at the gold lettering on the cover with the fingernails of his right hand. He brought the book closer to him now and continued scratching at the surface, the lettering crumpling beneath his nails. And for a few moments, his movements were torrid and uncontrolled. Then, as if ejecting it from a machine, he hurled the book across the room.

"Tom," came a voice from downstairs, "can you come down and help me put away some of this shopping?" It was his mother, Elaine.

Having spent so much time at home since his return from Big Town, Tom had come to love his mother all over again. He saw her through the clear eyes of grief, unobstructed by the veil of the wilfully blind.

After packing away the shopping, he made her a cup of tea. He sat down with her at the kitchen table and they both sipped their warm drinks in grateful silence. Not a word passed between them. During that time, their hearts and their souls continued to delve into one another, to soothe, to reconcile differences, to re-affirm love. They were in the same room together drinking tea.

George came into the house from the frozen garden and broke the profound silence. He closed the back door behind him and rubbed his cold hands together as if they might bring forth a spark between his palms that would ignite him in an instant.

"Tea nice is it?" he asked in mock earnest.

"Yes it is, George Spanner. Thank you," replied Elaine, smiling up at her husband.

"I'll do you one, Dad," said Tom, getting up from his chair.

The word 'Dad' melted into George. 'Dad.' He could not ever remember being called it before. Perhaps he hadn't. Not since Little Norman anyway. And it sounded so precious. He felt suddenly proud and exhilarated. There is my son. And there is my wife. And he began to grow again.

Whilst Tom was waiting for the kettle to boil, George sat down opposite Elaine.

"How's it going?" she asked, whispering just loud enough for Tom to hear.

George looked slowly from side to side and leaned towards her. "Not bad," he replied.

Tom looked up from the now steaming mug of tea before him and glanced quickly at his father who just smiled a sweet smile in return. He looked then towards his mother and just as he was about to speak to her, she rose and put her cup in the sink.

He knew he was beaten.

And he adored the moment.

That afternoon, the first snow fell. It swirled in ragged patterns, never really landing, just floating, dancing and floating. The garden became a glass ball filled with water and tiny white flakes, all shaken up by some unseen hand. As the hours passed, the white flakes began to settle on the hard ground, smothering it in a cold sheet, patching up the blemishes and adding purity to that which was rotting.

Tom watched from his bedroom window. Elaine watched from the kitchen. George peered out from the cracked, dusty window of his shed.

And each saw different patterns in the soft and silent storm.

From her flat in Big Town, Sandy too looked out upon the snow. The warmth within the flat caused mist to develop on the inside of the window and she had to continuously wipe it away with her hand in order to see.

It had been a long year for her. The insurance company had served her well and most of the stolen items had been replaced. She did have difficulty replenishing some of her father's old records but he had just smiled at her saying that he had heard them all before anyway. But she had never been able to understand how Tom could have done that to her. At times, she had even thought he had something to do with the attack on the shop. She had claimed for everything that had gone, except for the guitar, for he had surely taken that, taken it and ran.

You don't know me. Nobody knows me.

Sandy's mother had urged her to forgive Tom, to learn from the experience and to allow the bitterness to fall from her for she said bitterness was like a manacle to the soul. But she found it very hard to do. She had given everything. He had taken more. Not just the things in the flat, but her trust and her love. Even so, she tried to see him through the eyes of her mother. He is just a poor, lost boy. One day he will find that for which he is looking. Be proud of yourself Sandjreka. Be very proud.

As she was staring at the whiteness of the day, Sandy heard a key turn in the lock. She went into the kitchen and put the kettle on. And when she came back into the lounge, there was Javed. She moved behind him and slipped her arms about his neck as he sat there on the settee. He smiled up at her as he pulled away slowly, taking his coat off. She moved around now and stood before him, taking his cold hands in hers. And then she kissed him before going back into the kitchen to bring in their drinks.

"We'd better do the Christmas cards today," said Javed, as Sandy gave him his coffee. "It will be too late soon. And I tell you what, its bloody cold out there." He lifted the cup to his lips as he spoke to her and then recoiled in shock at the bitter taste. "Sandjreka," he gasped, "you didn't put any milk in it!"

"Oh, I'm sorry," she said. "I wasn't thinking."

But she was. She was thinking about Christmas cards. And she was thinking of Tom.

Time eased by and Tom awoke at ten o'clock the next morning. He had stayed up late the previous night watching an old black and white film. As he opened his eyes, he looked at the clock and realized he had only half an hour to get to the DSS to sign on. He grabbed the now clearly distressed ten-pound note from his bedside table, got dressed and stumbled out of the house.

At the DSS that morning, he was pleasantly surprised. The wire mesh that had separated the employed from the unemployed had been taken down. There was just a small gap now between them. The person who served him was real again, not some disfigured creature encased in metal. And he noticed how beautiful were her eyes, though she still remained unreceptive to pleasantries. But those eyes stayed with him and lit a fuse in him.

When he emerged from the DSS and into the town centre, the snow that had relented to the pale sun for a moment began to fall once more. As he walked, he promised himself that he would make one more effort to find a present for his parents. After an hour of toil, he had at least bought them a card each. As for a present, he could still find nothing sufficiently special. Not for less than a tenner.

Over dinner that evening, the arrangements were made for the Christmas weekend.

"Well," said Elaine, "we've got two choices." George and Tom listened in silence as they ate. "We can either spend Christmas Day here, or we can go up to Sheila's. She said she'd have us and that we could stay all weekend if we wanted to. Go up Christmas Eve."

"It's a long way," said George, turning to Elaine. "Are you thinking of going by train?" Elaine nodded. "Fine by me," he continued, "as long as it's okay with Sheila and Malcolm."

"What do you think, Tom?" asked Elaine.

"About what?" he replied quietly. For his mind had been on other things.

"Spending Christmas with your Auntie Sheila. All of us."

"Yes. Sure," said Tom looking up from his plate and recalling with a feint smile his rotund Aunt. "I don't reckon we'd go short of food, would we?"

"I don't know," interjected George quickly. "You don't get to that size by giving your food away."

Tom almost choked on his chips.

"Now stop it you two," said Elaine, trying to suppress a smile. "Tom, don't encourage your father," she added.

The young man looked at his father and saw in truth they were the same man. They had experienced different things and different times but, in essence, they were as one. And each had spent their lives watching the other from a distance.

"Is that settled, then?" asked Elaine, once her two boys had managed to control themselves. "Can I call Sheila and tell her we'll be up tomorrow?"

"Of course, love," said George, resisting the temptation to comment further.

"Tom?"

"Sure. No problem."

Elaine took the plates into the kitchen and went into the hall to call her sister. Tom washed up and George dried.

"Did you notice they've taken that wire stuff down at the DSS, you know, between the windows?" asked Tom as he passed a wet, stained plate to his father.

"Yes," replied George. "It looks a lot better."

But George knew that the wire mesh hadn't been taken away at all. It was just that you could see it before. And now you couldn't. Every fortnight, he would continue to receive that same look of pity and unintentional contempt. Maybe it came from within himself. He had begun to think so at times. And he would still want to get out of that place as quickly as if it were aflame. For he knew deep down that there are some barriers that will always remain.

Tom, like his father, did not receive many letters through the post that weren't either offers of loans or seductive advances from catalogue companies. But on this morning, there was one, a Christmas card on Christmas Eve. He was the first to rise that morning, so his parents had been unaware of the card.

Upstairs in his bedroom, he opened the envelope and pulled out the card. On the front, there was a robin sitting on a twig, watching the snowfall. Inside, it read 'To Tom, Happy Christmas, Love from Sandy.' When he had read it, he put it sharply down as if the words had not been written, but spoken. He then picked it up gently and looked at the front again. He eased his fingers across the red breast of the little robin and looked closely at the tiny flakes. He read the words over and over again. It was the word 'love' that lingered on. The very word made him ache for Sandy. Feelings and memories returned to him, washed over him. He could almost feel her beside him. He had been old then. He was so much younger now.

Tom hadn't thought about Sandy for weeks. At first, he had been so tempted to call her but he realized he didn't even know the number. He couldn't write to her for he only knew where she lived by sight, not by address. The time was right. He had sorted out his Mum and Dad's present that night. In fact, he had barely slept. It was Christmas Eve. And he would go and see her—a surprise, a Christmas surprise.

Tom was aware that he was supposed to take the five-thirty train from the station in Big Town with his parents and then travel on north with them, so he left a note on his bed telling them he would meet them on the platform. He was just going to see an old friend and wish them a happy Christmas.

On his way to Big Town, he bought a card for Sandy, a cute card that was similar in style to the one she had sent him. He intended to write it on the train but was unable to find an empty seat.

It was whilst her son was on his way to Big Town once again, that Elaine came down the stairs and found a piece of paper on the kitchen table. She felt a sudden, terrifying grip upon her chest. Fear and anger bore down upon her. Eventually, with shaking hands, she picked the note up and read it. Her sigh of relief continued to fill the room even as her husband entered some moments later.

"Have you seen this, George?" she asked him, her voice a little unsteady.

"Yes. It was on his bed. He knows we're leaving this evening. Don't worry."

"I did tell him the arrangements, didn't I?"

"Yes. He'll phone if he's not sure," said George, putting his gentle hands upon his wife.

"Yes. He will," she said. She so wanted to ask her husband the question that dare not leave her lips. Pain held it in, but it slipped through all the same. "He will be there, won't he?" she whispered meekly into her husband's chest. He held her tighter now.

George kissed the top of her head and stroked her tousled hair with his hand. He looked out of the kitchen window but could see no reflection in the glass. He strained his eyes, but all he saw was the garden and the shed. It was just too light outside.

So the mother and the father held onto one another as the winter sun looked down upon them in awe.

Tom walked to Sandy's flat from the station under the weight of strange emotions. A pendulum of sensations that swung between anticipation and fear struck him. And somewhere at the back of his mind, he wondered whether the Beautiful Guitar had been found.

When he finally stood outside the flat, he took the card from his pocket and crouched down. Resting the card on his knee and taking a cracked pen from his jacket pocket, he wrote 'To Sandy, have a great Christmas, Lots of Love, Tom.' He slotted the card back into the envelope and licked it secure before taking the steps to the flat in threes and fours, bounding up them like a rabbit, like poor Paul Regis.

Hearing the knock on the door, Javed rose steadily to answer it, but Sandy was closer and got there before him. When she opened the door, she had to look again before being capable of displaying any reaction other than shock.

Tom looked somehow so much cleaner, so much healthier than when she had known him. He had put on weight. Energy and excitement seemed to break from within him; sensations that at once thrilled and confounded her. "Tom," she said.

"All right?" he replied, all ebullience. "Thanks for the card. I've got one for you here."

Javed rustled the newspaper loudly and Sandy wavered for a moment.

"Come in, Tom," she said at last. "You must be cold."

"Cheers. I am a bit."

And Tom breezed in as if he'd never been away.

He was surprised then to see somebody else in the flat but he did not let it bother him. His mood was high now. He was bigger, stronger than last he was in this place.

Javed stood when Tom entered the room and the two men shook hands.

"Hello. I'm Javed."

"Tom. Good to meet you."

Sandy took Tom's jacket and he sauntered over to the window to warm himself by the radiator beneath it.

"Do you want coffee, Tom?" asked Sandy.

"Cheers," he said.

Once his hands had warmed a little, he moved to an armchair and sat down, Sandy had not been as excited to see him as he had hoped and he couldn't really think of anything purposeful to say to Javed. The coffee took forever.

"See you got your stuff back," he called out to the kitchen.

"Yes," replied Sandy, bringing in the black coffee.

"You've got quite a few cards."

"Yes, we have, haven't we," replied Sandy, sitting beside Javed on the settee.

Tom allowed the answer to pass him by and, putting his coffee down, leaned back over the chair to take a card off the shelf. It was from someone called Mark and it was addressed to Javed and Sandy. He put that one back and picked up another. That too was addressed to Javed and Sandy. He had assumed somehow that Javed was a friend or a cousin. And now the situation truly fell down upon him.

"Well," said Sandy, "where's my card?"

Her voice was sure now, confident. She felt safe next to Javed. She was not her mother yet.

Tom was in agony. He just wanted the word 'love' to fade out of the card, to disappear, never to emerge before the eyes of another. He gave the card to

Sandy as if it were a written confession of undreamed of guilt, just leaned across and handed it to her. He could not look at her as she opened it. He didn't want to look at Javed.

"Ah," said Sandy, passing the card to Javed. "That's nice. Thank you Tom. That's really sweet of you."

She leaned over the arm of the chair and kissed him on the cheek. And that kiss burned into his face setting his whole being on fire.

The air was thick and impenetrable. Everything was of stone, heavy, intense.

"I'd better be going in a minute," mumbled Tom, finally.

"Oh," said Sandy, "but you haven't finished your coffee."

"Sorry. It's just that I don't drink much of it anymore. I've kind of gone off it. Anyway, I've got to meet Mum and Dad in half an hour. We're going to my Aunt's for Christmas."

Sandy looked at him, searching his eyes. But they were cast down.

"I'll get your coat then," she said.

When Sandy left the room, Javed spoke.

"Tom," he said, "Sandy has told me about the summer and things that happened. She loves you a lot. She has told me. I want you to know that. But things happen and things change. I am with her now." He paused. His voice was low and captivating and Tom could not help but listen to him. "Sandy's father says you are a good man and that's good enough for me."

Tom looked up into Javed's dark eyes and could feel no anger, no pain. "Sure, mate," he said. "Cheers."

Sandy returned with Tom's jacket. She had put it on the radiator in her bedroom and it now felt warm upon his back.

So, he stood on the doorstep once more. He said goodbye to Sandy and he said goodbye to Javed.

"Have a good Christmas, Tom," called Sandy as he neared the bottom of the steps. He turned and looked up but all he saw was the empty spiral staircase down which he had descended.

And what Tom would have given to have somebody holding his cold hands as he walked to the station, to have felt the warmth of another. This yearning all but broke him.

Big Station was crowded and awash with panic. Nobody stood still. Movement was mindless and frenetic. Christmas Eve.

Tom wandered towards the platform and sat upon the ground amidst the slush and the damp and the dirt. A sudden thought came to him and he rummaged through his jacket pockets to see if Sandy had left a secret note like they do in films. But no, nothing. He sat there for an hour before his mother and father finally found him. They lifted him gently to his feet and together they boarded the train that would lead them away from all of this.

Chapter Twenty One

The night was clear and cold and the moon lit up the factories of Northern Town. Tom's Aunt Sheila and Uncle Malcolm met them all at the station with a hug and a handshake and everyone squeezed silently into Malcolm's Cortina. Sheila appeared to Tom even larger than he had remembered. He hadn't seen her for three years and his abiding memory of her was that she appeared never to have any ankles, how her sturdy legs just became feet after a certain point. He saw now that she had a kind, friendly face and a bright, appealing countenance. He was seeing through new eyes now. Uncle Malcolm, well, he was the same as ever. Tom liked Uncle Malcolm.

On their arrival at the small, end-terraced house, Tom volunteered to sleep downstairs on the settee. Sheila said she wouldn't hear of such a thing until George persuaded her that they were all very tired and that it would be easier on Tom's back than it would be on any of theirs. Thus placated, Sheila led her sister and her brother-in-law upstairs and showed them to the second bedroom. Malcolm followed them up, some steps behind.

There was much talk upstairs but Tom was unable to hear it clearly. He was weary now, in so many ways, and had not the will to concentrate. Eventually, he gave up trying to listen, sat back on the settee, and looked around the room. He noticed there were no curtains on the main window. A wooden curtain rail was propped against the wall behind the Christmas tree, the curtains falling from it like a flag of surrender. He recalled how Uncle Malcolm always used to say 'Why do today what she will do herself tomorrow?' and he smiled. This was a safe and a comfortable place.

"So, Tom," said Uncle Malcolm as they all gathered once more in the living room, their upstairs conspiratorial chat concluded, "how goes it?"

"Not bad," replied Tom. "It's all right."

"Still a Town supporter like your Dad?"

"I've kind of not got into it too much this season, to tell you the truth. Funnily enough, I'm looking forward to next season really. Just waiting for this one to finish."

"Next season? When they start doing a bit better you mean?" chuckled Malcolm.

"Something like that," replied Tom, looking down now. Talking was sometimes a great strain for him.

"Don't get at the boy, Malcolm," said Sheila, cutting off her husband mid-chuckle. "He's probably tired, aren't you love?"

"I'm okay," said Tom quietly, trying to smile. Malcolm winked at him and Tom did his best to return the boyish glance being hurled in his direction.

"Just let us know when you're ready to get your head down and we'll all disappear and leave you to sleep. I'll get your blankets in a minute. Now, you're sure you don't mind sleeping down here, love?"

"It's fine. Honest."

There was a silence in the room as each person gazed upon the other unnoticed. A family together, all good people, yet each engaged in their own private struggles.

"I think I'll go to bed now, Sheila," said Elaine after some moments. "I don't mean to be unsociable, it's just that tomorrow will be a long day."

"Me too," said George "yes. Big day tomorrow."

"Up you go then, you two. I'll bring you up a hot water bottle in a minute. It can get quite cold in that bedroom sometimes. The thermostat's not working properly is it Malcolm?" She looked at her husband with reproach leaving him to sail through on a battered ship of bravado, bolstered by the company around him.

"He's useless," she said to Elaine, shooting another glance towards her errant husband, "bloody useless. You're lucky. You've got a good one there. I've always said that."

They both looked over at George who was by the Christmas tree inspecting the forlorn curtain rail.

"Yes," said Elaine, "he's great." And in that moment, she fell in love with him all over again.

George and Elaine soon went upstairs, followed shortly afterwards by Sheila complete with hot water bottle. Tom felt she would probably tuck everyone in too until they were all tight and snug in their beds.

"So, Tom, my lad. It looks like it's just me and you now," said Malcolm. "Fancy a drink?"

But before Tom could answer, a stern voice called from the top of the stairs. "And don't have any ideas about getting the boy drunk, Malcolm. I want you up here in five minutes so he can get some sleep."

Malcolm shrugged and, leaning over to Tom as he stood, whispered, "Don't worry, lad. There's always tomorrow," before going up to his bed.

As Tom sat there alone in this house, so far from his own life, his mind began to nag at him, to throw images before his eyes. During his struggle to comprehend them, Sheila came down with his blankets and interrupted him. She laid them gently on the settee beside him.

"Are you okay now, love?" she asked in a voice almost quavering with compassion. Tom had to turn to check that it was indeed his Aunt. He didn't know what she had been told about the events of the summer, just that his Mum had stayed with her for a while. So he just nodded and yawned.

Sheila looked at her young nephew. She had wanted to hold him for years, to tell him that he was safe and loved and that his family would always be there for him. But he would learn that in time, she thought. Maybe tomorrow.

"Your blankets are here, love. We'll all see you in the morning."

But he was already asleep. So she covered him softly with the blankets, making him as comfortable as she could, comfortable and warm for the night. She sat there for an hour just looking at him, fearing for him, before turning out the light and lumbering solidly up the stairs to her room where her husband was snoring in simple bliss.

Tom awoke several times that night. The settee was rigid and unyielding and the heavy blankets irritated his skin. He had grown used to the luxury of his quilt. Oh it is strange how pauper can slip so swiftly into the fallen robes of the king. Eventually, he discarded the blankets and just curled himself up for warmth. In a way, he felt he needed to be cold, to keep struggling. He couldn't fully think it through. It was almost as if it were necessary at this time.

He soon lapsed into dreams, dreams full of wild images, distorted and vague. He saw faces of children from his infant school and faces of teachers long forgotten. All his childhood was thrown together in his sleep, presented before him like some incongruous montage of fears and hopes. And when he awoke, startled, there was just darkness and the sound of his own breathing. Sleep would take him once more only for different colours to be daubed upon the canvass of his night.

He became warm and sweaty even though the room itself was cold and his blankets were on the floor. At one point, he staggered aimlessly into the kitchen for a glass of water. His Aunt stirred upstairs.

"Tom?" she called in a whispered shout, "are you okay, love?"

Tom's mouth was dry and sore as he moved to the bottom of the stairs. "I'm just getting a drink," he croaked.

His Aunt drifted back to sleep and Tom sat there on the settee, his empty glass on the floor and the palms of his hands, damp from the glass, pressed against his eyes. He pressed harder and harder just to feel some tangible pain, not this furtive stinging that so constantly assailed him.

Outside, the snow began to fall again. Snow at Christmas. When he was younger, he and Little Norman would long for snow. Little Norman was always so sure it would snow. He would kneel on his bed and rest his chubby chin upon the windowsill. For hours he would stay there until, finally, his mother would cover him in his soft, warm covers. And then Tom would rush into his baby brother's room as the morning eased out of the shadows of the night and wake him saying 'Norm, it's snowed! Look! Look!' And he would lift Little Norman from the bed and hug him saying 'Happy Christmas, mate.' Little Norman would gaze over the shoulder of his big brother, who was so great by the way, just gaze at the snow-covered garden and the snow-covered rooftops, smiling proudly, wide eyes glistening as if each tiny snowflake had fallen straight from his dreams.

Tom thought of Little Norman as he sat there with his hands pressed against his eyes.

And it was only Little Norman that kept him from crying.

The pale morning sun glowed against the fresh snow and lit the windows like lanterns. It was Christmas Day at last. Tom was the last to wake and he opened his weary eyes under the gaze of the people that loved him.

"Who's for something to eat?" asked Sheila. "Sausages, eggs, bacon, beans, mushrooms, fried tomatoes and bread and butter for anyone who wants it."

Tom rubbed his eyes and nodded, feeling a strange relief. The long night was over and he felt something had changed somewhere deep down within him.

Elaine wasn't hungry and Malcolm was restricted with regard to fatty foods, so Tom, George and Sheila had their fill of the breakfast. Whilst they were wiping up the beans and egg with the thick buttered bread, Malcolm began to drink his Christmas bottle of whisky.

The tree in the corner was weighed down with decorations and chocolates. Tom sat back down on the settee, very full, and looked drowsily at the shimmering tinsel, losing himself at times in the gleaming plastic balls. The breakfast had just enhanced his feeling of weariness, though it had also brought with it a welcome satisfaction. He wanted to sit there all day without moving and just watch his family move and talk around him. But it was Christmas Day and he supposed he should make an effort. It wasn't that he was particularly miserable. He just felt a little weak.

"Tom, lad," called Malcolm from his ever growing armchair and his ever decreasing bottle of whisky, "fancy a drop?"

"Not yet, thanks," replied Tom. "I will do later, though," he added, hoping his Aunt Sheila would save him if it came to it. He really didn't fancy a drink.

Sheila finished washing up and they all sat together in the lounge. It was eleven thirty in the morning.

"Well, first of all," announced Sheila, "I'd like to wish everyone a happy Christmas." There was general agreement and a nodding of heads before she continued. "And I would like to say how lovely it is to spend Christmas with family. We haven't done that nearly enough over the past few years. I think we should all agree to see more of each other." Again, everyone assented to this point of view. You didn't argue with Sheila. She always managed to say what everyone else was feeling.

"Come on Sheila," interjected her husband. "It's Christmas. Let's get to the presents."

Sheila gave her husband a look so beautifully expressive that a page would not do justice to describing it. And he genuinely thought for a moment that this could actually be his last Christmas. Then the look transformed into a loving smile almost instantly. "Okay, then," she said, "shall I give the presents out?"

There was no audible reply, just a collective thought that passed between Tom and George that she was not unduly suited to the role of present distributor.

The presents beneath the tree were all but obscured by the branches and the decorations. To Tom, momentarily, they seemed pitiful. He was still young, after all. He knew that some children always awoke on Christmas Days where the whole floor was covered with boxes and wrapping paper and so many presents that they wouldn't be able to move. He knew that Malcolm did not work and that Sheila was a cleaner of some sort and he was angry with himself at this unconscious pang of disappointment. He felt a distance between himself and his family at this moment. Maybe it was age. Maybe it was Little Norman. The whole occasion began to sadden him.

"George," said Sheila, handing him a present, "this is from Malcolm and I."

George took the present with bashful unease and unwrapped it, all eyes upon him.

"Sheila chose it," chirped Malcolm from his chair, trying to wink as he said it but had great difficulty in doing this. Simultaneous movement was becoming something of a chore for him now.

The present was a packet of hacksaw blades and a hammer. George thanked Malcolm and Sheila and the latter nodded her acceptance of his honest gratitude.

And so it went on.

Elaine received an embroidery kit that she liked immensely. Tom saw her face soften and ignite as she opened it. He saw the beauty in her. He saw the little girl in her.

Uncle Malcolm received a handkerchief and a diary from his wife who pointedly instructed him to use them both as she was, frankly, beginning to lose patience with him. He smirked at her knowingly before swapping his presents for his glass of whisky.

"Tom," said Sheila, at last, handing a present to Tom, "this is from your Uncle Malcolm and myself. If you don't like it, we can take it back."

As Tom took the present, a shiver ran through him. It was soft. Was it something to wear? He strengthened himself. It was a time for courage and for fortitude. He could feel himself reddening even before the final wrapper was torn away. But his fear was a fear misplaced. When he saw what was there upon his lap, he smiled with instinctive pleasure. It was a Town scarf. He would go to every game next season. That's what he needed. He thanked his Aunt and grinned at his Uncle Malcolm who continued grinning long after the moment had passed.

Whilst Sheila was tidying up the wrapping paper, Tom told his parents that he hadn't been able to find a present for them but he had got them each a card. They said a card was just wonderful for in truth, he was their Christmas.

Tom watched them open their cards, his mother and his father, and he saw the look upon their faces as each read the words inside. He had written in each a poem, expressing his love for them simply and beautifully. His mother could not speak lest she cry. His father put his hand upon his son's shoulder and just looked at him. He had touched them more deeply than he would ever know, for he was still their little boy, the very reason for their lives. His simple words, scrawled down during a night of pain had freed them all. Their love for each other was the love of three good people just trying to keep a hold on life.

The Christmas dinner was massive. Plates were covered with so much food that the task of eating it all seemed at first an impossible one. Gradually, though, the mountains decreased and the plates were cleared. It was all Tom could do to sit up straight afterwards. Uncle Malcolm's green paper hat had slipped over his left eye and his chair was slowly nudging him beneath the table. Sheila looked at her husband and whispered something to her sister. And they both giggled like schoolgirls.

Malcolm slept all afternoon. He missed the Queen's speech. He missed 'The Guns of Navarone."

As the evening sketched it's darkness upon the town, everybody felt at peace. They all sat together in the lounge waiting for the next program to start on the television. Elaine spoke quietly to George and then turned to Sheila. "I think we should give Tom his present now," she said.

Sheila turned off the television and woke Malcolm up with a rough shove. George went upstairs, returning moments later with a present the size of a shoebox wrapped in gold paper. Tom saw now that they were all looking at him. A moment of confusion came over him for he had been far away, thinking of birds, of parks, of libraries and of dark, endless rooms. And there before him stood his father.

"Tom," he said, "this is for you. It's from me and your Mum." He passed the present to his son and went to stand beside his wife. In fact, they were all standing now, all except for Tom, standing and staring down upon the young man whom they all loved so much.

The box felt light. Tom slid the wrapping paper off easily and now held a white shoebox before him. At this point, he felt nothing, no emotion. Not yet. He lifted the lid gently from the box and there, resting softly on a bed of cotton wool, was the most beautiful wooden guitar he had ever seen. It was just ten inches long and perfect in every way, precise, elegant, intricate and wonderful. And then it came to him—those evenings of banging in the shed, those furtive glances. This Beautiful Guitar had been carved in wood by the hands of his father. And a tear dropped from his eye and fell upon it.

George and Elaine held each other tight. Sheila held her hands to her cheeks and Malcolm stumbled back unnoticed into his chair.

Tom looked up from the Beautiful Guitar at his mother and father. He wanted to kiss them both, to hold them and to never let them go. But he just sat there with the Beautiful Guitar upon his lap. That for which he had searched for so long, the very receptacle of his dreams, was with him now. H e had been presented with his perfect soul, there, straight from his father's heart.

Ron, strong and sturdy, sits in a park watching the children play. He watches them on the swings and the slides. He sees them run. He sees them fall and pick themselves up again. He watches the way they move, the young girls. He sits in the park, watching the children play.

And what of that little girl? What of Laura?

She never sleeps without waking in the pure blackness with tears in her eyes and fists clenched tight. And this will go on maybe forever.

The years pass now. Come with me. Look.

She has grown and has such eyes, as you never have seen before. And when she smiles you just break. She is so perfect, so entirely perfect.

And when she marries, her husband will wonder that ever such a woman should want him.

She will still wake in the night, trembling in fear but her husband will put his arms about her and he will brush back the sodden hair from her forehead and whisper into her ear such words of love until she falls back once more to sleep. And he will gently kiss her forehead and listen to the beating of her heart in the clear, cool night and allow the tears to fall from his own frightened eyes.

But the words that she hears as she falls to sleep are not the words of her husband, but those written on that old and tattered crossword grid that she keeps with her always, knows by heart, the words of her Dad. 'You are an angel, pure and clean and untouched, soft and beautiful.'

As the sky darkens and the night creeps in, the snow starts its mischievous transformation into ice. The roads become more hazardous than they already are and the pavements spew sand.

In the small house in Northern Town, Tom stands at the window looking at the sky. His mother and father are asleep in adjoining armchairs facing the window. Malcolm is stretched out on the settee in a drunken stupor, his head on the lap of his somnolent wife.

The moon is full and big and the stars shine brightly. Tom is faced in the blank window by his own reflection and the reflection of his family behind him. All is dark outside. And the glass becomes a mirror, framing himself and his family. Tom wants to keep the image alive, to protect it, and retain it forever. His eyes begin to moisten a little. He blinks. And when his sight is returned to him, there is Little Norman. He is there, reflected in the window, standing in the middle of the room between the armchairs where his parents lay sleeping.

Tom is frightened. He puts his hand upon the window and touches only glass. He dares not look around lest the vision slip away. Little Norman is smiling at him now, giggling the way he used to. His tiny body shakes as he giggles. And then he sees Little Norman begin to cough and to splutter. A strange expression passes across the small boy's face. And a bag of sweets drops from his chubby hand to the floor. And he sees those big eyes close tightly and that beautiful face go red then white. In a moment, the body of Little Norman is on the floor, shaking and writhing and Tom still touches only glass. And then the body is still. Little Norman is dead.

Tom is about to call out his brother's name but he cannot speak, is not allowed to speak. And the image in the window begins to fade and distort. Then slowly, very slowly, Little Norman stirs on the floor. He clambers to his feet, sighs and grins at his big brother, the most playful, captivating grin you ever saw.

And then the vision slips away. The room behind Tom holds its reflection but Little Norman is gone now. His body has turned to silver, gleaming in the night.

And Tom watches it glide up to Heaven like a star.

For two hours, he stands alone at the window, looking out upon the night, the beautiful guitar held gently in his hand. He watches over his Mum and he watches over his Dad. And he can't help but smile, thinking thoughts of Little Norman.

The End

978-0-595-45479-2
0-595-45479-8

Printed in the United Kingdom
by Lightning Source UK Ltd.
124726UK00001B/446/A